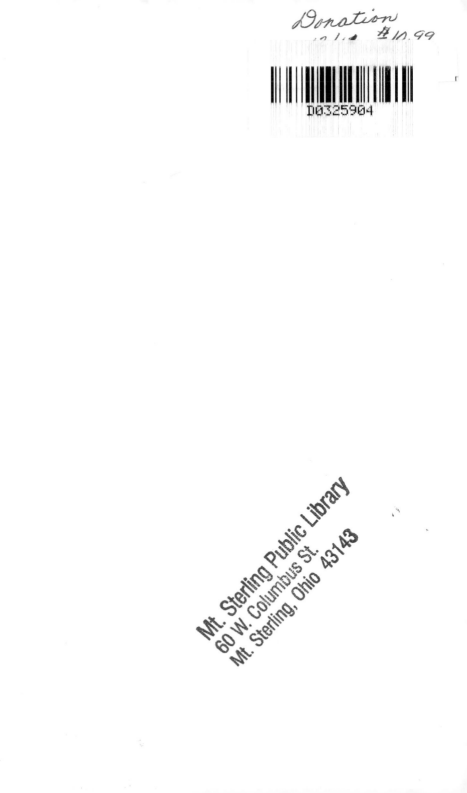

D0325904

THE FIRES OF
MERLIN

T. A. BARRON

THE FIRES OF
MERLIN

Book III of
THE LOST YEARS OF MERLIN

Philomel Books

Patricia Lee Gauch, editor

PHILOMEL BOOKS

A division of Penguin Young Readers Group.
Published by The Penguin Group.
Penguin Group (USA) Inc., 375 Hudson Street, New York, NY 10014, U.S.A.
Penguin Group (Canada), 90 Eglinton Avenue East, Suite 700, Toronto, Ontario
M4P 2Y3, Canada (a division of Pearson Penguin Canada Inc.).
Penguin Books Ltd, 80 Strand, London WC2R 0RL, England.
Penguin Ireland, 25 St. Stephen's Green, Dublin 2, Ireland
(a division of Penguin Books Ltd).
Penguin Group (Australia), 250 Camberwell Road, Camberwell, Victoria 3124,
Australia (a division of Pearson Australia Group Pty Ltd).
Penguin Books India Pvt Ltd, 11 Community Centre, Panchsheel Park,
New Delhi - 110 017, India.
Penguin Group (NZ), 67 Apollo Drive, Rosedale, North Shore 0745,
Auckland, New Zealand (a division of Pearson New Zealand Ltd.)
Penguin Books (South Africa) (Pty) Ltd, 24 Sturdee Avenue,
Rosebank, Johannesburg 2196, South Africa.
Penguin Books Ltd, Registered Offices: 80 Strand,
London WC2R 0RL, England.

Library of Congress Cataloging-in-Publication Data
Barron, T. A. The fires of Merlin / by T. A. Barron.
"Book three of 'The Lost Years of Merlin.' "
p. cm. Summary: Having voyaged to the Otherworld in his quest to find
himself, the young wizard must face fire in many different forms and deal with the
possibility of losing his own magical power.
1. Merlin (Legendary character)—Juvenile fiction. [1. Merlin (Legendary
character)—Fiction. 2. Wizards—Fiction. 3. Fantasy.] I. Title.
PZ7.B27567Fi 1998 [Fic]—dc21 97-49561 CIP AC
ISBN 978-0-399-25022-4
1 3 5 7 9 10 8 6 4 2
First Impression

This book is dedicated to
__Madeleine L'Engle__
who has kindled the fires of inspiration in so many

with special appreciation to
__Larkin__
age two, whose own fires burn so bright

W · E · S

THE · LOS

be there giants?

Ruins of Varigal

dwarves last seen here

Lake of the Face

living stones

Tuatha's Grave

crossing

Crystal Cave of the Grand Elusa

orcha

THE MISTED HILLS

Cobbler's Rowan

Arbassa, Home of Rhia

The River Unce

DRUMA WOOD

Forgotten Island

Treelings once lived here

The Last Shomorra

shore of the speaking shells

Trouble found here

dunes

Emrys' Landing

I·SCHOENHERR·MCMXCVI

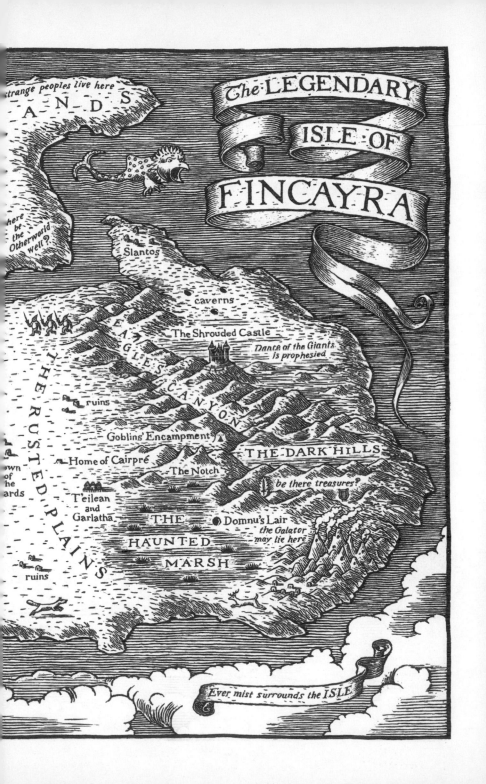

A·Detail·of·Southeastern·FINCAYRA

To·THE·DARK·HILLS·

be·there Kreelixes?

• Domnu's·Lair· the·Galator·may·lie·here

THE HAUNTED MARSH

The·Wheel·of·Wye

hidden·caves

This·way·to THE RUSTED PLAINS

The·Legendary Carpet·Caerlochlann· found·here

The·Region·of

THE·SMOKING·CLIFFS

Ancient·home·of·the·Mellwyn=bri=Meath·clan

IAN·SCHOENHERR

MCMXCVIII

CONTENTS

AUTHOR'S NOTE

Once again, this wizard is full of surprises.

As those who have read the first two volumes of *The Lost Years of Merlin* epic already know, Merlin first surprised me long ago. In his typically mysterious way, he pointed out that despite all the books, poems, and songs that have been written about him over the centuries, virtually nothing had been told about his youth. For there to be such an enormous gap in the lore about a character so rich, complex, and intriguing was strange indeed. So when Merlin invited me to serve as his scribe while he revealed at last the story of his lost years, I could not refuse.

Even so, I hesitated. I wondered whether it was really possible to add a new strand or two to the already wondrously woven tapestry of myth surrounding Merlin. And, even if it were possible, would the newly created threads feel integral to the rest of the weaving? Would their color, weight, and texture, while original, still feel part of the whole? Would they, in short, feel true?

Somehow, I needed to hear Merlin's voice. Not the voice of the worldly enchanter, all-seeing and all-knowing, whom the world has come to celebrate. Far from it. Down inside of that legendary wizard, buried beneath centuries of struggles, triumphs, and tragedies, was another voice: the voice of a boy. Uncertain, insecure, and utterly human. Possessed with unusual gifts—and with a passion as great as his destiny.

In time, that voice at last came clear. Although it rang with vulnerability, it also carried deeper undertones, full of the mythic and spiritual richness of ancient Celtic lore. The voice sprang partly from those Celtic tales, partly from the mysterious hooting of the owl in the cottonwood tree outside my window—and partly from somewhere else. And it told me that, during those years of his youth, Merlin did not merely disappear from the world of story and song. Indeed, during those years, Merlin *himself* disappeared—from the world as we know it.

Who was Merlin, really? Where did he come from? What were his greatest passions, his highest hopes, his deepest fears? The answers to such questions lay hidden behind the shroud of his lost years.

To find the answers, Merlin must voyage to Fincayra, a mythic place known to the Celts as an island beneath the waves, a bridge between the Earth of human beings and the Otherworld of spiritual beings. Merlin's mother, Elen, calls Fincayra an *in between place*. She observes that the swirling mist surrounding the island is neither quite water nor quite air. Rather, it is something akin to both and yet something else entirely. In the same sense, Fincayra is both mortal and immortal, dark and light, fragile and everlasting.

On the first page of Book One of *The Lost Years of Merlin,* a young boy washes ashore on an unknown coast. Almost drowned, he has no memory of his past—not his parents, not his home, not even his own name. Certainly he has no idea that he will one day become Merlin: the greatest wizard of all time, the mentor of King Arthur, the captivating figure who strides across fifteen hundred years of legend.

That book begins Merlin's search for his true identity, and for the secret to his mysterious, often frightening, powers. To gain a little, he must lose a lot—more, even, than he comprehends. Yet somehow, in the end, he manages to unravel the riddle of the Dance of the Giants. As his journey continues in Book Two, he searches for the elixir that could save his mother's life, following the winding path of the Seven Songs of Wizardry. Along the way, he must surmount his share of obstacles, though one remains far more difficult than all the others. For he must somehow begin to see in an entirely new way, a way befitting a wizard: not with his eyes, but with his heart.

All this Merlin had revealed to us when the time came to begin Book Three—the final installment, I had thought, of the story. Then came the wizard's latest surprise. He told me in no uncertain terms that the tale of his lost years could not possibly be told in just three volumes. When I reminded him that in the beginning he had promised me this would be a trilogy, itself at least a five-year project, he merely waved away my concerns. After all, he said with his unfathomable grin, what is a little extra time to someone who has already lived fifteen centuries? Let alone someone who has learned the art of living backward in time?

I could not object. This is, after all, Merlin's story. And like Merlin himself, the other characters in the tale—Elen, Rhia, Cairpré, Shim, Trouble, Domnu, Stangmar, Bumbelwy, Hallia, Dagda, Rhita Gawr, and others yet to come—have taken on lives of their own. Thus, a projected trilogy has become a five-book epic.

In this volume, Merlin must confront fire in many different forms. He feels the fires of an ancient dragon, of a mountain of lava, and for the first time in his life, of certain passions of his own. He may find that fire, like himself, holds an array of opposites. It can consume and destroy, but it can also warm and revive.

In addition, Merlin must explore the nature of power. Like fire, power can be used wisely or abused terribly. Like fire, it can heal or devour. The young wizard may even need to lose his own magical power in order to discover where it truly resides. For the essence of magic, like the music of the instrument he has made with his own hands, may lie somewhere else than it appears.

The more I learn about this wizard, the less I really know. Even so, I continue to be struck by the remarkable metaphor of Merlin himself. Like the boy who washed ashore with no memory, no past, and no name, without any clue about his wondrous future, each of us begins anew at some point in life—or, indeed, at several points over the course of a lifetime.

And yet, much like that half-drowned boy, each of us harbors hidden gifts, hidden talents, hidden possibilities. Perhaps we also harbor a bit of magic, as well. Perhaps we might even discover a wizard somewhere inside of ourselves.

As in the prior volumes, I am grateful for the advice and support of several people, most especially my wife, Currie, and my editor, Patricia Lee Gauch. In addition, I would like to thank Jennifer Herron, for her bright spirit; Kathy Montgomery, for her contagious good humor; and Kylene Beers, for her unwavering faith. Without them, Merlin's surprises would surely have overwhelmed me by now.

T. A. B.

Splendour of fire . . .

Swiftness of wind . . .

I arise today
Through the strength of heaven:
  Light of sun,
  Radiance of moon,
  Splendour of fire,
  Speed of lightning,
  Swiftness of wind,
  Depth of sea,
  Stability of earth,
  Firmness of rock.

—From a seventh-century hymn
  by Saint Patrick called
  THE CRY OF THE DEER

PROLOGUE

The mists of memory gather, the more with each passing year. Yet one day remains as clear in my mind as this morning's sunrise, although it happened those many centuries ago.

It was a day darkened by mists of its own, and by smoke thick and wrathful. While the fate of all Fincayra hung in the balance, no mortal creature suspected. For the mists of that day obscured everything but the fear, and the pain, and only the slightest hint of hope.

As still as a mountain for years beyond count, the massive gray boulder quite suddenly stirred.

It was not the fast-flowing water of the River Unceasing, slapping against the base of the boulder, that caused the change. Nor was it the sleek otter whose favorite pastime had long been sliding down the cleft between the boulder and the river's muddy bank. Nor the family of speckled lizards who had lived for generations in the patch of moss on the boulder's north side.

No, the stirring of the boulder on that day came from an entirely different source. One that, unlike the lizards, had never been seen at the spot, although it had in fact been present long before the first lizard ever arrived. For the source of the stirring came from deep within the boulder itself.

As mist gathered within the banks of the river, resting on the water like a thick white cloak, a faint scraping sound filled the air. A moment later, the boulder wobbled ever so slightly. With shreds of mist curling about its base, it suddenly pitched to one side. Hissing with alarm, three lizards leaped off and scurried away.

If the lizards had hoped to find a new home in the moss atop one of the other boulders, they were destined to be disappointed. For more scraping sounds joined with the constant splashing of the current. One by one, each of the nine boulders lining the river began to wobble, then rock vigorously, as if shaken by a tremor that only they could feel. One of them, partly submerged by the rushing river, started rolling toward a grove of hemlocks on the bank.

Near the top of the first boulder to come to life, a tiny crack appeared. Another crack split off, and then another. All at once, a jagged chip broke away, leaving a hole that glowed with a strange orange light. Slowly, tentatively, something started pushing its way out of the hole. It glistened darkly, even as it scraped against the surface.

It was a claw.

♦   ♦   ♦

Far to the north, in the desolate ridges of the Lost Lands, a trail of smoke rose skyward, curling like a venomous snake. Nothing else moved on these slopes, not even an insect or a blade of grass trembling in the wind. These lands had been scorched by fire—so powerful that it had obliterated trees, evaporated rivers, and demolished even rocks, leaving behind nothing but charred ridges coated with ash. For these lands had long been the lair of a dragon.

Ages before, at the height of his wrath, the dragon had incinerated whole forests and swallowed entire villages. Valdearg—whose
name, in Fincayra's oldest tongue, meant *Wings of Fire*—was the
last and most feared of a long line of emperor dragons. Much of
Fincayra had been blackened by his fiery breath, and all its inhab-
itants lived in terror of his shadow. Finally, the powerful wizard
Tuatha had managed to drive the dragon back to his lair. After a
prolonged battle, Valdearg had at last succumbed to the wizard's
enchantment of sleep. He had remained in his flame-seared hollow, slumbering fitfully, ever since.

While many Fincayrans grumbled that Tuatha should have killed
the dragon when he had the chance, others argued that the wizard
must have spared him for a reason—though what that reason could
possibly be no one knew. At least, in slumber, Wings of Fire could
cause no more harm. Time passed, so much time that many people began to doubt that he would ever wake again. Some even ques-
tioned the old stories of his rampages. Others went further,
wondering whether he had ever really existed, although very few
indeed were willing to travel all the way to the Lost Lands to find
out. Of those who did set out on the dangerous trek, very few ever
returned.

Very little of what Tuatha had said at the conclusion of the Battle of Bright Flames had been understandable, for he spoke in rid-
dles. And many of his words had been long forgotten. Still, a few
bards kept alive what remained in the form of a poem called *The
Dragon's Eye*. Although the poem had many versions, each as obscure as the others, all agreed that on some dark day in the future,
Valdearg would awaken once more.

Even now, these lands reeked of charcoal. Near the hollow, the air shimmered with the unremitting heat of the dragon's breath. The low, roaring sound of his snoring echoed across the blackened ridges, while the dark column of smoke continued to pour from his nostrils, lifting slowly skyward.

◆ ◆ ◆

The claw pushed higher, tapping the edge of the rock-like shell as cautiously as someone about to step on a frozen pond would tap the ice. Finally, the dagger-sharp tip of the claw dug into the surface, shooting cracks in all directions. A muffled sound, part screech and part grunt, came from deep inside. Then, all at once, the claw ripped away a large section of shell.

The enormous egg rocked again, rolling farther down the riverbank. As it splashed in the surging water, several more pieces of the shell dropped away. Although the morning sun had started to burn through the mist, its light did not diminish the orange glow radiating from the gaping hole.

More cracks snaked around the sides. The claw, curved like a huge hook, slashed at the edges of the hole, spraying fragments of shell in the river and on the muddy bank. With another grunt, the creature inside shoved the claw completely out of the hole, revealing a twisted, gangly arm covered with iridescent purple scales. Next came a hunched, bony shoulder, dripping with lavender-colored ooze. Hanging limp from the shoulder was a crumpled fold of leathery skin that might have been a wing.

Then, for whatever reason, the arm and shoulder fell still. For a long moment the egg neither rocked nor emitted any sound.

Suddenly the entire top half of the egg flew off, landing with a splash in the shallows. Rays of orange light shot into the shredding mist. Awkwardly, hesitantly, the scaly shoulder lifted, supporting a thin, purple neck flecked with scarlet spots. Hanging heavily from the neck, a head—twice as big as that of a full-grown horse—slowly lifted into the air. Above the massive jaw, studded with row upon row of gleaming teeth, a pair of immense nostrils twitched, sniffing the air for the first time.

From the creature's two triangular eyes, the orange light poured like glowing lava. The eyes, blinking every few seconds, gazed through the mist at the other eggs that had also begun to crack open. Raising one of her claws, the creature tried to scratch the bright yellow bump that protruded from the middle of her forehead. But her aim was off and instead she poked the soft, crinkled skin of her nose.

With a loud whimper, she shook her head vigorously, flapping her blue, banner-like ears against her head. After the shaking ceased, however, her right ear refused to lie flat again. Unlike the left one, which hung almost down to her shoulder, it stretched out to the side like a misplaced horn. Only the gentle droop at the tip hinted that it was, in fact, an ear.

♦ ♦ ♦

Deep within the smoking cavern, the gargantuan form shifted uneasily. Valdearg's head, nearly as broad as a hill, jerked suddenly, crushing a pile of skulls long ago blackened by flames. His breath came faster and faster, roaring like a thousand waterfalls. Although his enormous eyes remained closed, his claws slashed ruthlessly at some invisible foe.

The dragon's tail lashed out, smashing against the charred wall of stone. He growled, less at the rocks that tumbled onto the green and orange scales of his back than at the torments of his dream— a dream that pushed him to the very edge of awakening. One of his vast wings batted the air. As the wing's edge scraped the floor of the hollow, dozens of jeweled swords and harnesses, gilded harps and trumpets, and polished gems and pearls flew in every direction. Clouds of smoke darkened the day.

◆　◆　◆

The creature in the egg, her nose still throbbing, flashed her eyes angrily. Feeling an ancient urge, she drew a deep breath of air, puffing out her purple chest. With a sudden snort, she exhaled, flaring her nostrils. But no flames came, nor even a thin trail of smoke. For although she was, indeed, a baby dragon, she could not yet breathe fire.

Crestfallen, the baby dragon whimpered again. She lifted one leg to climb the rest of the way out of the shell, then halted abruptly. Hearing something, she cocked her head to one side. With one ear dangling like a thin blue flag and the other soaring skyward, she listened intently, not daring to move.

Suddenly the hatchling drew back in fright, teetering in the remains of the egg. For she had only just noticed the dark shadow forming in the mist on the far bank of the river. Sensing danger, she huddled deeper in the shell. Yet she could not keep her one unruly ear from poking over the rim.

After a long moment, she raised her head ever so slightly. Her heart thumped within her chest. She watched the shadow draw slowly nearer, wading through the churning water. As it approached, it started to harden into a strange, two-legged figure— carrying a curved blade that gleamed ominously. Then, with a start, she realized that the blade was lifting to strike.

PART ONE

I

THE LAST STRING

Just one more."

Even as I spoke the words, I could scarcely believe them. I slid my hand across the scaly, gray-brown bark of the rowan tree whose massive roots encircled me, feeling the gentle slopes and curves of the living wood. In one hollow, as deep as a large bowl, sat some of the tools I had been using over the past several months: a stone hammer, a wedge of iron, three filing rods of different textures, and a carving knife no bigger than my little finger. I reached past them, past the knobbed root that served as a hanging rack for my larger saws, to the thin shelf of bark that had so recently held all eight strings.

Eight strings. Each one cured, stretched, and finally serenaded under the full autumn moon, according to ancient tradition. Thankfully, my mentor, Cairpré, had devoted weeks before that night to helping me learn all the intricate verses and melodies. Even so, the moon had nearly set before I finally sang every one of them correctly—and in the right order. Now seven of the strings gleamed on the little instrument propped on the root before me.

Grasping the last remaining string, the smallest of the lot, I brought it closer. As I twirled it slowly, its ends twisted and swayed—alive, almost. Like the tongue of someone on the very verge of speaking.

Late afternoon light played on the string, making it shine as golden as the autumn leaves speckling the grass at the base of the rowan tree. It felt surprisingly heavy, given its short length, yet as flexible as the breeze itself. Gently, I draped it on a cluster of dark red berries hanging from one of the rowan's lower boughs. Turning back to the instrument, I inserted the last two knobs, carved from the same branch of hawthorn as the others, whose month-long kiln drying had ended only yesterday. Rubbing against the oaken soundboard, the knobs squeaked ever so slightly.

At last, I retrieved the string. After tying the seven loops of a wizard's knot on each of the two knobs, I began twisting, one to the right and the other to the left. Gradually, the string tightened, straightening out like a windblown banner. Before it had grown too tight, I stopped. Now all that remained was to insert the bridge—and play.

Leaning back against the trunk of the rowan, I gazed at my handiwork. It was a psaltery, shaped something like a tiny harp but with a bowed soundboard behind all the strings. I lifted it off the root, studying it admiringly. Though it was barely as big as my open hand, it seemed to me as grand as a newborn star.

My own instrument. Made with my own hands.

I ran my finger along the strip of ash inlaid at the top of the frame. This would be much more than a source of music, I knew. Unless, of course, I had bungled any of the steps in making it. Or, much worse, unless . . .

I drew a slow, unsteady breath. Unless I lacked the one thing Cairpré couldn't teach me, the one thing he couldn't even describe—what he could only call *the essential core of a wizard*. For, as he had so often reminded me, the making of a wizard's first instrument was a sacred tradition, marking a gifted youth's coming of age. If the process succeeded, when the time finally came to play the instrument, it would release its own music. And, simultaneously, an entirely new level of the youth's own magic.

And if the process did not succeed . . .

I set down the psaltery. The strings jangled softly as the soundboard again touched the burly roots of the tree. Among these very roots, Fincayra's most famous wielders of magic—including my legendary grandfather, Tuatha—had cobbled their own first instruments. Hence the tree's name, written into many a ballad and tale: the Cobblers' Rowan.

Placing my hand over a rounded knob of bark, I listened for the pulse of life within the great tree. The slow, swelling rhythm of roots plunging deeper and branches reaching higher, of thousands of leaves melting from green to gold, of the tree itself breathing. Inhaling life, and death, and the mysterious bonds connecting both. The Cobblers' Rowan had continued to stand through many storms, many centuries—and many wizards. Did it know even now, I wondered, whether my psaltery would really work?

Lifting my gaze, I surveyed the hills of Druma Wood, each one as round as the back of a running deer. Autumn hues shone scarlet, orange, yellow, and brown. Brightly plumed birds lifted out of the branches, chattering and cooing, while spirals of mist rose from hidden swamps. I could hear, weaving with the breeze, the continuous tumble of a waterfall. This forest, wilder than anyplace I had ever known, was truly the heart of Fincayra. It was the first place I had wandered after washing ashore on the island—and the first place I had ever felt my own roots sinking deeply.

I smiled, seeing my staff leaning against the rowan's trunk. That, too, had been a gift of this forest, as its spicy scent of hemlock reminded me constantly. Whatever elements of real magic that I possessed—outside of a few simple skills such as my second sight, which had come to me after I lost the use of my eyes, and my sword with some magic of its own—resided within the gnarled wood of that staff.

As did so much more. For my staff had, somehow, been touched by the power of Tuatha himself. He had reached out of the ages, out of the grave, to place his own magic within its shaft. Even with the blurred edges of my vision, I could make out the symbols carved upon it, symbols of the powers that I yearned to master fully: Leaping, between places and possibly even times; Changing, from one form into another; Binding, not just a broken bone but a broken spirit as well; and all the rest.

Perhaps, just perhaps . . . the psaltery would take on similar powers. Was it possible? Powers that I could wield on behalf of all Fincayra's peoples, with wisdom and grace not seen since the days of my grandfather.

I took a deep breath. Carefully, I lifted the little instrument in my hands, then slid the oaken bridge under the strings. A snap of my wrist—and it stood in place. I exhaled, knowing that the moment, my moment, was very near.

II

THE ROOT CHORD

Done," I announced. "It's ready to play."

"Done, you say?" Cairpré's shaggy gray head poked around from behind the trunk of the great rowan. He looked frustrated, as if he couldn't find the one remaining word he needed to complete an epic poem about tree roots. As his dark eyes focused on my little instrument, his expression clouded still more. "*Hmmm.* A fair piece of work, Merlin."

His tangled eyebrows drew together. "But it's not done until it's played. As I've said someplace or other, *For the truth shall be found, Not in sight but in sound.*"

From behind him, on the brow of the knoll, came a hearty laugh. "Never mind that your poem referred to a meadowlark instead of a harp."

Cairpré and I swung our heads toward my mother as she stepped lightly over the grass. Her dark blue robe fluttered in the breeze that smelled so strongly of autumn, while her hair draped her shoulders like a mantle of sunlight. It was her eyes, though, that drew my attention. Eyes more blue than sapphires.

Watching her approach, the poet straightened his smudged white tunic. "Elen," he grumbled. "I should have guessed you'd return just in time to correct me."

Her eyes seemed to smile. "Somebody has to now and then."

"Impossible." Cairpré did his best to look gruff, but could not hide his own fleeting smile. "Besides, it's not a harp the boy has made. It's a psaltery, though a small one, after the Greek *psaltérion*. Did no one ever teach you about the Greeks, young lady?"

"Yes." My mother stifled another laugh. "You did."

"Then you have no excuse whatsoever."

"Here," she said to me, pouring some plump, purple berries into the hollow in the root holding my tools. "Rivertang berries, from the rill across the way. I brought a handful for you." With a side-long glance at Cairpré, she flicked a single berry at him. "And one for you, for agreeing to give me a tutorial on Grecian music."

The poet grunted. "If I have time."

I listened, curious, to their bantering. Whatever the reason, their conversations often took such turns lately. And this puzzled me, since their words themselves didn't seem to be what mattered. No, their bantering was really about something else, something I couldn't quite put my finger on.

Watching them, I popped a few berries into my mouth, tasting the zesty flavor. Here they were, talking as if Cairpré thought he knew everything, more perhaps than the great spirit Dagda himself. Yet my mother realized, I felt sure, that he had never lost sight of how little he really did know. As much as he had taught me during the past year about the mysteries of magic, he never began one of our tutoring sessions without reminding me of his own limitations. He had even confessed that, while he knew that I must follow a series of intricate steps in making my first instrument, he wasn't at all certain of their meaning. Throughout the process—from choosing the proper instrument to shaping the wood to firing the kiln—he had behaved as much like my fellow student as my mentor.

Suddenly something nipped the back of my neck. I cried out, brushing away whatever insect had taken me for a meal. But the culprit had already fled.

My mother's blue eyes gazed down at me. "What's wrong?"

Still rubbing the back of my neck, I rose and stepped free of the burly roots. In the process, I almost tripped over my scabbard and sword that lay in the grass. "I don't know. Something bit me, I think."

She cocked her head questioningly. "It's too late for biting flies. The first frost came weeks ago."

"That reminds me," said Cairpré with a wink at her, "of an ancient Abyssinian poem about flies."

Even as she started to laugh, I felt another sharp nip on my neck. Whirling around, I glimpsed a small, red berry bouncing down the grass of the knoll. My eyes narrowed. "I've found the biting fly."

"Really?" asked my mother. "Where?"

I spun to face the old rowan. Raising my arm, I pointed to the boughs arching above us. There, virtually invisible among the curtains of green and brown leaves, crouched a figure wearing a suit of woven vines.

"Rhia," I growled. "Why can't you just say hello like other people?"

The leafy figure stirred, stretching her arms. "Because this way is much more fun, of course." Seeing my grimace, she added, "Brothers can be so humorless at times." Then, with the agility of a snake gliding across a branch, she slid down the twisted trunk and bounded over to us.

Elen watched her with amusement. "You are every bit a tree girl, you are."

Rhia beamed. Spying the berries in the hollow, she scooped up most of what remained. *"Mmmm,* rivertang. A bit tart, though." Then, turning to me, she indicated the tiny instrument in my hand. "So when are you going to play that for us?"

"When I'm ready. You're lucky I let you climb down that tree on your own power."

Surprised, she shook her brown curls. "You honestly expect me to believe that you could have lifted me out of the tree by magic?"

Tempted though I was to say yes, I knew it wasn't true. Not yet, at least. Besides, I could feel the deep pools of Cairpré's eyes boring into me.

"No," I admitted. "But the time will come, believe me."

"Oh, sure. And the time will come that the dragon Valdearg will finally wake up and swallow us all in a single bite. Of course, that could be a thousand years from now."

"Or it could be today."

"Please, you two." Cairpré tugged on the sleeve of my tunic. "Stop your battle of wits."

Rhia shrugged. "I never battle with someone who is unarmed." Smirking, she added, "Unless they boast about magic they can't really use."

This was too much. I extended my empty hand toward my staff resting against the trunk of the rowan. I concentrated my thoughts on its gnarled top, its carved shaft, its fragrant wood that carried so much power. Out through my fingers I sent the command. *Come to me. Leap to me.*

The staff quivered slightly, rubbing against the bark. Then, suddenly, it stood erect on the grass. An instant later it flew through the air, right into my waiting hand.

"Not bad." Rhia bent her leaf-draped body in a slight bow. "You've been practicing."

"Yes," agreed my mother. "You've learned a lot about controlling your power."

Cairpré wagged his shaggy mane. "And much less, I'm afraid, about controlling your pride."

I glanced at him bashfully as I slid the staff into my belt. But before I could speak, Rhia chimed in. "Come now, Merlin. Play something for us on that little whatever-it-is."

My mother nodded. "Yes, do."

Cairpré allowed himself a grin. "Perhaps you could sing with him, Elen."

"Sing? No, not now."

"Why not?" He regarded me thoughtfully, his face both anxious and hopeful. "If he can, indeed, make the psaltery play, it will be true cause for celebration." For some reason, his expression seemed to darken. "No one knows that better than I."

"Please," urged Rhia. "If there's any celebrating to do, there's no better way to do it than with one of your songs."

My mother's cheeks flushed. Turning toward the rippling leaves of the rowan, she pondered for a moment. "Well . . . all right." She opened her hands to the three of us. "I shall sing. Yes, a joyful song." Her eyes darted to the poet. "For the many joys of the past year."

Cairpré brightened. "And of the years to come," he added in a whisper.

Again my mother blushed. Just why didn't concern me, for I,

too, shared her joy. Here I stood, with family, with friends, increasingly at home on this island—all of which would have seemed utterly impossible just over one year ago. I was now fourteen years old, living in this forest, a place as peaceful as the autumn leaves I could see drifting downward. I wanted nothing more than to stay in this very place, with these very people. And, one day, to master the skills of a wizard. Of a true mage—like my grandfather.

My fingers squeezed the psaltery's frame. If only it would not fail me!

I drew a deep breath of the crisp air buffeting the hilltop. "I am ready."

My mother, hearing the tautness in my voice, brushed her finger against my cheek—the same cheek that, long ago, had been scarred by a fire of my own making. "Are you all right, my son?"

I did my best to force a grin. "I'm just imagining how my strumming is going to compare to your singing, that's all."

Although I could tell she didn't believe me, her face relaxed slightly. After a moment, she asked, "Can you play in the Ionian mode? If you will just strike the root chord, and play for a while, I can fit my song to your melody."

"I can try."

"Good!" Rhia leaped up to catch hold of the rowan's lowest branch. She swung to and fro, releasing a bell-like laugh as golden leaves rained down on us. "I love to hear a harp, even a tiny one like yours. It reminds me of the sound of rain dancing on the summer grass."

"Well, the summer has passed," I declared. "Yet if anything can bring it back, it will be Mother's voice, not my playing." I turned to Cairpré. "Is it time, then? For the incantation?"

Even as the poet cleared his throat, his expression darkened again—this time more deeply, as if a strange, contorted shadow had fallen across his thoughts. "First there is something I must tell you." He hesitated, selecting his words. "Since time beyond memory, any Fincayran boy or girl with the promise of deep magic has left home for an apprenticeship similar to yours. With a real wizard or enchantress, preferably, but if none could be found, with a scholar or bard."

"Like you." What was he leading up to? All this I knew.

"Yes, my boy. Like me."

"But why are you telling me this?"

His brow grew as wrinkled as his tunic. "Because there's one more thing you should know. Before you play your psaltery. You see, that apprenticeship—the time of mastering the fundamentals of enchantment, before even starting to make a musical instrument—normally takes . . . a long time. Longer than the eight or nine months it has taken you."

My mother cocked her head at him. "How long does it usually take?"

"Well," he fumbled. "It, ah, varies. Different, you see, from one person to the next."

"How long?" she repeated.

He observed her glumly. Then, under his breath, he answered. "Between five and ten years."

Like Elen and Rhia, I started—nearly dropping the psaltery.

"Even Tuatha, with all his gifts, needed four full years to complete his own apprenticeship. To do it all in less than one year is, well, remarkable. Or you could say . . . unheard of." He sighed. "I've been meaning to tell you this, really, but I wanted to find the proper time and setting. *The opportune time, As rare as good rhyme.*"

Elen shook her head. "You have another reason."

Sadly, he nodded. "You know me too well."

He looked at me imploringly, as he ran his hand over a root of the Cobblers' Rowan. "You see, Merlin, I haven't wanted to tell you because I haven't been sure whether your speed, your swiftness in mastering whatever lessons I gave you, was due to your own gifts—or to my deficiencies as your tutor. Did I forget any steps? Misread any instructions? It's been nagging at me now for some time. I've checked all the ancient texts—oh yes, many times—just to make sure that you've done everything right. And I truly believe that you have, or I would not have let you go this far."

He straightened. "Even so, you ought to be warned. Because if the psaltery doesn't work, it may be my fault instead of yours. That's right. And, as you know, Merlin, a youth gets just one chance at making a magical instrument. Only one. If it should fail to summon high magic, you will never have another."

I swallowed. "If my training really moved that fast, it's possible that the reason is something else altogether. Something unrelated to how good you might be as a mentor—or I might be as a student."

His eyebrows lifted.

"Maybe I had some help. From someplace neither of us suspected. Just where, I'm not sure." Pensively, I ran my thumb over the handle of my staff. Suddenly it struck me. "My staff, for example. Yes, yes, that's it! Tuatha's magic, you know." I rolled the tapered shaft under my belt. "It's been with me from the start, and it's here with me now. Surely, in playing my instrument, it will help again."

"No, my boy." Cairpré held my gaze. "That staff may have helped you in the past, it's true—but it's no use to you now. The texts are as clear as autumn air on this. Only the psaltery itself, and whatever skills you may have brought to its making, will determine whether you pass this test."

My hand, holding the tiny frame, began to perspire. "What will the psaltery do if I fail?"

"Nothing. It will make no music. And bring no magic."

"And if I succeed?"

"Your instrument," he said while stroking his chin, "should start to play on its own. Music both strange and powerful. At least that's what has happened in the past. So just as you have felt magic flowing between you and your staff, you should feel it with the psaltery. But this should be a different level of magic, like nothing you have ever known before."

I worked my tongue to moisten it. "The trouble is . . . the psaltery hasn't been touched by Tuatha. Only by me."

Gently, the poet squeezed my shoulder. "When a musician—no wizard, just a wandering bard—plays the harp skillfully, is the music in the strings, or in the hands that pluck them?"

Confused, I shook my head. "What does that matter? We are talking about magic here."

"I don't pretend to know the answer, my boy. But I could show you tome after tome of treatises, some by mages of enormous wisdom, pondering that very question."

"Then someday, if I'm ever a mage myself, I'll give you my answer. Right now, all I want to do is pluck my own strings."

My mother looked from me to Cairpré and back to me again. "Are you sure it's the time? Are you really ready? My song can certainly wait."

"Yes," agreed Rhia, twisting one of the vines that circled her waist. "I'm not so much in the mood for music now."

I studied her. "You don't think I can do it, do you?"

"No," she replied calmly. "I'm just not sure."

I winced. "Well, the truth is . . . I'm not sure myself. But I do know this. If I wait any longer, I may lose the courage to try." I faced Cairpré. "Now?"

The poet nodded. "Good luck, my boy. And remember: The texts say that if high magic does come, so, too, may come other things—surprising things."

"And song," added my mother gently. "I will sing for you, Merlin, whatever happens. Whether or not there is any music in those strings."

I lifted the psaltery, even as I lifted my gaze to the boughs of the ancient rowan. Hesitantly, I placed the instrument's narrow end against the middle of my chest. As I cupped my hand around the outer rim, I could feel my heart thumping through the wood. The breeze slackened; the rustling rowan leaves quieted. Even the gray-backed beetle on the toe of my boot ceased crawling.

My voice a whisper, I spoke the ancient incantation:

> *May the instrument I hold*
> *Usher forth*
> > *A magic bold.*
>
> *May the music that I bring*
> *Blossom like*
> > *The soul of spring.*
>
> *May the melody I play*
> *Deepen through*
> > *The passing day.*
>
> *May the power that I wield*
> *Plant anew*
> > *The wounded field.*

Expectantly, I turned to Cairpré. He stood motionless but for his roving eyes. Behind him, the lush hills of Druma Wood seemed frozen—as fixed in place as one of the carvings on my staff. No light swept across the branches. No birds fluttered or whistled.

"Please," I said aloud, to the psaltery, to the rowan, to the very air. "That's the only thing I want. To rise as high as I possibly can. To take whatever gifts, whatever powers, you can give me, and use them not for myself, but for others. With wisdom. And, I hope, with love. *To plant anew the wounded field.*"

Feeling nothing, my heart began to sink. I waited, hoping. Still nothing. Reluctantly, I started to lower the psaltery.

Then, ever so slightly, I felt something stir. It was not the leaves above me. Nor the grasses at my feet. Nor even the breeze.

It was the smallest string.

As I watched, my heart drumming against the wooden rim, the remotest tip of one end of the string began to twirl. Slowly, slowly, it lifted, like the head of a worm edging out of an apple. Higher it rose, pulling more of the string with it. The other end also awoke, curling about its knob. Soon the other strings started to move as well, their ends coiling and their lengths tightening.

Tuning itself! The psaltery was tuning itself.

In time the strings fell still. I looked up to see Cairpré's growing smile. At his nod, I prepared to pluck the root chord. Wrapping my left hand more firmly around the rim, I curled the fingers of my right. Delicately, I placed them on the strings.

Instantly, a wave of warmth flowed into my fingertips, up my arm, and through my whole body. A new strength, part magical and part musical, surged through me. The hairs on the back of my hands lifted and swayed in unison, dancing to a rhythm I could not yet hear.

A wind arose, growing stronger by the second, waving the branches of the Cobblers' Rowan. From the forested hills surrounding us, leaves started drifting upward—first by the dozens, then by the hundreds, then by the thousands. Oak and elm, hawthorn and beech, shimmering with the brilliance of rubies, emeralds, and diamonds. Spinning slowly, they floated toward us, like a vast flock of butterflies returning home.

Then came other shapes, swirling around the rowan, dancing along with the leaves. Splinters of light. Fragments of rainbow. Tufts of shadow. Out of the air itself, shreds of mist wove themselves into more shapes—wispy spirals, serpents, knots, and stars. Still more shapes appeared, from where I could not fathom, made not from light or shadow or even clouds, but from something else, something in between.

All these things encircled the tree, drawn by the music, the magic, to come. What, I wondered, would the power of the psaltery bring next? I smiled, knowing that the time to play my instrument had finally arrived.

I plucked the strings.

III

THE DARKEST DAY

At the instant my fingers plucked the chord, I felt a sudden blast of heat—strong enough to scorch my hand. I shouted, jerking back my arm, even as the psaltery's strings burst apart with a shattering twang. The instrument flew out of my grasp, erupting into flames.

All of us watched, dumbfounded, as the psaltery hung suspended in the air above us, fire licking its rim and soundboard. The oaken bridge, like the strings themselves, writhed and twisted as if in agony. At the same time, the shapes swirling around the rowan vanished in a flash—except for the multitude of leaves, which rained down on our heads.

Then, in the very center of the flaming psaltery, a shadowy image started to form. With the others, I gasped. For soon the image hardened into a haggard, scowling face. It was a face of wrath, a face of vengeance.

It was a face that I knew well.

There were the thick jowls, the unruly hair, and the piercing eyes I could not forget. The bulbous nose. The earrings made of dangling shells.

"Urnalda." The name itself seemed to crackle with fire as I spoke it aloud.

"Who?" asked my mother, gaping at the flaming visage.

"Tell us," insisted Cairpré. "Who is it?"

My voice as dry as the fallen leaves at our feet, I repeated the name. "Urnalda. Enchantress—and ruler—of the dwarves." I fingered the gnarled top of my staff, remembering how she had helped me once long ago. I remembered the pain of it. And how she had extracted from me a promise, a promise that I suspected would cause me greater pain by far. "She is an ally, maybe even a friend—but one to be feared."

At that, the blazing rim of my psaltery exploded in sparks, writhing even more. Shards of wood broke loose and sailed into the air, sizzling and sputtering. One ignited a cluster of dry berries on the overhanging branch, which burst into flames before shriveling into a fist of charcoal. Another flaming shard spun toward Rhia, barely missing her leaf-draped shoulder.

Urnalda, her face ringed with fire, scowled down on us. "Merlin," she rasped at last. "It be time."

"Time?" I tried to swallow, but couldn't. "Time for what?"

Tongues of flame shot toward me. "Time for you to honor your promise! Your debt be great to my people, greater than you know. For we helped you even though it be against our laws." She shook her wide head, clinking her earrings of fan-shaped shells. "Now it be our time of need. Evil strikes the land of Urnalda, the land of the dwarves! You must come now." Her voice lowered to a rumble. "And you must come alone."

My mother clasped my arm. "He can't. He won't."

"Silence, woman!" The psaltery twisted so violently that it snapped in two, releasing a fountain of sparks. Yet both halves remained in the air, hovering just above our heads. "The boy knows that I would not call on him unless it be his time. He be the only one who can save my people."

I shook free of my mother's grasp. "The only one? Why?"

Urnalda's scowl deepened. "That I will tell you when you be here at my side. But hurry! Time be short, very short." The enchantress paused, weighing her words. "This much, though, I will tell you. My people be attacked, this very day, as never before."

"By who?"

"By one long forgotten—until now." More flames leaped from the rim. The burning wood cracked and sizzled, almost burying her words. "The dragon Valdearg sleeps no more! His fire be kindled, as well as his wrath. Truly I speak, oh yes! Fincayra's darkest day be upon us."

Even as I shuddered, the flames suddenly vanished. The charred remains of my instrument twirled in the air for another instant, then fell to the grass and leaves in twisted trails of smoke. All of us stepped backward to avoid the shower of coals.

I turned to Cairpré. His face had hardened, like a craggy cliff, yet it showed the shadowed lines of his fear. His wild brows lifted as he repeated Urnalda's final words. *"Fincayra's darkest day be upon us."*

"My son," whispered Elen hoarsely. "You mustn't heed her demand. Stay here, with us, in Druma Wood, where it's safe."

Cairpré's eyes narrowed. "If Valdearg has truly awakened, then none of us is safe." Grimly, he added, "And our troubles are worse than even Urnalda knows."

I stamped my boot on a glowing coal. "What do you mean by that?"

"The poem *The Dragon's Eye*. Haven't I shown you my transcription? Took me more than a decade to tie together the pieces and fill in the gaps—most of them, at least. Rags and ratholes! I planned to show you, but not so soon. Not like this!"

My gaze fell to the remains of my psaltery, nothing more than broken bits of charcoal and blackened strings amidst the leaves strewn over the grass. Near one of the rowan's roots, I spied a fragment of the oaken bridge. It was still connected to part of a string—the smallest one of all.

Bending low, I picked up the string. So stiff, so lifeless. Not at all like the willowy ribbon I had held only moments before. No doubt if I tried to bend it now, it would shatter in my hands.

I raised my head. "Cairpré?"

"Yes, my boy?"

"Tell me about that poem."

He let out a long, whistling breath. "It's full of holes and ambiguities, I'm afraid. But it's all we have. I'm not even sure I can remember more than the last few lines. And you will need to know more, much more, if you are, in fact, going to confront the dragon."

At the edge of my vision, I saw my mother stiffen. "Go on," I insisted.

Doing his best not to look at her, Cairpré cleared his throat. Then, with a jab of his hand, he pointed to the distant, mist-laden hills. "Far, far to the north, beyond even the realm of the dwarves, lie the most remote lands of this island—the Lost Lands. Now they are scorched and reeking of death, but once they blossomed as richly as this very wood. Fruited vines, verdant meadows, ancient trees . . . until Valdearg, last emperor of the dragons, descended. Because the people of the Lost Lands had rashly killed his mate—

and, by most accounts, their only offspring—he set upon those people with the wrath of a thousand tempests. He tortured, plundered, and destroyed, leaving no trace of anything alive. He became, for all time, Wings of Fire."

Cairpré paused, looking up into the branches of the towering rowan. "Finally, Valdearg carried his rage southward, to the rest of Fincayra. It was then that your grandfather, Tuatha, engaged him in battle—driving him back into the wastelands. Although the Battle of Bright Flames lit up the skies for three years and a day, Tuatha finally prevailed, lulling the dragon into enchanted sleep."

I peered at the fragment of the psaltery in my hand. "Sleep that has now ended."

"Yes, which is why I spoke of *The Dragon's Eye*. That poem, you see, tells the story of their battle. And describes how Tuatha relied on a weapon of magic, great magic, to triumph in the end."

"What was it?" asked Rhia.

He hesitated.

"Tell us," she insisted.

The poet spoke softly, yet his words thundered in my ears. "The Galator."

Instinctively, my hand moved to my chest, where the jeweled pendant, possessing powers as mysterious as its strange green radiance, had rested so long ago. Rhia's eyes, I could tell, caught my movement. And I knew that she, too, was recalling the Galator— and its loss to the hag Domnu, that thief of the marshlands.

"The poem," continued Cairpré, "ends with a prophecy." Grimly, he studied my face. "A prophecy whose meaning is far from clear."

He seated himself on a bulging root, his gaze focused on something far distant. After a long moment, he began to recite:

When Valdearg's eye opens,
Too many shall close:
The darkest of days brings
The deepest of woes.
Together with terror
That swells into pain,
Disaster shall follow
His waking again.

By anger unending
And power unmatched,
The dragon avenges
His dreams yet unhatched.
For when he awakens
To find those dreams lost,
Revenge shall he covet
Regardless the cost.

Lo! Nothing can stop him
Except for one foe
Descended from enemies
Fought long ago.
In terrible battle
They fight to the last,
Reliving the furor
And rage of the past.

Yet neither opponent
Shall truly prevail.
The enemies' efforts
All finally fail.
Though striving to vanquish,
They perish instead:
The dragon's eye closes,
His enemy dead.

Then air becomes water
And water is fire;
Both enemies fall to
A power still higher.
Thus only when elements
Suddenly merge
Shall end the dragon,
Shall end the scourge.

But for the rustling of rowan leaves, there was no sound on the knoll. No one stirred, no one spoke. We stood as still as the charred scraps of my musical instrument. And as silent. Finally, Rhia stepped toward me and wrapped her forefinger around my own.

"Merlin," she whispered, "I don't understand what all that means, but I don't like its sound. Its feeling. Are you sure you want to go? Maybe Urnalda will find some way to stop the dragon without you."

I scowled, pulling my hand free. "Of course I don't want to go! But she did help me once, when I truly needed it. And I did promise to help her in return."

"Not to fight a dragon!" exclaimed my mother, her voice frantic.

I faced the woman who had, only moments before, been jubilant enough to sing. "You heard Urnalda. She said I'm the only one who can save her people. Why I'm not sure, but it must have something to do with the prophecy. No one can defeat the dragon except for one person—the one *Descended from enemies Fought long ago.* That means me, don't you see?"

"Why?" she implored. "Why must it be you?"

"Because I am the one descended from Tuatha, the only wizard— out of all those who must have battled him down through the ages—who finally bested him. Who defeated him, at least for a time." I tapped the top of my staff. "And I am the only one, it seems, who might have a chance to do the rest."

Her sapphire eyes dimmed as she turned to Cairpré. "Why didn't Tuatha kill the dragon when he had the chance?"

Slowly, the poet ran both of his hands through his hair. "I don't know. Just as I don't know what the prophecy meant by the dragon's lost dreams. Or by air becoming water and water merging with fire."

With an effort, he tore his gaze from Elen and turned to me. "Yet some of it seems plain. Too plain. It does, I fear, point to you as Valdearg's foe—and as the only one who can stop him from reducing most of Fincayra to ashes. For once he begins, he won't be satisfied just to wipe out the dwarves' realm, or even this forest. He will thirst to destroy everything he can. And so, Merlin, it may well be your part to confront the dragon, just as your grandfather did in the Battle of Bright Flames. But this time the outcome will be different. This time . . . both of you will die."

He swallowed. "Every bard I know understands the importance of this poem. That is why I spent so many years transcribing it, trying to piece it all together. While much remains debatable, no one—no one at all—disagrees on the outcome of the battle. *The dragon's eye closes, His enemy dead*. Whoever vanquishes the dragon will die as well."

Even as she tucked a loose vine back into her sleeve, Rhia examined him closely. "But there's more, isn't there? Something important that the other bards don't agree with you about?"

His cheeks flushed. "You have your mother's way of seeing right through my skin." He indicated the sphere, glowing softly with orange light, hanging from her woven belt. "Perhaps that is why Merlin gave you the Orb of Fire."

Thoughtfully, Rhia stroked the Orb. "The truth is I'm still not sure why he gave it to me." She glanced at me. "Even though I'm grateful. But that doesn't matter now. Tell us the rest."

The wind strengthened, rattling the branches above us as a warrior rattles sword and shield. The leaves rustled at our feet, while more leaves, twigs, and flakes of bark twirled downward. I felt a touch of winter chill in the air, even as my fingers still smarted from the heat of my burning psaltery.

Cairpré brushed a twig off his ear. "I'm not at all sure about this, but I think the key to the prophecy may be that obscure reference near the end: *A power still higher*. Whatever it means, it must be something stronger than the dragon. And stronger than . . ."

"Me. Someone whose magical instrument never played a single note."

"I know, my boy." He studied me anxiously. "Yet, even so, this power may be something you could still master. And if you could, perhaps you could use it somehow to overcome the dragon."

"What is it?" I demanded. "What could be more powerful than a dragon?"

"Rags and ratholes, boy! I wish I knew."

Rhia slapped her thigh. "Maybe it's the Galator! After all, we know it helped before."

I waved the idea away. "Even if you're right, there's no time now to try to get it back. It's all the way on the other side of the island. And Urnalda needs help right now! It's going to take several days, as it is, just to reach her borders. If only my Leaping were strong enough to send me there right away . . . But it's not." I rolled the blackened string between my fingers. "And probably never will be now."

Somberly, I shook my head. "No, let's hope that this higher power means something else besides the Galator. And that I can somehow find it."

Her voice weak, my mother protested once more. "But you don't even have a plan."

"Nothing unusual for him," observed Rhia. "He'll try to make one up as he goes along."

"Then I shall make a plan of my own," Elen replied grimly. "To pray. And to try not to grieve before I must."

Cairpré heaved a sigh. "Are you sure you want to do this, Merlin? No one would blame you if you chose to stay right here with us."

My gaze fell to the brittle string and shard of wood in my hand. All that remained of my psaltery. My failed attempt at higher magic. How could I, with only my staff and sword to help me, even hope to challenge a powerful foe? Let alone Valdearg himself? I lifted the lid of my satchel of healing herbs and precious objects, started to slip the charred remains inside—then caught myself. Why should I keep such a thing? It was useless to me, or anyone else. I let it fall from my grasp onto the ground.

At the same time, my fingertip, already inside the satchel, brushed against something soft. A feather. I smiled sadly, remembering the feisty young hawk who had given me so much, including my own name. Who had never shied away from a battle, even the one that finished his life.

At last my head lifted. "I must go."

IV

A DISTANT CHIME

Cairpré's hand brushed a pair of leaves from my shoulder. "Before you go, my boy, you should take this with you."

He bent to pick up the blackened string from my psaltery that I had discarded. Carefully, he retrieved it from the leaves and grass by my feet. Resting there in his open palm, it looked like the twisted, blackened corpse of a snake—killed in its very infancy.

I pushed his hand away. "Why would I want that?"

"Because you made it, Merlin. Crafted it with your own hands."

"It's worthless," I sneered. "It will only remind me that I failed the test."

His tangled brows climbed higher. "Perhaps. And perhaps not."

"But you saw what happened."

"I did indeed. *With my very own sight: Find the light, find the light!*" He brushed back some graying hair. "And I saw you never had a chance to play. You were interrupted by Urnalda before you—or the strings—could make any music. We don't know what might have happened if you had been allowed to finish."

I glanced at the gnarled roots of the great rowan tree, where I had worked for so many months to make the psaltery. And at the tools, of so many shapes and purposes, that I had finally learned to wield. "But now we'll never find out. You said yourself, I'll never get another chance."

Slowly, he nodded. "To make a magical instrument, yes. But it's just possible, though very unlikely, that your chance to play this one may not yet be over."

"He could be right, you know," said Rhia, stepping through the fallen leaves. "There's always a possibility."

I scowled at her. "You can't make music out of a burned ember!"

"How do you know?" replied Cairpré. "You may have powers you don't yet comprehend."

"Powers I'll never get to use—dragon or no dragon!" Angrily, I snatched the psaltery string from his hand. "Look at this, will you? You know as well as I do that unless a young wizard can make music flow from his instrument, his growth—his chance to become, well, *whatever* he might have become—is ended."

The poet's soulful eyes regarded me for a long moment. "Yes, my boy, that's true. Yet there is much about all this that we—most certainly I—don't understand."

"Remember all the leaves?" asked Rhia. "Even before you started to play, you were attracting things from all over. Not just the leaves, but magical things, too. Even Urnalda! Maybe the psaltery was already starting to show its power."

"That's right," added Cairpré. "And who can tell? Perhaps that power drawing all the leaves, all the magic, was also drawing something else. Something that hasn't yet arrived, that's on its way to you even now."

Skeptically, I studied the contorted string and what was left of the bridge. "I don't believe there is anything left in this. I just don't. But . . . I suppose there's no harm in keeping it for a while."

As I slipped the remains into my satchel, I cast a glance toward my mother, standing in silence by the rowan's trunk. "What I really need is something strong—very strong. To help me against Valdearg."

Cairpré touched my arm. "I understand, my boy. Believe me, I do."

Suddenly, Rhia pointed skyward. "What's that?"

The poet looked up—then hunched, as if struck by an invisible club. Like the rest of us, he gazed at a pair of dark, jagged wings emerging from a cloud. And the blood red mouth baring enormous teeth. Or fangs. As the shape circled high above us, we shrank toward the trunk of the old rowan.

"Not the dragon," prayed my mother, stepping over a massive root. Then, seeing the shape bank sharply to one side, she shook her head. "No, no, look! It's not big enough. It's more like a gigantic bat. What in Dagda's name is it?"

Cairpré made a choking noise. "It can't be! The last of them died ages ago." He rubbed his hand against the rowan's ragged bark. "Stay close to the tree, all of you! Don't move, lest it see us."

"What is it?" I grabbed his arm. "And why do I feel such fear, down inside? For more than our lives."

"Because, Merlin, that thing has come not for our lives, though it could easily take them. It has come . . . for your powers."

Before he could say anything more, a high, piercing shriek echoed across the wooded hills. It jabbed at me, slicing at my chest like a sword of sound. Then, as a wintry gust slapped the rowan, branches flailed, moaning and creaking, while more leaves and berries scattered across the knoll. In that instant, the winged beast wheeled sharply in the air. Downward it plunged, straight at us.

Rhia gasped. "It's seen us!"

"What is it?" I demanded.

Cairpré squinted to see through the waving branches. "A kreelix! Feeds on the powers—the magic—of others."

He tried to place himself in front of Elen, wedging her into a crevasse in the trunk. But she pushed him away. "Forget about me!" she cried. "Protect *him.*"

Cairpré's eyes stayed fixed on the bat-like creature. "Those fangs . . ."

Aghast, I stared at the dark shape descending, drawing closer by the second. Already I could see the three gleaming fangs. And the hooked claws jutting from the leading edges of the wings. I could almost feel them tearing at my flesh, my ribs, my thundering heart.

At least I could draw the beast away from the others! I glanced down at my sword, half buried by leaves at the base of the tree, then suddenly remembered a more powerful weapon. My staff! I tore it free from my belt.

Cairpré seized my arm. "No, Merlin."

I wrenched free. Clutching the staff, I leaped clear of the knot of roots.

The shriek of the kreelix cut through the air, drowning the poet's own shout. At the same instant, its enormous, hook-winged shadow fell across the rowan. The beast skimmed the very top of the tree, shearing off dozens of smaller branches as it passed. Debris showered me.

I brandished my weapon, calling on all the powers embedded in its wood. *Now. I need your help now!*

The kreelix careened, ripping at the air with its wings. Then it plunged toward me, the thick brown fur that covered its head and body flattened from the force of the wind. Its mouth opened even wider, thrusting its fangs outward. I realized that the creature lacked any eyes—that, like me, its ability to see came from some other source.

As the three fangs arched toward me, I stepped back, catching my heel on one of the rowan's roots. Though I struggled to keep my balance, I tumbled over backward. The staff flew from my hand, rolling down the hillside.

I started to push myself to my feet—when my hand struck the leather belt of my scabbard. The sword! I grasped the hilt. As I pulled the blade free, it rang faintly, like a faraway chime.

Scrambling to my feet, I had barely enough time to raise the sword before the kreelix struck. It flew straight at me, its wings and voice screaming as one. Now I could see the veined folds of its ears, the dagger-like edges of its claws, the scarlet tips of its fangs. Its shadow raced over the trees below the knoll, then up the grassy slope.

Planting my boots, I reared back. *Do not fail me, sword!* I braced myself. *You are all that stands between us and death.* I swung.

All at once, a blaze of scarlet light exploded inside my head. At the same time, a powerful force slammed into me. Even as it threw me backward, it seemed to reach deep into my chest. To rip the strength from my body, and the sword from my hands. I spun through the air, unable to breathe. With a thud I landed, then rolled to a stop.

I found myself on my back. On grass. And leaves. Yes, it felt like leaves. But where was this place? A short, labored breath. Air at last! I tried to rise, but could not. The clouds spun above me. And something else, something darker than a shadow.

"Merlin, watch out!"

Though I couldn't tell whether the cry came from within me or without, I forced myself to obey it. Weakly, I rolled to the side. A split second later, something slashed into the ground, barely missing my head. It rang softly, like a distant chime. Like . . . something else, something I could not quite remember.

Straining, I sat up. Blurred, unconnected shapes swam before me. A branch . . . a claw . . . or a blade? The broad trunk of a tree—no, it looked more like . . . I wasn't sure. Hard as I tried, I could not focus. Could not remember. Why was I so dizzy? Where was this place, anyway?

With great effort, I concentrated on the blood red shape that was growing steadily larger before me. It had two, no three, gleaming points in its center. It was round, or almost round. It was hollow, and very deep. It was . . .

A mouth! All of a sudden, my memory flooded back. The kreelix was almost upon me! It stood on the knoll, its back to the rowan tree, its wings spread wide. Its fangs glistened, as did the sword it held in a clawed fist. My own sword!

I made an effort to stand, but fell back to the ground, exhausted. The mouth drew nearer. I tried to wriggle away. My body felt heavier than stone.

There was no strength left in my limbs. Nor in my mind. The cavernous mouth started to blur at the edges. Everything looked red. Blood red.

I heard a crack, like splitting wood. The piercing shriek came again. Then silence—along with total darkness.

V

NEGATUS MYSTERIUM

I awoke to find myself, once again, on the leaves. Something brittle and tasteless clung to my tongue. I spat it out. A twig! Someone—my mother—lifted her head from my chest, where she seemed to have been listening. Tears stained her cheeks, but her sapphire eyes shone with relief.

Lightly, she stroked my brow. "You have awakened, at last." She looked up into the rustling boughs of the rowan tree and closed her eyes in thanks.

At that instant, I glimpsed just behind her a pair of huge, bony wings. The kreelix! I rolled to the side, smacking into her full force. She cried out, tumbling down the slope like an apple dropped from a branch. With a single leap, I landed on my feet. Wobbly though I was, I positioned myself between her and the dreaded beast.

Then I caught myself: The kreelix hung as limp as a discarded scarf, suspended by the branches of the rowan tree. Thick, gnarled boughs wrapped around each of its wings, while several more pinned the furred body against the trunk. Its claws, once so threatening, dangled lifelessly, while its head drooped forward, obscuring the fangs. A deep gash, stained with purple blood, cut across its neck.

"Don't worry." Cairpré's hand closed on my shoulder. "It's quite dead."

My mother puffed up behind us. "So am I, almost."

I whirled around. "I'm so sorry! I thought . . ."

"I know what you thought." She forced a grin, even as she rubbed a tender spot on her shoulder. "And I am glad to know beyond doubt, my son, that your strength has returned."

I turned again to the kreelix, draped against the tree. "How . . . ?" I began. "But . . . it was—how?"

"I do so love someone who can ask a clear question." Rhia emerged from behind the trunk, grinning sassily at me. In her hand she held my sword, gleaming in the scattered sunlight of the knoll. She lifted the scabbard from the ground, thrust in the blade, and handed them to me. "I thought you'd prefer your sword without all that blood. Such a ghastly purple color. Reminds me of a rotten fish."

Seeing the confusion on my face, she glanced at Cairpré and Elen. "I suppose we ought to fill him in. Otherwise he'll be peppering us with unfinished questions all day long."

"Tell me!" I roared. "What in the world happened? To me—and that flying maggot over there."

Cairpré's head wagged. "I tried to warn you. It all happened too fast. A kreelix lives on magic, you see. Eats it. Sucks it right out of its prey, as a bee takes nectar from a flower. Since I, like everyone else, thought the last kreelix died centuries ago, I never bothered to tell you about them before. *Foolish error, Greatest terror.* A better tutor would have taught you that the only way to battle one— as the wizards of old learned the hard way, I'm afraid—is slyly. Indirectly. The worst thing you can do is to confront it head-on, exposing all your magic."

"As I did." Buckling the sword, I shook my head. "I had no idea what hit me. There was this flash of scarlet light . . . Then all my strength, all my life it seemed, was ripped away. Even my second sight felt crippled."

The eyes beneath the bushy brows gazed at me solemnly. "It could have been worse. Far worse."

I tried to swallow, but my throat felt rougher than the rowan's bark. "I could have died, you mean. So why didn't I? Right then?"

His hand reached over and tapped my wrist. At first I noticed nothing. Suddenly I spied the puncture, smooth and round, in the sleeve of my tunic. A thin ring of charcoal surrounded it. Something seemed to have melted—not ripped—right through the cloth.

"The fang," he declared, "struck here. A finger's width to the side and you would have died. Without question. Because even the tiniest contact with the fang of a kreelix will destroy the power, as well as the life, of any magical creature. No matter how strong, or large."

Pensively, he ran a hand through his mane. "That was why the ancient wizards and enchantresses tried so hard to avoid face-to-face battles. Especially with weapons that held their own magic, which simply gave the kreelixes more to dine upon."

"Like my sword here."

"Yes, or like the great sword Deepercut you rescued some time ago. One of the island's oldest legends tells how Deepercut was hidden, buried somewhere, for more than a hundred years—just so no kreelixes could find it." He chewed his lip. "Now you see, my boy, why I didn't want you to wield your staff. For it carries, I suspect, more magic than a dozen Deepercuts."

I glanced toward the magical staff lying among the leaves. "How then did they fight the kreelixes? If they couldn't do it face-to-face?"

"That I don't know. But I can promise you this: I intend to find out." His eyes narrowed. "In case there are any more left."

I blanched. "So how did you stop this one?"

He glanced gratefully at the Cobblers' Rowan. "Thanks to your friend over there. And your talented sister."

All at once, I understood. "Rhia! So you did it! Using tree speech! You spoke to the tree, and it snatched the kreelix from behind."

She gave a nonchalant shrug. "Barely in time, too. Next time you try to get yourself killed, at least give us a little warning."

Despite myself, I grinned. "I'll do my best." Then, as I glanced at the giant, bat-like form hanging limply from the branches, the grin disappeared. "Even a tree as powerful as this one couldn't have held any creature that could fight back with magic. So why didn't the kreelix? Surely, if it lived on others' magic, it must have had some of its own."

"Magic?" Cairpré rubbed his chin thoughtfully. "Not as we normally think of it. But it did possess something. What the ancients called *negatus mysterium*, that strange ability to negate, or swallow up, the magic of others. That was the scarlet flash—*negatus mysterium* being released. If directed at you, it can numb some of your magic, at least temporarily. But it won't kill you. That part is left to the fangs."

He scooped up a handful of leaves, then let them drift back to the ground. "Yet the kreelix's own powers ended there. Leaping, Changing, Binding—all the skills you've been trying to develop—the beast itself couldn't command. So it had no power to strike back once caught by the tree."

I indicated the corpse. "Or to keep you from using my sword to finish it off."

"No," answered Rhia, her face clouded. "Before any of us could try to get the sword, it used the blade on itself."

Cairpré nodded. "Perhaps it feared us so much that it chose to slit its throat before we could. Or perhaps," he added darkly, "it feared we might learn something important if it had lived."

"Like what?"

"Like who has kept it alive, and in hiding, all these years."

I shot him a questioning look. The poet's face, already grave, grew more somber still. He fingered the air, as if turning the pages of a book that only he could see. "In ancient times," he half whispered, "there were people who feared anything magical—from the merest light flyer to the most powerful wizard. They saw all magic as evil. And, too often, wizards and enchantresses would abuse their powers, justifying such fears. These people formed a society—Clan Righteous, they called themselves—that met secretly, plotting to destroy magic wherever they found it. They wore an emblem, concealed most of the time, of a fist crushing a lightning bolt."

He drove his own fist into his palm. "Eventually, they started to breed the kreelixes, beasts as unnatural as their appetites. And to train them, as well—to attack enchanted creatures without warning, to wipe out any magical powers completely. Even if the kreelixes themselves died in the process, their victims would usually also die."

Soulfully, he gazed at me. "Their favorite targets, I'm afraid, were young enchanters like you. The ones whose powers were only just ripening. A kreelix would be assigned to watch each of them, to stay hidden until the very moment those powers began to emerge. It might have been the youth's first Changing, first triumph in battle—or first musical instrument. At that moment, the beast would sweep down from the sky, hoping to prevent the young wizard or enchantress from ever growing up."

Seeing Elen's morose expression, he grimaced. "This, truly, is Fincayra's darkest day."

I cringed, as if the shadow of the kreelix had passed over me again. I knew now that whoever had sent it had done so for one particular purpose. To destroy me. To keep me from using whatever powers I possessed. Or—was such a thing possible?—to keep me from ever facing Valdearg.

VI

TWO HALVES OF TIME

Unable to sleep, I rolled from one side to the other on the bed of pine needles. I tried crooking an arm beneath my head, bunching the tunic under my knees, or staring at the thick web of branches above me. I tried thinking about the evening mist, filtering through stands of trees at sunset; or the starlit sea, sparkling with thousands of eyes upon the waters.

Nothing helped.

Again I rolled over. Eh! A spiky pinecone jabbed the back of my neck. I brushed it aside, nestled my shoulder deeper into the needles, and tried once again to relax. To rest, at least a little. To move beyond the doubts, the wonderings—so vague I couldn't even put them into words—that poked at me like a pinecone of the mind.

I drew a deep breath. The fragrance of pine, sweet and tangy, flowed over me like an invisible blanket. Yet this blanket lacked enough warmth to ward off the chill night air. I shivered, knowing that before long the first snow would fall in this forest.

Another deep breath. Normally the smell of pine calmed me right away. Perhaps it reminded me of the quieter days of my childhood, long before the pieces of my life began to shift like river pebbles under my feet.

In those days I often climbed up to my mother's table of healing herbs. Sometimes I simply watched her sifting and straining, while the wondrous aromas filled my lungs. Other times, though, I mixed my own combinations, meshing whatever colors and textures pleased me. All the while—the smells! Thyme. Beech root. Sea kelp. Peppermint (so strong that one whiff popped open my eyes and tingled my scalp). Lavender. Mustard seed, straight from the meadow. Dill—which always made me sneeze. And, of course, pine. I loved to crush the needles, so that my fingers would smell like a pine bough for hours.

So why, tonight, did they do so little for me? They only pierced my shoulders, my back, and my legs like so many little daggers. Curling myself into a ball, I tried again to relax.

Something nudged the middle of my back. Rhia's foot, no doubt. Maybe she, too, was having trouble sleeping.

The nudge came again. "Rhia," I grumbled, not bothering to roll over. "Isn't it enough you insisted on following me—" I paused, correcting myself before she could. "Guiding me, I mean, when it made things that much worse for our mother? You don't have to come over here and kick me, as well."

Again—this time harder. "All right, all right," I admitted. "I know you promised her you'd turn back at Urnalda's lands. And, yes, I did agree to the idea! But I agreed because you could save me half a day or more. Not because you'd keep me up all night!"

When I felt another nudge, I flipped over and angrily grabbed—

A hedgehog. Hardly bigger than my fist, it curled itself even tighter, burying its face in a mass of bristles. Embarrassed, I grinned. Poor little creature! It was clearly frightened. Probably cold, too.

I hefted the prickly ball. Though I couldn't see its face, I recognized the darker markings of a male. No more than a few months old, most likely. The little fellow could have been lost, separated from his family. Or simply cold enough that he had abandoned any caution for the warmth of my back.

Holding his belly in my palm, I started gently stroking along his spine. While I had learned much in the last year about the language of trees (having moved well beyond the simple swishing of beeches, I could now carry on a rudimentary chat with an elm or even an oak), I still knew practically nothing about the speech of animals. Even so, I managed to produce a piping *yik-a-lik, yik-a-lik,* which I had once heard a mother hedgehog sing to her brood.

Very slowly, while I continued stroking, the ball began to un-curl. First came the leathery pads of the rear feet, each no bigger than my thumbnail. Then came the front feet. Then the belly, swelling like a dark bubble in a peat bog. At last an eye emerged, then the other, blacker than the shadows of night surrounding us. Finally came the nose, sniffing the skin of my thumb. As I stroked more vigorously, he released a tiny, throaty sigh.

Rhia would enjoy this little creature. Even if it meant waking her—and admitting my own folly. I could already hear her bell-like laugh when I told her that I had mistaken him for her foot.

Sitting upright on the bed of needles, I turned my second sight toward the cluster of fern where she had fallen asleep. Suddenly my heart froze. She was gone!

Setting down the hedgehog, I ignored his plaintive whimpers as I clambered to my feet. My second sight stretched to its fullest, peering through the shadowy branches and dark trunks of the grove. Where had she gone? Having trekked with her so often, I was accustomed to her daytime roamings, whether to forage for food, follow a deer's tracks, or plunge into the cool water of a tarn. But she had never before left camp at night. Had something sparked her curiosity? Or . . . brought her harm?

I cupped my hands around my mouth. "Rhia!"

No reply.

"Rhia!"

Nothing. The forest seemed unusually quiet. No branches clacked or groaned; no wings fluttered. Only the continuing whimpers of the hedgehog broke the silence.

Then, from somewhere beyond the ferns, came a familiar voice. "Do you need to be so loud? You'll wake every living thing in the forest."

"Rhia!" I grabbed my staff, sword, and leather satchel. "Where in Dagda's name are you?"

"Out here, of course. Where else did you expect me to watch the stars?"

Buckling the belt of my sword, I hurried through the mass of ferns. As often as I ducked to avoid the pine boughs, a jagged limb would clutch at my tunic. All of a sudden, the trees parted. A chill breeze splashed my face. I stood at the edge of a small, rock-strewn meadow.

To my left, a spring bubbled out of the ground, forming a pool enclosed by reeds. Beside it rested a flat slab of moss-rimmed stone. There, her arms wrapped around her shins and her face turned skyward, sat Rhia.

As I approached, whatever frustration I harbored melted away. She seemed so at peace, so at home. How could I blame her? I leaned my staff against the stone, sat down beside her—and gazed.

Stars, an immense swath of them, arched above us. Like singers in a grand, celestial chorus, they marched across the sky, linked through outstretched arms of light. It reminded me of the phrase, carved into the wall of the great tree that was Rhia's home—as well as my own memory: *The great and glorious Song of the Stars.*

Rhia continued scanning the sky, her curls sparkling with starlight. "So you couldn't sleep? Neither could I."

"You found a better way to spend the night than I did, though. I was just tossing around on pine needles."

"Look there," she cried, pointing to a plummeting star. Brightly it burned for an instant, then swiftly vanished. "I've often wondered," she said wistfully, "whether a star like that one falls somewhere in our world, or in someone else's."

"Or into a river beyond," I offered. "A great, round river that carries the light of all the stars, flowing endlessly into itself."

"Yes," she whispered. "And maybe that river is also the seam binding the two halves of time. You remember that story? One half always beginning, the other half always ending."

Propping my elbows on the stone, I leaned farther back. "How could I forget? You told it to me on the same night you showed me how to find constellations not just in the stars themselves, but in the spaces between them."

"And you told me about that horse—what was his name?"

"Pegasus."

"Pegasus! A winged steed, prancing from star to star. With you hugging his back." She laughed, a bell pealing in the forest. "How I'd love to fly like that myself!"

I grinned. "It reminds me of the thrill—the freedom—of my first time on horseback."

"Really?" For the first time since my arrival, she turned from the glittering vista. "When did you ever ride horseback?"

"Long ago. So long ago! It was a great black stallion, belonging to our . . . father." I didn't say the rest: before Rhita Gawr corrupted him, filling him with the wicked spirit's lust to control Fincayra. Those words still left such a hateful taste in my mouth. "I don't remember much about that horse, except that I loved to ride him—with someone holding me, of course. I was so small . . . but I loved the sound of his hooves beneath me, pounding, pounding. And the warm breath from his nostrils! Every time I visited him at the castle stable, I brought him an apple, just so I could feel his warm breath on my hand."

Softly, she touched my shoulder. "You really loved that horse."

I sighed. "It's all so blurry now. Maybe I was just too young. I can't even remember his name."

"Maybe it will come back to you in a dream. That happens sometimes. Dreams can bring back the past."

My teeth clenched, as I thought about the only dream that brought back the past for me. Over and over and over again. How I hated that dream! It struck at unpredictable times—but always carried me to the same place. Beyond the swirling mists surrounding Fincayra, across the sea, to a ragged village in the land called Gwynedd. There, a powerful boy—Dinatius by name—attacked me. In my rage I called upon my hidden powers and caused a fire, a fire that exploded out of the very air. The blaze! It scorched my face, searing the skin of my cheeks and brow. I lost my own eyes in those flames—while Dinatius, I fear, lost his life.

The dream always ended in the same way: Dinatius, shrieking in mortal agony, his arms crushed beneath the blazing branch of a tree. I always woke up the same way, as well. Sobbing, clutching at my sightless eyes. Feeling the pain of those flames. And what made the dream worse was that it was true.

Even as I shuddered, Rhia twirled one of her fingers around my own. "I'm sorry, Merlin. I didn't mean to upset you. Were you thinking about . . . the dragon?"

"No, no. Just dragons of my own."

She released my finger and ran her hand across the stone's rough surface. "The worst kind."

I swallowed. "The very worst."

"Sometimes those dragons are different from what they seem."

"What do you mean?"

She faced me squarely. "The Galator. You know it could help you defeat Valdearg. Why, it could be your only chance! So why aren't you going after it first? Before you have to face him?"

My cheeks grew hot. "Because there's no time! Why, you heard—"

"Is that all?" she interrupted. "Your only reason?"

"Of course it is!"

"Really?"

"Of course!" I pounded the stone with my fist. "You don't think I'm doing this because I'm scared of . . ."

"Yes?" she asked gently.

"Of Domnu." I stared at her, amazed. How could she have known? Just the thought of that treacherous old hag made me shudder. "Cairpré was right. You really do know how to see under someone else's skin."

"Maybe," she replied. "Sometimes it's easier to see someone else's dragons than your own, that's all. As to this one, I don't know whether you should go right to Urnalda's lands, or not. Time is short, as you said. But I do know that you're scared of Domnu. Very scared. And you need to know it's affecting your thinking. And, more than likely, your sleeping."

I couldn't help but grin. "You're a lot of trouble, you know. But every once in a while . . . you're almost worth it."

"Thanks," she said, returning the grin.

My brow furrowed. "I think, though, I still should go straight to Urnalda. There's my promise to her—and she needs the help now. Remember her words? *My people be attacked, this very day, as never before.*"

"If you do manage to help her somehow, she doesn't seem the kind of person who's going to give you any thanks."

"Oh, she would—in her own way. She's crusty, all right. And easily angered. But you can trust her, at least. Not like Domnu! All Urnalda really wants is to keep her people safe." I reflected for a moment. "Even if I could regain the Galator, I couldn't possibly do it in time to help her. On top of that, I never did find out how it works. So even if I found some way to get it back from Domnu, how much better off would I be?"

I glanced at the sea of stars above us. "There's also this: Maybe Urnalda knows something about the dragon that could help. In the same way the Galator helped win the last battle. She is, after all, an enchantress."

My gaze met Rhia's. "And, finally, there's one more thing." I took a long, slow breath. "I'm scared of Domnu. Just as much as I am of that dragon."

Sparks danced on her head as she nodded sympathetically. "Her name—what does it mean?"

"Dark Fate. That's all anyone needs to know about her! She calls on magic so ancient that even the most powerful spirits—Rhita Gawr, or Dagda himself—just leave her alone. And as much as I'd like to see her humbled, that's exactly what I'm going to do."

Just then my staff slid off the stone. I reached down among the grasses to fetch it—when something pricked the back of my hand. I jumped, startling Rhia so much that both of us nearly tumbled off.

At that instant, I started to laugh. I lowered my hand into the grass. And I picked up the little hedgehog, stroking his bristly back.

VII

STONE CIRCLE

Through most of the following day, we trekked north through Druma Wood. Thanks to Rhia's knowledge of the hidden pathways made by fox paws and deer hooves, we covered much ground. And quickly. Only twice did our speed slacken: in crossing a thick stretch of thorny brambles, as high as our hips in places, that ripped our clothing and raked our shins; and in climbing a buttress of rock whose shadowed face already wore a slick layer of ice.

Most of the time, though, Rhia's relentless pace left me breathless. She charged up hills, leaped across rivulets, and ran effortlessly through glades of oak, beech, and hemlock. Half deer herself she seemed, as I struggled to keep up with her. Whenever she spotted some tangy mushrooms or sweet berries, I felt doubly grateful—since they staved off our hunger and also gave us a chance to pause.

Yet I never complained about our pace. Urnalda's urgent plea still rang in my ears. Time leaned on me, as heavily as a toppled tree. If only I could get there faster! And if only I had a better idea what to do once I arrived.

Early that afternoon, we entered a grove of cedars that skirted the base of a hillside. Suddenly, the wind grew stronger. Branches waved wildly, slapping and scraping. Trunks twisted and moaned.

Rhia halted, listening intently to the cacophony around us, looking grimmer by the minute.

At length, she turned to me. "The trees—I've never heard them so agitated before."

"What are they saying?"

"Turn back! Over and over they keep saying *the boy of the wizard's staff will* . . ." She paused, working her tongue. *"Will die. As surely as a sapling smothered in flames."*

I cringed, touching the still-tender scars on my face. "But I can't turn back. If I don't face Valdearg, then you and everyone else—including every tree in this forest—will have to face him. The Druma will be a graveyard." The spicy scent of cedar pricked my nostrils. "If I must die, though, I only wish . . ."

I paused, listening to the clacking and creaking of the trees. "That I could be certain I will slay him, too."

Rhia's gray-blue eyes narrowed, but she said nothing.

"The question," I said gravely, "is how. I'm not ready to battle a dragon. Let alone slay one! Never will be, probably. Not after what happened . . . back there at the rowan. No, I'm still just *the boy of the wizard's staff*. Not a true wizard."

A branch snapped just above us, splintering as it struck the ground at our feet. Rhia, biting her lip, turned to go. Buried in my thoughts, I followed.

In time, the sound of our boots squelching through muddy soil replaced the wailing of the branches. Puddles filled every path. Trees grew sparser, except for the whitened skeletons of those whose roots had long ago drowned. Water birds whistled in the rising mist, while the first traces of a rotting smell fouled the air.

I turned to Rhia as we walked. "Is this the great swamp at the Druma's northern edge? Or a different one?"

She planted her boot of woven bark against a mound of peat, testing its firmness before plodding across. "It's part of the great swamp. But more than that I can't say. We're much farther east than the stretch I usually cross, since I took the most direct route. I thought it would save some time." Her voice dropped. "I hope I was right."

The mud sucked at my boots. "So do I."

The swamp, I knew, was not the only treacherous land ahead. When we reached the other side, we would find the fog-laden gullies of the living stones. Too often I had heard tales of travelers whose legs, arms, or heads had been suddenly removed from their bodies, crushed in jaws of rock. Nor could I shake the memory of the time when the lips of a living stone had nearly swallowed my own hand.

We began sloshing through a flooded stretch, stepping over decaying trunks and branches. By the time we reached a thick stretch of bog grasses, the sun had vanished behind a sheath of clouds. I looked over my shoulder at the western horizon. Rhia glanced in the same direction, then at me.

"Clouds are gathering, Merlin. There won't be any stars to guide us tonight. If we haven't reached the other side before nightfall, we'll need to rely on your second sight to find our way."

I took a deep breath, though the air reeked of things rotting. "That's not what worries me. It's what lives in this swamp. And what stirs after dark."

Silently, we trekked on, slogging through water up to our knees. In the waning light, strange sounds began to bubble up from the bog. From one side came a thin, unsteady hum; from behind us, a sudden splash—though we whirled around to see nothing. Then a *thwack,* and a screech of pain, as if someone's skull had been split. Soon the darkening mists echoed with distant wailing.

Without warning—something slithered past my shin. I jumped, leaving behind my boot in the process. Whatever it was quickly vanished, but we lost several minutes extracting my boot from the muck.

Sunset came and went without any change in the gloom. As dusk deepened around us, the wild sounds swelled. Suddenly Rhia stumbled, falling into a reeking pool. When she climbed out, I saw a huge leech, as long as my forearm, clinging to the dripping leaves on her back. It squirmed toward her neck. With a swipe of my staff, I knocked it away. The creature hissed shrilly before landing with a splash.

The light faded steadily. I began probing with my staff to help us avoid pits of quicksand—and whatever else lurked in the depths. We slogged on, trying always to head northward. But how could we keep our bearings without sun, moon, or stars? Each stumble, each twist in the route, took its toll. Merely staying together proved more difficult by the minute.

In the deepening darkness, strange shapes, twisting and writhing, rose out of the marsh. At first I tried to convince myself they were nothing but gasses bubbling up from below. Or shadows—a trick of the waning light. But their ghoulish forms didn't move like gasses. Or shadows. They moved . . . like things alive.

The shapes began sighing, almost weeping. Then came sudden cries of anguish—cries that jabbed like icicles in my ears. As fast as we tramped, the shapes pressed closer. A hand, or what seemed to be a hand, grasped at my tunic. I dodged it, nearly tripping in the process.

Just then, in the near blackness, I detected a vague, sloping contour ahead. But for the high mound in its center, it looked as rounded as the back of a great turtle. An island! Though the writhing shapes hampered my vision, the island seemed devoid of life.

"Rhia," I called. "An island!"

She halted. "Are you sure?"

"Looks that way."

She leaped to the side to avoid one of the shapes. "Let's go, then! Before these things—get away, you!—drown us in the muck."

Taking her by the elbow, I rushed forward. The shapes writhed more frantically, swirling about us, but we eluded them. Finally, we reached the edge of the island. While the wailing cries continued, we trudged ashore, leaving the eerie shapes behind.

Total darkness embraced us as we climbed higher. Despite the squelching of slick vines underfoot, the land seemed fairly dry. And solid. With my second sight, I surveyed the area. Only the massive mound, brooding and mysterious, broke the island's smooth surface.

"Nothing lives here," I noted. "Not even a lizard. Why, do you think?"

Rhia stretched her back wearily. "I don't know. I'm just glad those *things* aren't here."

I approached the mound. It was, I realized, a great boulder, about as high as a young oak tree. I froze. "There are no living stones around here, are there?"

"No. They keep to the higher ground, in the hills beyond. Here, in the swamp, we have other creatures to worry about."

Cautiously, I drew nearer to the boulder. I tapped it with my staff. A flake of moss broke off, spinning lazily to the ground. I placed my hand upon the surface, leaning into it until I felt certain of its solidity. Its stoneness.

"Well, all right," I declared. "But it still seems odd—a huge boulder, sitting all by itself in the middle of a swamp like this. As if someone placed it here for some sort of reason."

Rhia squeezed my arm. "If it's all by itself, then at least you can be sure it's not a living stone. They always travel in groups, five or six together." She yawned. "Merlin, I'm about to drop. How about a little rest? Until dawn?"

"I suppose so." I yawned myself. "We're not going back out there until the light returns anyway. Go ahead and rest. I'll take the first watch."

"You'll stay alert?" She waved at the swamp, whose chorus of harrowing sounds continued. "We don't want any visitors."

"Don't worry."

In unison, we collapsed at the base of the boulder. Tired though I was, I propped myself stiffly against the rock, determined to stay awake. A sharp knob pushed into the tender spot between my shoulder blades, but I didn't move. Better to have the security of something solid behind me. No more swamp creatures would surprise us this night.

Rhia, stretched out by my feet, gave my ankle a squeeze. "Thanks for taking the first watch. I'm not used to having someone look after me on a trek."

I grunted wearily. "That's because nobody can keep up with you on a trek." Then I added, "It's our mother, I'm afraid, who needs looking after. She must be so lonely right now."

"Mother?" Rhia rolled to her side. "She's upset, worried sick about us probably—but not lonely. She has Cairpré. He'll stick to her like resin to pine."

"Do you really think so?" My fingers slid down the shaft of my staff. "He always has so much to do. I thought he would get her settled somewhere, then go on his way."

Rhia's laughter joined the noises bubbling out of the swamp. "Haven't you noticed what's been happening to them? Really! You must be as thick as this boulder to have missed it."

"No," I snapped. "I haven't missed anything. You're not telling me they . . . well, have some *interest* in each other, are you?"

"No. They're well beyond that already."

"You think they're falling in love?"

"That's right."

"Come now, Rhia! You're dreaming even before you've fallen asleep. That sort of thing doesn't happen to . . . well . . ."

"Yes?"

"To mothers! At least not to *our* mother."

She giggled. "Sometimes, dear brother, you amaze me. I do believe you've been so wrapped up in your training the past few months that you've missed the whole thing. Besides, falling in love could happen to anyone. Even you."

"Oh, sure," I scoffed. "Next you'll try to convince me that we'll find a tasty meal in a pool of quicksand."

A despairing sigh was her only response. "I'm too tired to convince you of anything right now. In the morning, if you like, I'll enlighten you."

Tempted as I was to reply, I held my tongue. Right now we needed to rest. I adjusted my back against the boulder. Enlighten me, indeed. How could she be so sure of herself?

Even as I grumbled silently about Rhia, I stretched my second sight all the way across the island. Nothing stirred; nothing approached. The night progressed, full of the ongoing cacophony of the swamp. Yet no creatures joined us on this shore. I began to wonder whether the boulder itself might somehow deter visitors, though I could not understand why. Still, in an eerie way, it seemed more than it appeared.

Perhaps it was some quality of the rank air of the marsh, or the result of my own exhaustion. Or perhaps it was some silent magic of the living stone itself. Whatever the cause, it was only when I felt Rhia's hand pulling wildly on my foot that I realized that I had been swallowed by a mouth of stone.

And by then it was too late.

VIII

CIRCLE STONE

First, *silence.*

No wind whispering, no swamp voices echoing, no gasses bubbling. No shrieking, chattering, or hissing. No thumping of my living heart. No whooshing of my very breath.

No sound. No sound at all.

What sound can I remember? Quickly! I must not forget. The stream we crossed this morning? Yes! I heard it long before I saw it. Spraying sound as well as vapor, it pounded down the banks. Ice, touched by the first finger of dawn, crackled and burst. Water spilled and splashed, thrummed and gurgled, singing like a chorus of curlews.

Yet . . . this silence, so complete, so enormous, slowly overwhelms the singing. With each passing moment, the sound of the stream grows more distant. I begin to hear instead the quiet, in all its richness. Soft enough to roll in, deep enough to swim in. No more clanging, no more dissonance. Only silence. Who could desire more than to hear the heartbeat of the void?

I could! I must struggle to remember. I must. Yet all the sounds I would remember feel so separate, so strangely far away.

Second, darkness.

Light is gone. Or never existed? Oh, but it did! I can still call it back, still see its glow. Luminous. Eternal. First light on the clouds, radiant footsteps ascending the sky. A gleam on the horizon, a flame on the candle, a tremble on the star. And another kind of light, bright in the eyes: Rhia laughing, Mother knowing, Cairpré probing.

Still, darkness pulls on me, coaxes me to sleep, to let go. Why fight for the wavering flame? So easily it fails, returns to the dark. So gracefully the night ever follows the day. Darkness is all; all is darkness.

Light! Where are you? I am so lost . . . so frightened . . .

Third, stillness.

As long as I can move, I am alive. As long as I can feel—the wind against my cheeks, the earth under my toes, the petal between my fingers. Yet all I feel now is hardness. Everywhere. Closing in, crushing me. Move, fingers! Move, tongue! They do not respond. They do not exist. Gone are my bones. My blood. My flesh. Squeezed into nothingness.

I cannot move, cannot feel, cannot even breathe. Whatever is left of me is pressed and condensed. I long to snap like a whip, to spin like a leaf. Yet, even more, I long to rest. To be still.

Now I hear only silence. I see only darkness. I feel only stillness. I begin to accept, to understand, to become. I am solid and strong; I have the patience of a star. I am ageless, unyielding.

For now I am stone.

Almost. Something remains of that former self, that former me. I cannot touch it—cannot name it—yet it stays with me still. Down, deep down, in the center of my core. Too small to see; too large to hold. Snarling. Flaming. Twisting. It prods me to remember. To escape if I can! I have a longing. A life. A self. Yes, I can still hear my own voice, even as another, ancient voice swells around me, urging me to let go of all the rest.

Be stone, young man. Be stone and be one with the world.

No! I am too much alive, even now, encircled in rock. I want to change, to move, to do all the things stones cannot.

You know so little, young man! A stone comprehends the true meaning of change. I have dwelled deep within the molten belly of a star, sprung forth aflame, circled the worlds in a comet's tail, cooled and hardened over eons of time. I have been smashed by glaciers, seized by lava, swept across undersea plains—only to rise again to the surface upon a flowing river of land. I have been torn apart, cast aside, uplifted and combined with stones of utterly different origins. Lightning has struck my face, quakes have ripped my feet. Yet still I survive, for I am stone.

And I answer: I want to know you. Nay, more than that, I want to be you! But . . . I cannot forget who I was. Who I am. There are things I must do, living stone!

What is this strange magic that surrounds you, young man? That makes you resist me? You should have succumbed to my strength long ago.

I know not. I only know that my own self clings to me still, even as clusters of moss cling to you.

Come. Join me. Be stone!

I yearn even now to join you. To feel your depth; to know your strength. And yet . . . I cannot.

Ah, the stories I could tell you, young man! If only you would release yourself completely, allow yourself to harden. Then I could share with you all that I know. For a stone, while separate, is never far from the mountains and plains and seas of its birth. A stone's power springs not from itself alone, but from all that surrounds, all that connects.

I want to learn from you, living stone. Truly, I do. Yet I want still more to live the life I was born to live. Though it may be futile, and fleeting—it is nonetheless mine. You must set me free!

You are a strange one, young man. Although I have very nearly destroyed you, I cannot seem to consume you. There is something in you I cannot reach, cannot crush. That leaves, I am saddened to say, but one possibility.

What is that?

It is not the best for you, nor the best for me. Yet it is, alas, my only choice.

IX

SMOKE

With a thud, I landed on my back on the ground at the base of the living stone. Although Rhia's sudden shriek would normally have chilled my blood, I was glad to hear it. I was glad to hear anything at all.

"Merlin!" She threw her arms around me and squeezed.

"Not so hard, will you?" I wriggled free, patting my sore chest. It ached, as did my arms, legs, and back. Even my ears. In fact, I felt as if one gigantic bruise covered my whole body. Then, seeing Rhia's tear-stained face, so relieved, so thankful, I beckoned her to embrace me again.

She gladly accepted the invitation—more gently this time. "How?" she blurted. "How did you do it? I've never heard of a living stone releasing anyone it's caught."

Despite my sore cheeks, I grinned. "Most people don't taste as bad as I do."

She released me, her laughter echoing across the swamp. Then, for a long moment, she observed me. "There must be something in you that even a living stone couldn't crush."

"My thick head, perhaps."

"More likely, your magic."

Although my ribs throbbed, I drew a deep breath. "As little as there is, I suppose you could say it's my core. Essential—and undigestable."

With her leafy forearm, she brushed some chips of stone off my shoulder. "Well now, look at you! Your tunic is ripped, and there's so much dust in your hair that it's more gray than black." She smiled. "But you're alive."

"How long was I in there?"

"Two or three hours, I'd guess. The sun came up just before you returned."

Warily, I gazed up at the enormous boulder that had ejected me. I stepped slowly toward it, my heart pounding. Rhia tried to hold me back, but I waved her away. Placing a tentative hand on a flat, mossy spot, I whispered, "Thank you, great stone. One day, when I am stronger, I should like to hear more of your stories."

Though I could not be sure, I felt the rock beneath my fingers shiver ever so slightly. Removing my hand, I bent to retrieve my staff, still lying on the ground. The shadow of the living stone did not diminish the wood's lustrous sheen. I grasped the gnarled top—which, as always, fit my hand perfectly. For a few seconds, the scent of hemlock pushed aside the reeking smells of the swamp.

Rhia gasped. "Your sword! It's gone."

I started. Indeed, my sword, scabbard, and belt had vanished. They must have remained inside the living stone!

Whirling around, I pleaded, "My sword, great stone! I need it! For Valdearg."

The stone did not stir.

"Please . . . oh, please, hear me! That sword is part of me now. And it has magic of its own. Yes! I've been entrusted to bear it—

until the day, far in the future, when I shall give it to a boy. A boy born to be king. A boy of great power. So great that he will pull that very sword from a scabbard of stone."

The boulder remained motionless.

"It's true! The sword will be held—not by you, not by a living stone, but by a stone that will guard it, awaiting that very moment."

No response.

My nostrils flared. "Give it back."

Still, no response.

"Give it back!" I demanded. Grasping the shaft of my staff, I raised it to strike the living stone. Then, noticing my thumb on top of the carved image of a sword—symbol of the power of Naming—I halted. The name! The sword's name! Which, like all true names, held a magic of its own. Perhaps, just perhaps . . . I leaned toward the stone.

Abruptly, I caught myself. I had not used any magic since—since plucking my psaltery. If I called on my powers again, would another kreelix attack? And succeed where the other one had not? I cringed, remembering the gaping red mouth, the jagged wings, the ruinous fangs. Yet . . . if I let the elemental fear of another attack rule my actions, then what was I? A coward. Or worse. Whether or not another kreelix appeared, it would have already robbed me of my powers.

I gritted my teeth and bent closer to the stone. Mist, rank with decay, blew off the marsh, shrouding us completely. The swamp's eerie gasping, hooting, and wailing pressed closer. I could hardly hear my own thoughts for the noise.

Concentrating, I cupped my hands over my mouth. So that no one, not even Rhia, might hear the sword's true name, I spoke it softly. Then, with my full voice, I added: "Come to me, from the depths of stone. Wherever you are, I summon you."

Glancing nervously over my shoulder, I saw nothing but the curling trails of mist. Suddenly I heard a rumbling, growing louder by the second. It swelled steadily, like an approaching wind, until it obscured even the sounds of the swamp.

The living stone suddenly wrenched. Chips of rock broke loose, along with flakes of yellowish moss. Small cracks appeared all over its weathered surface. The whole stone rocked from side to side, as if struck by a violent tremor. An instant later, the surface split open, pursed, then spat out my sword and scabbard. They thudded on the ground.

I lunged for the prize, even as the living stone rolled to cover it. Rhia shouted, leaping aside. Together we ran across the island. As we reached the shore, vines squelched and popped under our boots. The mist grew thinner, shredding rapidly, revealing again the swamp.

Before plunging into the mire once more, I quickly strapped on the sword's leather belt. Then I gazed back at the living stone, rocking sullenly on the ground, and called to it. "Do not be angry, great stone! This sword would be difficult for you to digest. No less than its master! Someday, perhaps, you and I shall meet again."

With a deep rumble, the boulder started rolling toward us. Not wanting to wait to learn more about its mood, Rhia and I splashed into the putrid waters of the swamp. Yet as the ooze seeped into my boots, splattered my legs, and assaulted my nose, I felt somehow grateful even as I felt repulsed. Grateful to smell and hear again. And grateful to move freely—my legs pushing through bog grasses, my arms swinging by my side.

For most of that morning, we slogged northward through the marsh. Except for the pool of quicksand that tried to tear my staff from my hand, we had no great difficulties. Still, our hearts leaped when we reached drier ground at last. Eagerly, we shook the mud off our boots. An old apple tree, springing from the side of a low hill, offered us the remains of its autumn harvest. Withered and small as they were, the apples burst with flavor. We ate all we could hold. Nearby, Rhia found a clear, cold stream where we washed away the lingering odor of the swamp.

Continuing north, we trekked rapidly toward the realm of the dwarves. The land rose gradually in a series of grassy plains, lifting like stairs to the high plateau where the River Unceasing bubbled out of the ground. There, I knew well, we would enter the dwarves' terrain. Valdearg's terrain. If only I could find Urnalda before the wrathful dragon found me! Maybe I really could help her somehow. And maybe . . . she could also help me.

In midafternoon, we paused to feast on some shaggy gray mushrooms sprouting among the roots of a leaning elm. And to take advantage, for a moment at least, of the chance to sit down. Wiping the perspiration off my brow, I stretched my legs and surveyed the grassy plains surrounding us. While the River Unceasing flowed well to the east, my second sight could still make out the twisting corridor of mist that marked its channel.

I knew well the river's path: After gathering in these plains, it grew steadily wider and stronger, surging straight through the heart of Fincayra. Along most of that way, steep banks and pounding rapids made crossings difficult. In fact, between the headwaters and the Shore of the Speaking Shells far to the south, I had found only one reliable place to cross—a shallow stretch marked by nine rounded boulders. We couldn't be far from that spot now. For some inexplicable reason, I felt a gnawing urge to go there again.

After tossing another mushroom to Rhia (which she popped right into her mouth), I pointed toward the mist. "What about crossing the river over there? At the place with the boulders."

Still chewing, she shook her head. "I've had enough of boulders for one day! Besides, the shortest route is to keep going due north, up the plateaus, until we meet the headwaters. Crossing there won't be difficult, especially at this time of year when the waters are low."

Though I knew she was right, I continued to stare at the snaking mist. "I don't know why, but I feel drawn to that crossing."

"Whatever for?" She eyed me skeptically. "That would cost us half a day. As it is, the light will only last another couple of hours." She sprang to her feet. "Let's go."

"You're right. Haste is everything." With a final glance at the misty corridor, I followed her through the tall grasses.

A large flock of geese passed overhead, so close we could hear the rhythmic creaking of their wings. Like all the other birds we had seen that day, they were traveling in the opposite direction from us. After them came what looked at first like a spinning knot of dust—until we heard the buzzing and realized it was, in truth, an immense swarm of bees. Following close behind came a wide-winged heron, a pair of tattered gulls, a sandpiper, several swallows, and an elderly raven, flapping arduously. Then, hidden by the grass, a family of foxes nearly charged straight into us. Seeing their wide eyes glowing with terror, Rhia shot me a worried glance. Though we continued to ascend the terraced meadows, her pace slackened a little.

As late afternoon light brushed the grasses with gold, we reached the lip of another plateau. Both of us halted, struck by the same sight. The sky ahead of us loomed unusually dark. A heavy veil draped over the horizon . . . yet it seemed thinner, flatter than any thundercloud. Could it be a shadow caused by the lowering sun? At that moment, a gust of wind fluttered my tunic. I caught the first whiff of a scent that smote me like a broadsword.

Smoke.

I released a groan. The sky ahead had been darkened not by clouds, nor by shadows, but by Valdearg.

Rhia turned to me. Her face, usually so bright, looked utterly grim. "Until now, Merlin, I've been able to push aside my doubts. Because I thought it was right to help you. But now . . . I'm not so sure. Look there! The land burns, like Valdearg's angry heart. It seems so—well, *foolhardy* to walk right into his mouth like this."

"Have faith," I countered bravely. But my croaking voice betrayed how little faith I had myself. I shook my head. "Foolhardy it is, I admit. What else can I do, though? The longer I wait to confront Valdearg, the more he's sure to destroy. My only hope is to reach Urnalda soon. Perhaps she knows something useful. She might even know what the prophecy meant by *a power still higher.*"

Rhia set her clenched fists upon her hips. "All I remember about that prophecy is that, even if you do somehow slay this dragon, you're going to die with him! So either he kills you and survives, or kills you and dies himself. Either way, I lose a brother."

With my staff, I jabbed at a mound of grass. "Don't you think I know that already? Look. Here we are, at the very edge of the dwarves' realm, and what weapons can I really count on? My staff, my sword—and whatever magical powers, still unformed and untrained, that I carry inside me. Put together, they don't amount to a single scale on Valdearg's tail."

I scanned the smoky horizon. "And that's not the worst of it."

She cocked her head. "Meaning?"

"Meaning I just can't rid myself of the idea that Valdearg isn't all I need to worry about."

Incredulous, she stared at me. "Wings of Fire himself isn't enough? What are you talking about—the kreelix? Or whoever might have secretly raised it?"

"No. Though they might also be part of this, for all I know."

"Who, then?"

My voice lowered. "Someone who longs to take Fincayra in his hand. To squeeze it like a gemstone. To make it his own."

For an instant, Rhia's face went as white as birch bark. "Not . . . Rhita Gawr? What makes you think he's involved?"

"I, well . . . I'm not really sure. It's vague. But I wonder why the dragon woke up now, after sleeping for so many years. And who might know enough about magic—or *negatus mysterium*—to have caused such a thing. I don't know whether it's Rhita Gawr or someone else . . . or if I'm just imagining things. Yet I can't help wondering."

She scowled at me. "You're hopeless, really! Listen, Merlin. Rhita Gawr has not set foot on this island since the Dance of the Giants routed him and his forces over a year ago! You'd be better off worrying about the enemies you know—rather than creating any more for yourself."

I twisted my staff into the turf. "All right, all right. You speak wisely, I'm sure. It's just that . . . well, forget it. Here, what do you say we stop talking about enemies—of all kinds—for just a moment. Let's dine on some of these astral flowers."

"Before Valdearg dines on you?"

Ignoring her comment, I picked a fistful of the yellow, star-shaped flowers speckling the grass. As she looked on glumly, I rolled them into a compact mass that produced a sharp, tangy aroma. "I remember when you first showed me how to eat these. You called them *a trekker's sustenance.*"

"Now I'll call them my brother's last meal."

Tearing the mass in half, I handed one part to her. "None of us will eat many more meals unless Valdearg is stopped."

She nodded, her curls ignited by the golden light. "True." She took a bite of the astral flowers, chewed thoughtfully, and swallowed. "That's why I'm coming with you."

"You are not!"

"You will need help." Her eyes bored into me. "I don't care if Urnalda wants you to come alone! I've saved your skin before."

I fingered my staff. "That you have. This time, though, we're talking about Wings of Fire. He could wipe out every single life we know." Wrapping my forefinger around hers, I added gently, "Including our mother's. She is the one who needs you most, Rhia. She is the one you must protect. Not me."

Her head bowed.

"Remember, you promised her that you would come back. That you would take me no farther than the dwarves' borderlands."

Rhia lifted her head slowly. "At least . . . let me give you something." She reached for the Orb of Fire at her side.

"Not the Orb. That's yours to keep."

"But I don't know how to use it!"

I squeezed her finger. "You will, someday."

Releasing me, she deftly unwove a bit of vine from her sleeve. Then, without a word, she tied the bracelet of vibrant green around my wrist.

"There," she said at last. "This will remind you of all the life around you, and the life within yourself." She studied me sternly, though I could see the clouds in her eyes. "What it won't do is help you stay out of trouble."

Now it was my turn to bow my head. "Nothing can do that, I'm afraid."

Numb as I was, I could still feel her leafy arms wrap around me. Then I strode off without her, my future as dark as the veil of smoke on the horizon.

PART TWO

X

HUNTER AND HUNTED

Within the hour, shafts of glowing crimson streaked the sky, like the strings of a celestial psaltery. I soon reached a winding stream, flowing red in the waning light: the headwaters of the River Unceasing. Crossing the narrow channel, a mere trickle of water compared to the torrent it would become in the spring snowmelt, proved easy. Just as Rhia had predicted.

As my boots ground against the rounded stones in the channel, I wondered if her other, more fearful predictions would also prove true. And whether I would ever see her again. Like the nameless horse from my childhood we had talked about under the stars, Rhia was more than a companion, more than a friend. She was part of me.

Stepping onto the northern bank, I surveyed the lands of the dwarves. Somewhere out there, in those rolling, rocky plains, lay the hidden entrances to their underground realm. While Urnalda would, I knew, be grateful for my help, I doubted that she guessed how much I would also need hers. It still puzzled me why she had declared that I, and I alone, could help her people. Perhaps she, too, knew the prophecy of *The Dragon's Eye:*

> *Lo! Nothing can stop him*
> *Except for one foe*
> *Descended from enemies*
> *Fought long ago.*

I shuddered, for while I did indeed carry Tuatha's blood in my veins, I did not possess either his wisdom or his weaponry. And I shuddered again to think of the unmatched power of Valdearg. *Disaster shall follow His waking again.* Slaying the dragon, in itself, would be difficult enough. Evading the prophecy, and somehow surviving the battle, would be—I felt sure—impossible.

Squeezing the shaft of my staff, I debated how best to find Urnalda. Or, more likely, to help her find me. If I made myself too visible, Valdearg might well spot me first. If, on the other hand, I hid too well, I might waste valuable time. Keep to the open, I decided at last. And stay ever alert.

Soon the stench of smoke grew stronger. My eyes began to water. I entered a stretch of plain that looked more like an abandoned fire pit than a field. The base of my staff no longer swished through tall grasses, but rather crunched against brittle stems and parched soil. Scorched brambles clawed at the smoky air. Boulders, scattered over the plain, resembled lumps of charcoal. And always the smell!

With my second sight, I frequently scanned the darkening sky for any sign of the dragon. As large as he would be, giving me the chance to spot him at a distance, I expected he would also be fast. Terrifyingly fast. And even while watching for him, I also watched the shadowy terrain at my feet, for I preferred not to tumble into one of the dwarves' cleverly disguised tunnels. Every indentation, no matter how slight; every unusual shadow, no matter how small—all these I checked carefully.

Just then a gruff voice barked a command. It came from just behind a mass of brambly gorse to my left. Cautiously, I crept closer.

Crouching behind the charred thorns, I spotted a pair of dwarves, their leather leggings and red beards catching the last rays of light. Although they stood not much taller than my waist, their stout chests and burly arms gave warning of their surprising strength. Heavily armed, each of them bore a double-sided axe, a long dagger, and a quiver of arrows. They had just drawn their bows, in fact, and were hurriedly nocking their arrows.

I turned to see a pair of deer, a doe and a stag, cowering at the back of a steep gully rimmed by blackened boulders. No doubt the dwarves had driven them into this trap, hoping to fell one or both of them before they could escape. The doe, tensing her powerful thighs, tried to leap up the side of the gully, but slid back down with a clatter of rocks and a cloud of ash. The stag, meanwhile, lowered his massive rack and prepared to charge straight at the hunters. The points of his antlers gleamed dangerously, yet I knew they would prove worthless against speeding arrows.

The peril of the deer made my stomach clench. Myself, I never ate venison—ever since the day long ago when Dagda himself, disguised as a stag, had rescued me from certain death. Yet I had never deigned to interfere with anyone else's enjoyment of deer meat. Still . . . I had never before stumbled upon one of the graceful creatures' execution.

At the instant the arrows nocked into the bowstrings, the doe suddenly turned in my direction. Whether she saw me or not through the brambles, I could not tell. Yet the sight of her wide, intelligent, brown eyes—stricken with terror—hit home.

"Stop!" I shouted, leaping into the air.

Startled, the dwarves jumped. Both of their arrows went wide, skidding off the rock-flaked walls of the gully. At the same instant, the doe and the stag bolted across the turf before the dwarves could reach for their quivers again. In a single, magnificent leap, their forelegs tucked tight against their chests, the deer sailed over their attackers' heads and bounded out of range.

"What fool are you?" demanded one of the dwarves, pointing his reloaded bow straight at my chest.

"I come in peace." Emerging from the tangle of gorse, I lifted my staff into the smoky air. "I am Merlin, called to join you by Urnalda herself."

"Pshaw!" The dwarf scowled at me. "Did she also command you to ruin our hunt?"

I hesitated. "No. But I couldn't do otherwise."

"Couldn't *what?*" The other dwarf stomped angrily, threw his bow to the ground, and pulled out his axe. "You miserable, long-legged oaf! Methinks we should bring back man meat instead of deer."

"A fine idea," snapped the first. "These days meat of any kind is hard to come by. You won't taste nearly as good as venison—the first we've found in many days, mind you—but you'll do. Did Urnalda never tell you that your race is forbidden to enter these lands?"

"Go ahead," urged his companion. "Shoot him now. Before he tries one of his man tricks on us."

"Wait," I protested, my mind racing to find some way to escape.

"You say these lands are forbidden, yet I have been here before." Although my knees were wobbling, I stood my tallest on the charred soil. "And I have come back to help your people, even as you helped me."

"Pshaw!" He drew back his bow. The arrow point glinted darkly. "Now I know you're a liar as well as a thief. Our laws tell us to kill human trespassers, not help them! Not even Urnalda, whose memory is as short as her plump little legs, would forget that."

"Be that so?" demanded a sharp voice from the shadows.

Like myself, both dwarves whirled to face a squat figure standing beside one of the boulders. Urnalda. She wore a hooded cloak over her black robe that glittered with an embroidery of runes. Her ragged red hair, surging out of the hood, held many jeweled clasps, ornaments, and pins. She wore earrings of conch shells, each almost as large as her bulbous nose. One of her thickset hands curled around her staff, while the other hand pointed at the dwarf holding the bow. Her eyes, as bright as the flames that had consumed my own psaltery, burned with rage.

"Urnal-nalda," fumbled the first dwarf, lowering his bow. "I didn't mean to insult you."

"No?" The enchantress eyed him for a long moment. "An insult be an insult even if the person it maligns be out of hearing."

"B-b-but you are mis-mistaken."

"Be I?" Urnalda stepped fully out of the shadows. "Far worse than your insult to me, huntsman, be your threat to our friend here." She nodded toward me, swaying her shell earrings. "You be about to skewer him before I arrived."

My own chest relaxed, even as the dwarf panted in fright. Nervously, he pawed his beard. "But he—"

"Silence! He may be a man, but he still be a friend. Oh, yes! A valued friend. And more than that, he be our only hope." She glared at him. "You seem to be forgetful of my command to keep him safe after he came to our realm. Be that so?"

"Y-yes, Urnalda. I forgot."

A flash of light burst from Urnalda's hand. At the same instant the dwarf yelped in surprise. He stood in his same leggings, though they fell like loose sacks around his boots. I thought his pants had fallen—then realized the truth.

"My legs!" he wailed. "You shortened them!" He tried standing on his toes, though he still only reached his companion's elbow. "They're only half as long as they were."

"Yes," agreed the enchantress. "So now your memory be no longer than your legs."

He dropped to his knees, now only a little higher than the tops of his boots. "Please, Urnalda. Please give me back my old legs."

"Not until you give Urnalda back her faith in your loyalty." Her eyes flicked toward the other dwarf, who stood shivering. "I would do the same to you, but I be short of huntsmen just now."

Slowly, Urnalda turned to me. Her face, though still wrathful, seemed a touch softer. "I be sorry your return be so unpleasant."

I bowed respectfully. Then, with a grateful sigh, I leaned against my staff. "I am glad you arrived when you did. Very glad."

The conch shells swayed as Urnalda bowed her head slightly. "Your timing be just as good as my own, Merlin. You see, this be the night that Valdearg will come back here."

Stiffening, I glanced at the sky, darkened both by twilight and the hovering streaks of smoke. Gradually, my puzzlement overcame my fear, and I asked, "You know he will come back tonight?"

"That be true."

"How can you be sure?"

Her cheeks pinched. "Because, my young friend, I made a pact with him. Oh yes! A dragon be a most intelligent beast, aware of what he really wants. And in this case, I be sorry to say, what the dragon really wants . . . be you."

XI

THE PACT

Before I could begin to move, Urnalda waved her hand. A flash of scarlet seared my mind. I flew backward from the impact, landing with a thud on the charred turf. For an instant I felt my heart had been ripped away, and my lungs crushed completely. The pain in my chest! The shadowy sky, tinged with scarlet, careened above me.

Haltingly, I took a breath of smoky air. My throat stung. I forced myself to sit up. There—the swirling face of the enchantress, smirking confidently. So dizzy . . . Not far away, my unsheathed sword lay on the ground. Much farther away, my staff. I could barely keep the images distinct; everything blurred together. Hadn't I felt this way before? Recently? I vaguely recalled . . . but when? I couldn't quite remember.

My sword, I told myself. *If I can just get it back, I can protect myself.*

Stretching out a trembling hand, I tried my hardest to halt the spinning, to concentrate my thoughts. *Come to me, sword. Leap to me.*

Nothing happened.

Although I could hear Urnalda sniggering in the background, I did not let my thoughts veer from the sword. *Leap to me, I say. Leap!*

Still nothing.

Once again I tried. Gathering all of my power, I poured every drop of it into the sword. *Leap!*

Still nothing.

"Sorry to say, Merlin, you be a little lighter now." Grinning broadly, the enchantress stepped over to the sword and snatched it. "I be taking something that once be yours."

"My sword." I tried to rise, but fell back weakly. "Give it back to me!"

Urnalda's eyes flamed. "No, it not be your sword I mean." Bending toward me, she spoke in a chilling whisper. "I be taking not your sword, but your powers."

Suddenly I remembered when I had felt this way before. With the kreelix! My stomach twisted in knots; my mind whirled. Gasping for breath, I forced myself to stand. Though I felt as wobbly as a newborn colt, I faced her.

"Urnalda. You can't! I am your friend, aren't I? You said so yourself! How can you do this?"

"Easily," she answered. "A bit of *negatus mysterium* be all it takes."

My legs buckled, and I fell back to the sooty ground. "Why, though? I could help you! I'm the only one who can defeat Valdearg. That's the prophecy of *The Dragon's Eye.*"

"Bah!" scoffed the enchantress. "Such prophecies be worthless. What matters be my pact with Valdearg himself." Her stubby fingers played with one of her earrings as she studied me darkly. "You see, the dragon awoke from his spell of sleep because someone destroyed the most precious part of his waking life, the one thing he treasured over everything else."

I shook my spinning head. "What was that?"

"I think you be pretending, Merlin. I think you already know."

"I don't! Believe me."

"All right, then. I shall humor you. Valdearg awoke because someone—someone most clever—found the secret hiding place of his eggs. His only offspring! Then that bloodthirsty someone killed his young ones. Every last one of them. That be a most dangerous thing to do."

Angrily, she slashed at the air with my sword. "Since the dragon eggs be hidden near the land of the dwarves, Valdearg blamed this deed on my people. The innocent, upright people of Urnalda! So he flies down here, burns my lands, pounds the ground with his tail to make my tunnels collapse, roasts alive dozens of my huntsmen." Her slashing grew more violent. "Ruin! Devastation! Until finally—yes, finally—I convinced him that the killer be not a dwarf after all."

I started to speak, but her torrent of words overwhelmed me.

"Urnalda, so clever, so wise, examined what be left of the eggs most carefully. And I found proof that the killer be not a dwarf, but a man. A poison-hearted man! It be no easy task to convince Valdearg himself to look close enough to see the proof, since even flying high above the remains fills him with rage. Uncontrollable rage." She jabbed at the air with a vengeance. "Even so, I persisted—and finally succeeded. When Valdearg realized the killer be a man, he decided that only his old foe Tuatha—or a descendant if Tuatha no longer be alive—would be capable of doing such a terrible thing."

My cheeks burned. "Where did he get such an idea?"

"That be simple." Her taut lips scowled at me. "It be true."

"But it's not!" I started to stand, but she slashed at me with the blade until I sat down again.

"So I, Urnalda, made a pact with Wings of Fire. Indeed I did! We agreed that if I could deliver you to him, he would leave my people in peace. Forever. But dragons be not patient. He refused to wait very long."

She stabbed at the ashen earth. "We agreed to meet tonight. If I did not yet have you as my prisoner, he promised me just one more week—seven days, no more. If, on the night of the seventh day, I could not produce you—then he vowed to annihilate every last one of my people. And anyone else in his path until he found you."

"But I never killed his young! How could I? For months, I haven't done anything but work on my instrument."

"Bah! You could be slipping away quite easily, with no one ever knowing."

"It's not true."

She looked at me skeptically, her eyes glowing like a dragon's flame. "In many ways, it be a bold and visionary act. Rid this land of dragons! Destroy their despicable race altogether!" She twisted the sword into the ground beside me. "Yet you should be knowing that it bring harm to the dwarves. The people of Urnalda."

"I didn't do it, I tell you!"

Raising the weapon, she swung it over my head, barely missing me. "It be in your blood to kill! Do you deny it? You relish the feeling of power, of strength. You know my words be true, Merlin! Look what Tuatha's only son—your father, Stangmar—did to the dwarves and the rest of Fincayra! He poisoned our lands. He murdered our children. How can you tell me that you, his own son, be any different?"

"But I am!" I pushed myself into a crouch. My second sight, no longer spinning, focused on Urnalda's flashing eyes. "I am the one who finally defeated him! Haven't you heard that? Ask Dagda himself if you doubt me."

The enchantress grunted. "That means nothing. Only that you be still more ruthless than your father." She pricked the edge of my sword with her fingernail. "Answer me truly. Do you deny that you would be glad to see Fincayra rid of dragons forever?"

"N-no," I admitted. "I can't deny that. But—"

"Then how can I believe you be not the killer?" She thrust the sword at my neck, holding the tip just a finger's width away. Her lips curled in a snarling grin. "Now, however, you must understand. Whether or not you really did it be unimportant. Yes, irrelevant."

"Irrelevant?" I slammed my fist on the charred soil, sending up a cloud of ash. "It's my life you're talking about."

"And the life of my people, which be much more important." She nodded, clinking the conch shells dangling from her ears. "What counts be that the dragon *believes* that you be the man who killed his young. Whether or not you really be him—that be meaningless. All he needs be a few bites of man flesh to ease his appetite for revenge." She leaned closer, pressing her bulbous nose against mine. "You be the man."

In desperation, I started crawling toward my staff. Urnalda, though, moved too quickly. Waving her hand in the direction of the staff, she caused it to rise off the ground and twirl in the smoky air. The two dwarves looking on gasped in amazement.

"Now," she snapped, "do you doubt that I stripped you of your powers? Do you think to use your wizard's staff against me?" Before I could answer, she spat out a strange incantation. With a sizzling flash of scarlet light, my staff completely disappeared.

My chest ached with emptiness. *My powers. Gone! My staff, my precious staff. Gone!*

Urnalda examined me severely. "Undeserving as you be, I still be merciful. Oh yes! I be leaving you with your second sight so that you will give the dragon the satisfaction of believing you can defend yourself—at least for a minute or two. That way, after he slays you, he be more likely to keep his bargain. For the same reason, I give this back to you."

She hurled my sword high into the air, at the same time barking a command. It fell back toward me, before suddenly swerving in midair and sliding straight into the scabbard at my waist. "Be warned, though," she growled. "If you be thinking about trying that blade against me, I be using it to cut your legs as short as my huntsman's over there."

The recently shortened dwarf, clasping his baggy leggings, released a whimper.

Urnalda drew in her breath. "Now be the time. Up, I command you!" She pointed with her staff toward a rocky, pyramid-shaped rise across the plateau. "March to that hill. The dragon be arriving there soon."

Weakly, I struggled to my feet. My mind reeled, even as my body ached. I had feared—even expected—that I would lose my life in the end to Valdearg. But not like this. No, not at all like this.

And although some of my strength had returned, I felt more than ever that emptiness in the middle of my chest. As if my very center had been torn away. My future as a mage was already clouded—bad enough. But now whatever powers I possessed, those gifts of magic I barely even understood, had vanished. And with them, something more. Something very close to my soul.

XII

To Circle a Story

Just then one of the huntsmen cried out. All of us turned to see a large doe bounding across the darkened plateau. With grace and speed, she sprinted over the rolling plain like a flying shadow. I could not tell whether it was the same wide-eyed doe from the gully. I could only hope that her legs would soon carry her far away from this land of ruthless hunters—and traitorous allies.

"*Mmmm,* venison." Urnalda clacked her tongue. "Quick! Before it be gone."

Before she had finished her sentence, the arrows were already nocked. Both dwarves, brawny arms bulging, drew back their bows. This time, I felt sure, at least one of their arrows would find its mark. And this time I could do nothing to prevent it.

An instant before they let fly, the doe leaped high into the smoke-streaked air. For a heartbeat she hung there, floating, the perfect target.

"Shoot!" commanded Urnalda. "I said—"

An immense bulk suddenly plowed into her from behind. With a terrified screech, she flew into the pair of dwarves, sending their arrows skittering across the ground. The huntsmen, just as surprised as Urnalda, collapsed under her weight. Apparently stunned, she lay on top of them, moaning. The recently shortened dwarf tried to free himself and stand, but tripped over his loose leggings. He landed directly on Urnalda's face, crushing one of her shell earrings.

Simultaneously, a huge rack of antlers scooped me up and lifted me into the air. I toppled backward, falling across an enormous neck, bristling with fur. The stag! All at once we were bounding across the plain. It took all my strength just to hold on, my legs entwined with the antler points and my arms wrapped around the powerful neck. Coarse fur scratched my cheeks as the great body bounced beneath me. Soon the cries of the dwarves faded away and all I could hear was the pounding, pounding of hooves.

I have no idea how long I rode this way, though it seemed half the night. The muscles of the stag's neck felt as hard as stone. Pound, pound, pound. At least once I fell off, thudding into the ground. In a flash, the antlers scooped me up again and the brutal ride continued.

Finally, dazed and bruised, I tumbled off again. This time, no rack of antlers retrieved me. Rolling onto my back, I felt the coolness of wet grass against my neck. My battered body gave way, at last, to exhaustion. Vaguely, I thought I heard voices, almost human but different somehow. Finally, my head pounding as incessantly as the hooves, I fell into heavy slumber.

When I awoke, it was to the sound of a stream. Water bounced and splattered somewhere nearby. Finding myself facedown in a bed of grass, I turned over stiffly. My neck and back ached, especially between my shoulders. Bright light! The sun rode high above, warming my face. The air, while still mildly smoky, seemed lighter and clearer than last night.

Last night! Had all that really happened? Despite the painful stiffness of my back, I sat up. Suddenly, I caught my breath. There, seated on a toppled tree trunk beside the bubbling stream, sat a young woman about my own age.

For a long moment she and I sat in silence. She seemed to be looking past me, at the stream, perhaps out of shyness. Even so, I could tell that her immense brown eyes were watching me cautiously.

Handsome did not describe her—just as, I well knew, it did not describe me—yet there was a strong, striking air about her nonetheless. Her chin, unusually long and narrow, rested upon her hand. She seemed relaxed, yet poised to move in a fraction of a second. Her braided hair glinted with the tans and auburns of marsh grasses. The braid itself swept across her shoulder and over the back of her yellow robe that seemed to have been woven from willow shoots. She wore no shoes.

"Well, well," declared a deep, resonant voice. "Our traveler has awakened."

I spun around to see a tall, broad-chested young man approaching us through the grass. Wearing a simple, tan-colored tunic, he stepped with long, loping strides. His chin, like the girl's, jutted strongly. He possessed the same rich brown eyes, though not quite so large as hers. And he, too, had bare feet.

At once, I knew that these two were brother and sister. At the same time, I felt the gnawing sense that they were somehow more, and less, than they appeared. Yet I couldn't quite identify how.

Pushing myself to my feet, I nodded to both of them. "Good day to you."

The young man nodded in return. "May green meadows find

you." He held out his hand, although the motion seemed slightly awkward for him. We clasped, his sturdy fingers curling around my own. "I am Eremon, son of Ller." He cocked his head toward the trunk. "That is my sister, Eo-Lahallia. Though she prefers to be called just Hallia."

She said nothing, but continued to watch me warily.

He released his grip. "We are, you could say, people of these parts. And who are you?"

"I am called Merlin."

Eremon brightened. "Like the hawk?"

Sadly, I smiled. "Yes. I had a friend once—a dear friend. A merlin. We . . . did much together."

Eremon's wide eyes gleamed with understanding. He seemed to know, somehow, what I had left unsaid.

"Unlike you," I went on, "I am not from this region. You could, as you did before, call me a traveler."

"Well, young hawk, I am glad your travels brought you here. As is my sister."

He glanced toward her hopefully. She did not speak—although she shifted uneasily on the trunk. And while she continued to avoid my own gaze, she shot a direct look at Eremon: a look of mistrust.

Turning back to me, he indicated the patch of matted grass where I had been sleeping. "Your travels have drained you, it seems. You might have slept a full week if your fitful dreams hadn't wakened you."

A full week. All that remained—and now, less! Valdearg would return one week from last night. To devour me. And if not me, everyone and everything in his path.

Seeing me suddenly tense, Eremon placed his hand upon my

shoulder. "I have not known you long, young hawk. Yet I see you are troubled." His gaze flowed over me like a wave washing over a rocky shore. "I have the feeling, somehow, that your troubles are also ours."

Hallia sprang to her feet. "My brother!" She paused, hesitant, before saying any more. At last, in a voice quieter but no less resonant than Eremon's, she asked, "Shouldn't you . . . wait? You are, perhaps, too quick to trust."

"Perhaps," he replied. "Yet the feeling persists."

Still without looking straight at me, Hallia waved in my direction. "He only just awoke, after all. You haven't even . . . circled a story with him."

Puzzled, I watched Eremon close his brown eyes thoughtfully, then reopen them. "You are right, my sister." He turned to me. "My people, the Mellwyn-bri-Meath, have many traditions, many rhythms, some of which have come down to us all the way from Distant Time."

With the agility of a sparrow turning in flight, he moved to the stream's edge and knelt by a strip of soft mud. "One of our oldest traditions," he continued, "is to circle a story, as a way of introducing ourselves. So in meeting someone from a different clan, or even a different people, we often invoke it."

"What does it mean, to circle a story?"

Eremon reached into the stream and pulled out a slender, gray stone. He shook the water from it, then drew a large circle in the mud. "Each of us, starting with you as the newcomer, tells part, but only part, of a tale." Using the stone, he divided the circle into three equal portions. "When we have finished, the parts combine, giving us a full circle."

"And a full story." I stepped to the stream bank and knelt beside him. "A wonderful tradition. But must we do it now? I am, well, much better at listening to stories than telling them. And right now my thoughts are . . . elsewhere. My time is short. Too short! Indeed, I really should go." Under my breath, I added, "Though I'm not quite sure where."

Hallia nodded, as if my reaction had confirmed her suspicions. "Now . . . see there?" she said to her brother, her voice still hesitant, but urgent all the same. "He does not like stories."

"Oh, but I do!" I pushed some hair off my brow. "I have always loved stories. It's miraculous, really, where they can take you."

"Yes," agreed Eremon. "And where they can keep you." He studied me. "Come, young hawk. Join our circle."

Something behind the rich brown of his eyes told me that staying a moment longer, in this particular place with these particular people, could be important. And that my part of the story would be heard with interest—and judged with care.

"All right, then," I replied. "How do I begin?"

"However you like."

I bit my lip, trying to think of the best way to start. An animal— yes, that felt right. One who lived as I did now: alone. I filled my lungs with air. "The story begins," I declared, "with a creature of the forest. A wolf."

Hallia started at my choice. Even her brother, whose wide eyes continued to scan me, flinched. I knew, beyond doubt, that I had chosen poorly. Yet I could not be sure why.

"This wolf," I went on, "called himself Hevydd. And he was lost. Not on the ground, but in his own heart. He wandered through the high hills, exploring and sleeping and hunting wherever he liked. He sat for hours upon his favorite stone, howling to the pearls of the night sky. Yet . . . his forest felt more like a prison, with every tree another bar on his cage. For Hevydd was alone—in ways he could not fathom. He hungered for answers, but he didn't even understand the questions. He longed for companions, but didn't know . . ." My dry throat made me cough. "Didn't know where to look."

Eremon frowned—whether from sympathy or dismay, I could not tell. Yet I knew, as did he, that my portion of the story had finished. Deftly wielding the stone, he began to draw in the upper third of the circle. A symbol, I realized, of my part of the story. But instead of the head or body of a wolf, as I myself would have drawn, he drew a paw print. The wolf's track.

Looking not at me, nor at Hallia, but at the circle, Eremon began to speak. "Hevydd did not realize," he intoned, "that the forest was no cage of bars—but an endless maze of overlapping trails. Where one trail ended, another one began. Deer loped this way; badgers ran that. A spider dropped from one branch; a squirrel climbed another. Along the floor slithered a newborn snake; across the sky soared a pair of eagles. Each of these trails connected to each other, so that when the wolf padded along the ridge by himself, he was really traveling alongside all the others. Even when he veered from his path to stalk his next meal, the trails of hunter and hunted became one."

His voice fell until I could hardly hear it above the splattering stream. "So Hevydd did not notice when the last oak perished, causing the squirrels to move away. Nor did he mourn when plague struck the rabbits' warren, killing every single one of them. Nor did he mark the day when the yellow-backed butterflies stopped flitting through the groves, along with the jays and ravens who dined upon them."

He stopped, drawing a dozen different tracks in his portion of the circle—the prints of all the animals he had named, and more. As he was finishing, Hallia stepped closer, still avoiding me with her round eyes. For a moment she peered thoughtfully at the drawing in the mud, while playing with her auburn braid.

"The forest," she began, "grew quieter . . . by the day. So very quiet. Fewer birds chattered in the branches; fewer beasts strolled through the underbrush. From his stone on the ridge, though, Hevydd howled more often. He howled from greater hunger, since food was more scarce. And he howled, as well, from greater loneliness."

Bending gracefully, she took the slender stone from Eremon's hand. She started to speak again, then paused for a while before the words finally came. "The day arrived . . . that a new creature entered the forest." With deep, harsh strokes, she filled the remaining portion of the circle with another track: the booted foot of a man. "This creature came . . . with arrows and blades. Stealthily, craftily, he approached Hevydd's howling stone. No birds remained to rise skyward in warning. No animals scattered from his path. And no one was left to mourn when the man killed Hevydd . . . and cut out his heart."

XIII

To Run Like a Deer

Hallia, her portion of the story finished, gazed solemnly at the splattering stream. Though I had been struck by the brutality of her words, I had been struck even more by the anguish in her voice.

Eremon rose slowly to face her. "Would it be fair to say, my sister, that Hevydd might have lived if he had understood more?"

"Perhaps," she replied, pausing even longer than usual before she continued. "Yet it would also be fair to ask: Did the fault belong to him, or to the man who slew him?"

"Both," I declared, standing once more. "That's usually the way of it. With fault, I mean. I've seen how often my own faults combine with someone else's to make things worse."

While Hallia backed away, to the very edge of the stream, Eremon remained still, watching me quizzically. "And how, young hawk, do you know so much about your faults?"

Without hesitation, I answered: "I have a sister."

His whole face wrinkled in a smile—which vanished as soon as Hallia glanced at him sharply. "Tell us, now. What brought you here? And why do I feel so much of the lone wolf in you?"

Feeling the sudden urge to lean against my staff, I instinctively scanned the grass. All at once, I remembered. My staff was gone. Destroyed. Along with my powers.

The boy of the wizard's staff, the trees of the Druma had called me. I cringed at the memory. "I had something . . . unusual. Something precious. And now it's lost."

Eremon's thick eyebrows drew together. "What is this thing?"

I hesitated.

"Tell us, young hawk."

Gravely, I spoke the word. "Magic. Whether or not I might ever have become a true wizard, I still had some gifts. Gifts of magic." I paused, reading the doubt in both of their faces. "You must believe me. I came to the realm of the dwarves at Urnalda's request, to help her battle Valdearg—Wings of Fire. Then she turned on me. Stole my powers." I touched my chest. "I feel, well, this emptiness now. My magic, my essence, was just ripped away. If only you could feel it . . . you would know I speak truly."

Eremon's ears, slightly pointed at the top like those of all Fincayran men and women, quivered for an instant. "I can feel it," he said softly.

Turning to his sister, he asked by his expression whether or not she agreed. Yet Hallia's face showed only mistrust. Slowly, she shook her head, her long braid glinting in the sun.

My jaw tightened. "If you believe nothing else, at least heed this. In just six and a half days, all of Fincayra will know Valdearg's rage. Unless, that is, I can find some way to stop him."

Eremon's eyes widened.

"And I have no idea even where to begin!" My hand squeezed the air as it would have my staff. "Should I just submit to the dragon now? Let him devour me? It might satisfy him. Urnalda said it would. But it might not! He could just continue on his rampage, destroying whatever he likes. I've got to prevent that."

"You ask a lot of yourself," observed Eremon.

I sighed again. "One of my faults." My attention fell to the circle in the mud at our feet. "It's hopeless, really. Like the wolf in our story." In frustration, I struck my fist against my palm. "Those two deer should have just left me to die!"

Hallia started. "What did you say?"

I winced. "If you doubt the rest, then you'll never believe this part."

For the first time, she looked straight at me. "Tell us . . . about the deer."

"Well, it's enough to say that two brave deer—for whatever reason—risked their lives to save me last night. It was they who brought me here. No, it's true! I wish I could thank them—even though things would be simpler if they hadn't bothered. I haven't any idea where they are now."

Hallia's deep eyes probed me. It seemed to me that a new doubt, different than before, shone in them. Then, suddenly aware that I was returning her gaze, she turned shyly away.

Her brother bent toward her. "Say what you will about his words. I, for one, judge them true."

She took him by the arm. "Part of what he says may be true . . . but only part. Remember, he is a—" She caught herself. "A creature not to be trusted."

Her brother shook loose. "A creature not so different from ourselves." He pushed a hand through his nut brown hair and faced me. "That Wings of Fire has reawakened is no secret. Nor that he has done much recently to punish the dwarves. Because the dwarves have very few friends in other parts of Fincayra, most of us who live on their borders have just assumed they brought this trouble on themselves. But no—if your tale is true, Valdearg's anger must spring from another cause altogether."

Grimly, I nodded. "It does." A cold wind arose, ruffling the grasses. "His eggs—his only young—were murdered."

Hallia tossed her braid over her shoulder. "I feel . . . no sorrow for him. He has wasted so many lands, so many lives. Still, I can't help but feel sympathy for his hatchlings, murdered like that. Without even a chance to escape."

I frowned. "I feel no sympathy for them. They would have only grown up to be like . . ." My words trailed off as I realized what I was about to say. *Like their father.* How different was that from what Urnalda had said about me?

Eremon's voice resonated clearly. "For my part, I feel sympathy for them all. They did not seek to be born as dragons, but merely to be born." He paused, watching me. "Do you know who killed them?"

"A man."

His ears trembled once more. "And who was that man?"

I swallowed. "Valdearg believes it was me. Since I am descended from his greatest foe—Tuatha. But it was not. I swear it was not."

His brow knitted as he studied me for a long moment. At last he announced, "I believe you, young hawk." He drew a deep breath. "And I will help you."

"Eremon!" cried his sister, all her hesitancy gone. "You can't!"

"If his words are true, all of Fincayra should rise to help."

"But you don't know!"

"I know enough." He stroked his prominent chin. "Yet I wish

I knew one thing more: where those dragon eggs have lain hidden these many years. If only we could find whatever is left of them, we might find a sign. Something that could tell us who is the true killer."

"I've thought of that, as well," I replied. "But the remains of the eggs could be anywhere! We have no time to search. Besides, what we need to find most is not the killer—but some way to stop Valdearg."

At that, the wisp of an idea rose within me. A desperate, outlandish idea. And, with it, an overwhelming sense of dread. "Eremon! I know what I must do in whatever time remains. It's a foolish hope, yet I can think of no other." I faced him squarely. "And it's far too dangerous to ask anyone else to join me."

Hallia's somber face lightened. Eremon, for his part, regarded me gravely.

"One of the few things I know about my grandfather's battle with Valdearg, ages ago, is that he triumphed only with the help of an object of great power. A pendant—full of magic—known as the Galator."

Both pairs of brown eyes stared at me.

"For a time I myself wore it around my neck. Yet I learned very little of its secrets." My shoulders started to droop as I realized that, without my own powers, the Galator's magic might be useless to me. And yet . . . there was, at least, a chance. I tried to stand taller. "I must get it back somehow! If I can, it just might defeat the dragon once again."

"Where is it now?" queried Eremon.

I bit my lip. "With the hag Domnu—also called Dark Fate. She lives at the farthest reaches of the Haunted Marsh."

Hallia inhaled sharply through her nose. "Then you had best . . . devise another plan. You cannot possibly walk all the way there and back in just six and a half days."

I winced at her words. "You're right. It would be difficult enough even if I could run like a deer."

Eremon threw back his head. "But you can."

Before I could ask what he meant, he turned and started running across the grass, his feet moving effortlessly. He loped faster and faster, until his legs became a blur of motion. He leaned forward, his broad back nearly horizontal, his arms almost touching the ground. The muscles of his neck tightened as his chin thrust forward. Then, to my astonishment, his arms transformed into legs, pounding over the turf. His tunic melted away, replaced by fur, while his feet and hands became hooves. From his head sprouted a great rack of antlers, five points on each side.

He swung around, flexing his powerful haunches as he bounded back over the field. In an instant he stood before us again, every bit a stag.

XIV

EREMON'S GIFT

Astonished, I gazed into the deep brown eyes of the stag. "So it was you who saved me."

Eremon's antlered head dipped. "It was," he declared, his voice even richer than before. "My sister and I only wished to come to your aid, as you had come to ours."

Her brow creased in worry, Hallia reached up and, with her slender hand, stroked the thick fur of the stag's neck. Quietly, she said, "Once should be enough, my brother. The favor is exchanged. Do you really need to do more?" She glanced at me, and her expression hardened. "And for the sake of a man? Need I remind you that men stole our parents' lives? That they cut out our mother's and father's shoulders for a meal . . . and left the rest of their bodies to rot?"

Their eyes met. At length, Eremon spoke with a new softness. "Eo-Lahallia, your pain, like all you feel, is great. Yet I fear that instead of stepping through your pain, as you and I have stepped through many a marsh, you have let it cling to you, like the bloodthirsty tick that rides our backs for months on end."

Hallia blinked back her tears. "This tick will not fall away." She swallowed. "And . . . there is more. Last night, after we regained our two-legged forms, a dream came to me. A terrible dream! I entered . . . a dark and dangerous place. There was a river, I think, flowing fast. And right before me, the body of a stag. Blood everywhere! He quivered, at the edge of death. The very sight made me weep! Just as I came close enough to look into his eyes, I awoke."

Eremon kicked anxiously at the grass with his hoof. "Who was this stag?"

"I . . . can't be sure." She wrapped her arms tightly around his neck. "But I don't want you to die!"

As I listened, my heart filled with anguish. I remembered too well Rhia's parting embrace at the headwaters, and my longing to be with her again. "Heed her warning," I urged. "As much as I yearn for your help, Eremon, that would be too high a price. No, whatever I must do, I must do it alone."

Relief flickered in Hallia's eyes.

Eremon observed me. "Was it hard for you to part with your sister?"

His guess took me aback, though I managed a nod.

He tilted his rack so that one of the points lightly brushed Hallia's cheek. "Can a race whose brothers and sisters care so much for each other be entirely evil?"

She said nothing.

The stag lifted his mighty head and addressed me. "My own race, the deer people, have lived too long in fear and rage at yours. I do not know whether helping you will also help to bind us to the race of men and women. Yet I do know this: It is right to help another creature, no matter the shape of his track. And so I shall."

Hallia sucked in her breath. "Is . . . your path firmly set?"

"It is."

"Then," she declared with a shake of her whole torso, "I will join you."

She raised a hand as Eremon started to protest. "Is your choice to be respected, but not mine?" Sensing his anguish, she stroked his ear softly. "If I must weep, I would rather do so by your side than someplace far away from you."

Gently, the stag's moist nose touched hers. "You will do no weeping." After a pause, he added, "Nor, I hope, will I."

With that, Hallia stepped back from her brother. She glanced down at her hands, stretching her fingers in the sunlight. At length, she turned toward the open field, the meadowsweet poignant under the midday sun. In a flash she was running, then loping, then bounding through the green spears with the grace of a deer. She turned and pranced over to us, her hooves springing lightly off the turf.

Eremon flicked his ears, then faced me squarely. "Now for you."

I stepped back in surprise, slipping off the edge of the muddy bank. With a flop, I landed in the stream. Dripping wet, with a trail of mud rolling down my cheek, I clambered back to the grass.

Hallia's eyes averted me, but I could not miss her snickering. "He may be a wizard, but he could use some more practice walking on two legs before he tries four."

"He will learn quickly," predicted Eremon.

"B-but wait," I stammered, wringing out my sleeves. "I have no magic! And even when I did, the art of Changing was still new to me. I could no sooner change into a deer than into a puff of wind."

"There is a way. Although the magic will be mine, not yours, you still can share in it." He lowered his great rack. "Here. Take your sword."

"No!" cried Hallia, kicking her forelegs. "You can't do that."

"Would you rather carry him on our backs the whole way? I barely managed to bring him from the dwarves' land to this place. The lair of Domnu is much farther."

Speaking again to me, he commanded, "Cut off one of my points. A clean swipe will do it."

Gripping the hilt, I pulled the sword free of the scabbard. It rang distantly, like a shrouded bell. Aiming at the point farthest from Eremon's head, I brought down the blade with all my strength.

There was a sudden flash, and the point snapped off, dropping to the ground. A fresh, spicy smell, like a forest glade, enriched the air. I breathed deeply, remembering the hemlock grove that gave me my staff long ago. Eremon raised a rear hoof and stomped heavily on the point. Over and over again. When, at last, he stopped, a small pile of silver powder remained.

I sheathed my sword and kneeled to look more closely. The tiny crystals glistened in the light.

Eremon's foreleg nudged my shoulder. "By rubbing the powder into your hands and feet, young hawk, you will gain, for a time, the power of my people. You may change from a man to a deer and back again, simply by willing it." His voice took on an edge of warning. "Remember, though, that to survive as a deer you must not only look like one, but think like one, too."

Wondering at his words, I swallowed.

"And," he continued, "there is a risk you must understand. The power could last three months—or three days. There is no way to predict."

"And if it wears off while I am in deer form?"

"Then you will remain a deer forever. This gift can never be given to you again, so I cannot help you change back."

For a moment I gazed into his immense eyes. "I accept the gift.

And the risk, as well." Pulling off my boots, I spread the powder on my palms, and rubbed it thoroughly over both my feet and hands.

The stag's rack poked my thigh. "Don't miss a single joint of a single toe."

Finally, having finished, I stood. "When—if—I change into a deer, what will happen to my satchel? And my sword?"

"The magic will conceal them while you are a deer, and restore them when you are a man."

"Then I am ready."

Hallia huffed through her nose. "Not quite! You had better . . . put your boots back on. Otherwise, when you return to man form, you will have bare feet. And, before long, countless blisters."

As much as her tone irked me, I didn't reply.

Eremon gave a low, throaty laugh. "Now run, young hawk! Enjoy your own motion. Be as fluid as the stream over there, and as light as the breeze."

Through the grass I plodded, my wet boots clomping heavily on the ground. Water sloshed under my toes. I did not need to see Hallia to feel her critical gaze.

Faster I raced, and faster. As *fluid as the stream.* I leaned forward, dangling my arms. *As light as the breeze.* My knees bent backward. My strides felt surer, stronger. My chin stretched outward. Both hands—no, something else—met the turf. My back lengthened, as did my neck. All at once, I was bounding across the field.

I was a deer.

My sleek shadow flew across the grass. Atop my head rode a small rack with two points on one side and three on the other. *This is not so difficult,* I told myself. Glancing back over my shoulder, I saw the handsome stag and doe beside the tumbling stream. Deciding to lope back to them, I whipped around sharply. My left rear hoof struck the inside of my right foreleg. Caught off balance, I twisted and fell.

Barely had I righted myself, knees wobbling, before Eremon and Hallia were at my side. The stag nudged me with concern. My flank less bruised than my pride, I trotted a few steps to show him that I hadn't injured myself. As for Hallia—well, I really didn't care what she thought.

"Come," boomed Eremon, curling his long lips. "We must leave for the river crossing. With any luck, we can be well into the plains before dark."

He loped back toward the shining stream, ears cocked forward, and cleared the channel with a single leap. Hallia followed, the picture of grace. I bounded behind, far less smoothly. Although I tried to clear the stream as easily as the others, my hind legs splashed into the cold water, soaking my underside. I scuttled up the bank, doing my best to catch up.

Eremon led us due south for a while, reversing the route over the stairway of meadows that Rhia and I had crossed just the day before. In time, the rhythm of running through the tall grasses and late-blooming lupines began to seep into my muscles and bones. So gradually that I didn't notice it happening, I started to move less woodenly, less even like a body than like the air itself.

Bounding through the grasses, tinted rust by the onset of autumn, I realized that my sight was good. Very good. No longer relying on my second sight, which in daytime had never measured up to true eyesight, I relished the details, the edges, the textures. Sometimes I even slowed my running just to look more closely.

Dewdrops clinging to a spiderweb, tufts of grass bending as gracefully as a rainbow, airborne seeds drifting on the wind. Whether my eyes were still coal black, or brown like my companions', I could not tell. Yet that mattered not at all, for they were, at last, open windows to the world.

As good as my eyesight had become, my sense of smell had grown even better. Intimate aromas came to me from all around. I smelled, with relief, the diminishing traces of smoke as we moved farther from the dwarves' lands. And I drank in, unrestrainedly, the subtle aromas of this bright autumn day. A coursing rivulet. An old beehive in the trunk of a birch tree. A fox's den hidden among roots of gorse.

Yet the newest of all my senses, it seemed, was my hearing. Sounds that I had never known existed washed over me in a constant stream. I heard not only the continual pounding of my own hooves, and the distinctive weight and timing of the hooves of the two deer ahead of me—but also our echoing reverberations through the soil. Even as I ran, I caught whispers of a dragonfly's wings humming and a field mouse's legs scurrying.

As the sun drew closer to the western hills, I realized that my ability to hear went even beyond having sensitive ears. Somehow, in a mysterious way, I was listening not just to sounds, but to the land itself. I could hear, not with my ears but with my bones, the tensing and flexing of the earth under my hooves, the changing flow of the wind, the secret connections among all the creatures who shared these meadows—whether they crawled, slithered, flew, or ran. Not only did I hear them; I celebrated them, for we were bound together as securely as a blade of grass is bound to the soil.

XV

THE MEANING
IN THE TRACKS

The sun had nearly reached the horizon when Eremon turned his great rack toward the corridor of mist that I knew marked the banks of the River Unceasing. As I followed, the rush and splatter of rapids grew louder. Arms of mist encircled me. Slowing my gait, I realized that the stag had brought us to the crossing that I knew well. The same strange longing that I had felt before with Rhia, to see the great boulders at the river's edge, welled up in me again.

Though I could hear the crashing waters plainly, I could not yet see the river through the knotting mist. Eremon and Hallia, their tan coats shining with sweat, trotted to a patch of dark green reeds. Affectionately, Hallia nudged her brother's shoulder with her own. Then, lowering their heads, they began browsing on the shoots.

When I approached, the stag lifted his rack and greeted me with an approving nod. "You are learning to run, young hawk."

"I am learning to listen."

Hallia, seeming to ignore us, ripped out a tuft of reeds. Her jaws crunched noisily.

I, too, began nibbling at the reeds. Though they tasted almost bitter, I could feel new strength in my limbs almost instantly. Even the velvet covering of my antlers seemed to tingle. I took another, larger bite.

While munching, I nodded approvingly. "What is, *crunchunchunch,* this reed?"

"Eelgrass," Eremon replied between bites. "From the days when my clan of deer people lived by the sea. Feel the texture on your tongue? It's like the dried skin of an eel."

He tore out some more shafts and chewed pensively for a while. "Although we no longer live by the shore, we have kept the reed's name—and many uses. It is woven into our baskets, our curtains, and our clothing. Chafed, pounded, and mixed with hazelnut oil, it starts our fires on winter evenings. It greets our young as a blanket at birth, and sends them on the Long Journey as a funeral shawl at death." His black nose nuzzled another tuft. "Its best use of all, though, is simply as food."

Suddenly Hallia bellowed in pain. She leaped into the air, shaking her head wildly. Even as she landed, Eremon was at her side, stroking her neck with his nose. She continued to cast her head about, whimpering.

"What is it, my sister?"

"I must have bitten—ohhh, it aches! A stone or something. Broke . . . a tooth, I think." Quivering, she opened her mouth. Blood covered one of her rear teeth; a trickle ran down her lip. "Ohhh . . . it hurts. Throbs." She stamped her hoof. "Why now?"

Eremon glanced worriedly at me. "I don't know how to treat such a wound."

Hallia, still casting her head, kicked at the reeds. "I will go . . . ehhh! to Miach the Learned. He will—"

"Too far," interrupted the stag. "Miach's village is more than a full day from here."

A shudder coursed through her. "Then maybe it will—oh! heal on its own . . . in time."

"No, no," declared Eremon. "You must find help."

"But where? Do I just go . . . wandering?" She closed her eyes tightly. As she reopened them, tears gathered on her lashes. "I had wanted . . . to stay with you."

"Wait," I declared. "I may not have any magic of my own, but I do know a little about healing."

"No!" shrieked Hallia. "I won't be healed by . . . him."

Eremon fixed his gaze on hers. "Let him try."

"But he might . . ." She shivered. "He's . . . a man." Cautiously, she curled her tongue to caress the broken tooth. "Oh, Eremon!" Bobbing her head, she said nothing for a long moment. At last, she asked weakly, "You really . . . trust him?"

"I do."

"All right, then," she whispered. "Let him . . . try."

My hoof stomped hard. "Hands. I need hands. How do I change?"

"Just start walking," Eremon answered. "And will yourself to change back."

Though my heart ached at losing my newfound senses, even for a moment, I turned back toward the lands we had bounded across. I strode into the curtains of mist, trying to recall just where I had seen a mass of curled yellow leaves—the plant my mother called *hurt man's blanket*. Many times I had seen her use it to deaden pain, though never in a tooth. I could only try . . . and hope.

After a few steps, my hooves started to flatten, my back to arch upward, and my neck to shorten. My motions suddenly felt clipped, disjointed. And my breath—less deep. Soon my boots, still wet from their plunge in the stream, clomped on the grasses.

As the mist thinned somewhat, I started searching for the yellow cluster I had remembered. For several minutes, I looked—without success. Was my vision now too poor to spot it? Had the roving mist swallowed it completely? Finally—there it was. I hurried over and picked one of the curling, hair-covered leaves. Stiffly, I ran back to the others.

"Here," I panted, holding the leaf in my palm. "I need to wrap this around your tooth."

Hallia whimpered, her whole body quaking.

"It will help," I coaxed. "At least . . . it's supposed to."

She gave a fearful moan. Then, as Eremon gently nudged her neck, she opened her mouth and lifted her tongue, exposing the bloody tooth. Delicately, very delicately, I ran my fingertip along its surface. Suddenly my finger pricked a tiny pebble wedged into a crack. With a tug, I wrenched it free. Though Hallia bellowed again, she continued to hold her mouth open long enough for me to wrap the leaf over her tooth and gum. Just as I finished, she jerked her head away.

"That should do it," I said, sounding less sure than I would have liked.

Slowly, Hallia's lips pinched. She shuddered, tilting her head from one side to the other. I felt certain that she was about to spit out the leaf.

But she did not spit. Instead, her brown eyes flitted toward me. "This tastes terrible. Like rotting oak bark, or worse." She paused, hesitating. "Still . . . it does feel a little . . . better."

Eremon's great head bobbed. "We are grateful, young hawk."

Suddenly feeling as shy as the doe, I turned aside. "Not as grateful as I am, to have been a deer—for a while, at least."

"You shall walk with hooves again soon. And often, if the magic lasts." He glanced at his sister, whose tongue was playing lightly over the crumpled leaf. "For now, though, we are glad you have fingers."

Hallia took a step nearer. "And . . ." she began, taking a slow breath, "knowledge. Real knowledge. I thought men and women had forsaken the language of the land—of the plants, the seasons, the stones—for the language of written words."

"Not all men and women," I replied. Tapping the hilt of my sword, I half grinned. "Believe me, I've learned a few things from stones." My thoughts turned to Cairpré, forever finding treasures between the covers of books. "The written word has its own virtues, though."

She eyed me skeptically.

"It's true," I explained. "Reading a passage in a book is like—well, like following tracks. No, no—that's not it. More like finding the *meaning* in the tracks. Where they are going, why they are sprinting or limping, how they are different from the day before."

Hallia said nothing more, though she swiveled her ears as if she were intrigued. At that instant, the wind shifted. A gap opened in the mist around us, allowing a few gleaming shafts of light to burst through. The rays poured over the shoots of eelgrass, making them seem to glow from within.

She sighed. "How beautiful."

I nodded.

"Don't you love," she said quietly, "the way the mist moves? Like a shadow made of water."

I ceased nodding. "Myself, I was watching the sunlight, not the mist. How it paints the reeds, and whatever else it touches."

"Hmmm." Her ears twitched. "So you saw light, while I saw motion?"

"So it seems. Two different sides of the same moment."

Eremon released a throaty sound, almost a chuckle. Shredding mist wove through his antlers. All of a sudden, the wind again shifted. The stag stiffened, his nostrils quivering.

Hallia chewed nervously on the leaf. "That smell . . . what is it?"

For quite some time, he did not answer, did not move. At last, he lowered his rack. "It is the smell," he declared, "of death."

XVI

DREAMS YET
UNHATCHED

Stepping cautiously, we approached the bank of the rushing river. Rapids slapped and pounded. Strands of mist, tinted red from the setting sun, wound around our legs, curling like vaporous ropes. The soil grew soft and slippery under my feet—and the others' hooves.

At the lip of the bank, I paused to watch Eremon and Hallia descend. Despite the unstable ground, they moved as gracefully as a pair of dewdrops rolling down the petal of a flower. Unlike them, I stood upright and vertical—a young man, half human, half Fincayran. Two legs felt so narrow, so unsteady. Even as I curled my fingers, feeling their delicacy, I missed my own hooves. And, still more, I missed my own magic. Thanks to Eremon's gift I had, at least briefly, forgotten the emptiness in my chest.

Change back! Yes. Now. I turned to run along the edge of the bank—when I saw Eremon suddenly halt, his antlered head erect. Hallia, too, froze, the fur on her back bristling.

Like them, I stood motionless. For through the shredding mist, I could now see the edges of the opposite bank. And the scene of slaughter that scarred it.

The boulders that I remembered no longer marked this place.

Only broken shells, their reeking innards clotted with blood. In a flash, I comprehended that they had never been boulders at all. They had been eggs.

Dragon eggs.

Strewn across the muddy shore, the broken remains of the eggs lay in ghastly heaps. I spotted a section of throat, hacked brutally. And a ragged wing, streaked with scarlet and green. Except for the few strips of flesh that fluttered in the spray, everything seemed frozen in the moment of death.

No wolves had dragged away these carcasses. No vultures had carried off the meaty fragments, still glistening with newborn scales. At once, I knew why. For over the whole scene hung something as potent as the fetid odor of rotting flesh—the possibility that Valdearg himself might appear at any moment.

I clambered down the bank to join the others. Mud tugged at my boots, while a growing dread tugged at my heart. As we stepped into the shallows, frigid water slapped against our legs. Yet nothing chilled so much as the devastation before us. At least, I told myself, they were only dragons. Destroyed before they could do the same to anyone else. Even so . . . Eremon's words still nagged at me.

The stag bounded up the opposite bank, then veered sharply to the left. Forehoof raised, he bent over something, studying it intently.

As fast as I could, I scrambled up behind him. Below his hoof, I spied a slight indentation in the soil stained dark orange from blood. All at once, I realized that it was a footprint. The footprint of a man. Here, I felt certain, was the proof that Urnalda had used to turn the dragon's wrath away from the dwarves—and toward me.

Cautiously, Hallia approached. She lowered her head to sniff the print, her nose almost touching it. She glanced at me, the old mistrust back in her eyes. Working her tongue, she spat out the leaf that I had given her. Then, her voice barely audible above the river, she spoke. "This man, whoever he is, has brought much pain."

"And Valdearg will bring even more," added Eremon grimly. "Unless we are successful. Yet our time dwindles. Already the sun is setting on this day."

Sadly, I shook my head. "This print looks so much like my own."

Hallia snorted. "All men's footprints look alike. Heavy and clumsy."

Eremon struck the mud with his hoof. "Not so, my sister. See here? The edge of the heel is blunted, but with a sharp edge. Not in the normal, rounded way caused by walking on turf, or even hard floors."

Hallia turned toward one of my own footprints. After a long pause, she admitted, "There is, I suppose, a difference." Hesitantly, she glanced at me once again. "I'm sorry. I just . . ."

"It's all right," I replied. "Say no more." Facing Eremon, I asked, "So what does the shape of that heel tell you?"

"That it was cut, over time, by something jagged. Perhaps this person lives in some sort of cave, lined with rough stones. Or in a maze of tunnels under the ground."

"Urnalda lives in a realm of tunnels," I mused. "Yet she doesn't wear a man's boots. Besides, why would she ever attack Valdearg's young, knowing it might bring his wrath down on her people?" Slowly, I exhaled. "It doesn't make sense."

Hallia's ears twisted. "There is another possibility. This person, this man, could have left the print on purpose, trying to trick us somehow."

"Possibly," acknowledged the stag. "Men can sometimes be . . ."

"Deceitful," she finished.

His antlers tilted to one side. "Are you saying a deer is never deceitful? Would you never try to trick an enemy?"

The doe straightened her neck. "Only to defend myself." She glanced at the nearest of the heaps, swathed in mist. "Or, one day, my young."

I strode over to the demolished egg. Kicking aside a piece of shell, I froze. Before me lay a severed arm, its claws extended like fingers. Though the arm's shape was not much different from my own, it was at least twice the size. Its underside bore a crest of iridescent purple scales; its wrist seemed as delicate as the neck of a swan. The claws seemed to be reaching, groping for something just beyond their grasp.

Something about this lifeless arm made me want to touch it. With my own hands, my own fingers.

I kneeled and stroked its length. The arm felt soft, despite the rows of scales. Almost like the chubby leg of a newborn baby. Not long ago, it had been alive. And young. And innocent.

At last, I understood the full horror of this tragedy. No life, no creature, no future, deserved to be wasted like this. Murdered like this. No wonder Valdearg's rage knew no bounds.

To myself, I recited the lines from Tuatha's prophecy:

> *By anger unending*
> *And power unmatched,*
> *The dragon avenges*
> *His dreams yet unhatched.*
> *For when he awakens*

To find those dreams lost,
Revenge shall he covet
Regardless the cost.

Suddenly, Eremon jerked his head, his rack spraying drops of water. His body and Hallia's stiffened as one. They were sensing something, feeling something, that eluded me completely.

Then I heard a sound, deep and rasping, like a distant volcano erupting. It came from somewhere far beyond the river, yet it grew steadily louder. A wind stirred; the air felt almost imperceptibly warmer. I picked up the faint scent of smoke. All at once an enormous shadow darkened the reddening mist.

"The dragon!" cried Eremon. "Run!"

The two deer scattered, bounding into the mist, while I stumbled over to the slick bank. The sound of flying thunder rent the air as the shadow passed over again. Terrified, I thought of changing back into a deer myself—when suddenly I slipped in the mud, losing my balance. In a whirl, I rolled down to the river's edge. Frigid water coursed over my legs as well as my sword. Breathless, I regained my feet and dashed across the shallows.

On a steep section of the far bank, I spied an overhang. A thick curtain of grasses, soaked from spray, dangled over the edge. Yet behind the grasses loomed a dark place where the river had washed away the soil. A cavern!

Even as the sound above me swelled into a roar, I threw myself into the cavern, rolling over and over on the mud until I bumped into the arching wall of the bank. For a moment I lay in the darkness, panting. Feeling the chill of the river, I sat up and pulled my knees to my chest. As I gazed through the dripping curtain of grasses I felt a touch of satisfaction. I had eluded Valdearg. Only temporarily, of course. Yet even delaying the inevitable by a handful of days seemed cause enough for pride.

Listening to the rushing torrent outside, I felt grateful for the safety of this cavern. It was cramped, and smelled . . . rancid somehow. Yet who could ask for a better hiding place? Then, without warning, something brushed against my leg.

XVII

POWERLESS

I drew back in fright. Grasping the hilt of my sword, I struggled to wrench it from the scabbard. But the scabbard's mouth had been so caked with mud that the blade refused to come free. Hunched beneath the low ceiling, I pulled and pulled without success.

Hurl myself from the cavern! Now, while I still could. Before whatever had stirred did so again. Yet . . . I hesitated. Beyond the grassy curtain Valdearg himself might well be waiting for me. Again I tugged at my sword. Again it failed to move.

Suddenly a sound like I had never heard before echoed in the darkness. Part moan, part snarl, part whimper, it grew louder until at last it abruptly died away. I pressed myself against the earthen wall. Mud oozed down my neck, but I did not stir. I barely breathed—yet the rancid smell assaulted me, stronger than ever. I could only hope that this creature, whatever it was, might just ignore me and leave.

Then, very gradually, a faint orange glow began to illuminate the cavern. At first I could not tell where it originated, for its flickering caused strange, ungainly shadows to grow and wither on the walls: giants stalking, snakes writhing, trees crashing to the ground.

Finally, though, I located the source: a triangle of orange light, not far above the floor at the cavern's far end. The light flickered, quavering like a candle in a breeze.

Though fear gripped me, I did the only thing I could think to do. With both hands, I scooped a chunk of mud off the floor, pressed it into a ball, and hurled it straight at the glowing triangle. A splat—and instantly, the light went out. At the same time, the whining, moaning sound returned, this time swelling so loud that I had to cover my ears. I wriggled closer to the rear wall.

All at once, the entire wall shifted behind me. Mud poured over my head. For an instant I thought the riverbank was about to collapse on top of me. Yet the earthen wall did not collapse. Instead, it did the one thing I least expected.

It breathed. Shaking with effort, the whole surface drew a slow, halting breath. Foul-smelling wind rushed over me, swirling around the enclosure. Heedless of Valdearg, I rolled to the curtain of drenched grasses, hoping to escape in time.

Just as I was about to roll out of the cavern, back into the churning waters outside, the long breath choked off. As abruptly as it had started, it ceased. It was, I felt sure, one of the last breaths—if not the very last—of something at the edge of death. Or dead at last. Pausing at the entrance, I studied the path of a single shaft of light, as crimson as the setting sun, that slit the cavern from the place where my shoulder had pushed apart the grasses. It landed on the spot where I had seen the glowing triangle.

My heart froze. For there, tilted on its side in the black mud, lay an enormous head—twice the size of the head of a full-grown horse. It belonged to a dragon.

Its eye, whose eerie light had filled the cavern only a moment before, was now shut. Long lashes rimmed the eyelid. I could see, clinging to the lashes, a few fragments of broken shell. A dull yellow bump protruded from the forehead, while lavender scales ran down the full length of the wrinkly nose. Dozens of teeth, as sharp as daggers, glistened within the half-open jaws. Curiously, only the left ear flopped limply on the mud. The right ear, silvery blue in color, stretched stiffly into the air, like a misplaced horn.

A sudden rush of pity filled me. What vision of terror, I wondered, had driven this young hatchling from its egg and into hiding in this hollow? My skin tingled as I recalled the movement of the great body against my back, movement that was probably its final stirring of life. An inexplicable instinct made me guess that this dragon had been female. If so, she would never have the chance to lay any eggs of her own.

Reaching up, I pulled out several handfuls of the grass that hung over the entrance. More crimson light filtered into the cavern. Probing with my second sight, I spied a pair of sharp claws, flecked with purple, protruding from the mud. Not far from the place where I had momentarily rested, a tail with two hooked barbs lay coiled. Turning back to the head, I smiled sadly at the irrepressible ear. Nothing, not even death, could make it lie down.

I wondered about the dragon's wounds. Had she starved to death? Bled from some fatal gashes I could not see? Or, like any abandoned child, simply suffered from sorrow and fear—until she finally died?

At that moment, another deep moan, weaker than before, rose within the cavern. Still alive! The dragon's immense bulk shuddered, shaking the earthen floor. Clumps of mud dropped from above, splattering my head and shoulders. Her eye opened barely a sliver, fluttered, then closed once again, but not before I caught its look of anguish.

Biting my lip, I hesitated. Then . . . slowly, very slowly, I crawled closer. Gingerly, I lay my open hand over the eye, stroking its delicate lashes. It did not open again. Ever so gently, I moved my hand down the lavender scales of the nose, stopping at the immense nostrils. My whole hand barely covered them. A faint flutter of air warmed my fingers—reminding me of that horse from my childhood, whose name I could no longer recall, but whose misty breath I had never forgotten. But the breath of this creature, I could tell, was rapidly fading.

Yet what if a tiny spark of life still remained? Maybe I could . . . But no! I had no more magic. My jaw clenched, as I cursed Urnalda's treachery. Had she not stolen my gifts, I might have been able to call upon the sky above and the soil below—sources of the power of Binding, which could knit together the threads of the cosmos, and heal even the deepest wound.

Limply, my hand slid from the dragon's nose. I could not call upon that power—or any others. Nor could I do anything for this wretched beast. Helpless! I sighed, feeling more than ever that aching emptiness within my chest.

Something tugged against my hand. One of the dragon's scales had caught on the vine bracelet that Rhia gave to me as we parted. Even in the dying light, the bracelet shone with lustrous green. What had she said as she tied it on my wrist? *This will remind you of all the life around you, and the life within yourself.* I closed my eyes, hearing her voice again. *The life within yourself.*

Yet . . . what use was that to anyone else?

Almost out of habit, I reached into my leather satchel and pulled out a handful of herbs. Rubbing my palms together, I crushed them as best I could. Instantly, scents of rowan bark, beech root, and silver balm enriched the rancid air of the cavern. Then, with effort, I pulled off one of my boots. Using it as a makeshift bowl, I dropped in the herbs, gathering them at the heel. I squeezed some water from my soaked tunic into the boot, mixed the soup thoroughly with my finger, and leaned closer to the dragon. Since her head lay tilted in the mud, I was able to pour a few green, glistening drops into her partly open mouth.

As the drops struck her tongue, I waited for a swallow. But none came.

Once again, I poured some of the potion out of my boot. And I waited, hoping for some sign—any sign—of life. Yet she did not swallow. Or stir. Or moan.

"Swallow!" I commanded, my voice echoing dully in the dank walls. I poured another few drops, which slid off her tongue and fell to the floor.

Long after the last rays of twilight disappeared, and through the unforgiving night, I continued to try. My back ached, my bootless foot throbbed with cold, and my head swam from lack of sleep. Yet I refused to stop, hardly daring to hope that the eyelid might again flutter, that its orange glow might again illuminate the cavern. Or that the dragon might actually swallow something. But my hopes came to nothing.

When my herbal potion finally ran out, I tried rubbing the dragon's neck in slow circles, as my mother had once done for me— long ago, when I had thrashed from fever. It didn't help. Apart from the rare, halting breaths, which grew more frail by the hour, she showed no life at all.

When the first tentative rays of dawn drifted into the cavern, I knew that all my efforts had failed. I studied the motionless form, appreciating the subtle beauty of the scales, the savage curl of the claws. The hatchling lay utterly still, utterly silent.

Glumly, I turned away. The feeling of this hollow now revolted me. Like the devastation across the river, it stank of untimely death. Heedless of whatever danger lay outside, I rolled through the curtain of wet grasses.

XVIII

VEIL OF MIST

Rolling down the slick bank, I slid across the mud, finally stopping at the edge of the river. The surging water pounded in my ears. Cold spray drenched my face. Once again thick bands of mist twined themselves around me.

Cautiously, I scanned the opposite bank for any sign of Valdearg. Or of my companions. I found nothing but the remains of the eggs—broken shells, clotted innards, and hacked pieces of rotting flesh. The twirling columns of mist, and the river itself, were all that moved.

Full of regret, I glanced back at the cavern that held the last of the hatchlings. The last of Valdearg's offspring. Had whoever slaughtered these creatures intended to rouse the sleeping dragon of the Lost Lands, as well as his anger? And had the killer also intended that a man—whether myself or someone else—would be blamed? There was no way to tell. Perhaps simply murdering Valdearg's offspring was enough to serve the killer's purposes.

But what could those purposes be? To eliminate the hatchlings? Or to awaken Wings of Fire and send him on a deadly rampage? Yet that made no sense. Unless . . . perhaps the killer was an enemy of the dwarves, someone who hoped that Valdearg would show them the brunt of his wrath. Or an enemy of my father's race, the men and women of Fincayra. And there were many such enemies, I knew too well. Such a scar on this island, Stangmar's time on the throne! A scar that refused to heal.

I kneeled by the water's edge. Cupping my hands, I dipped them into the chill torrent, then washed my mud-splattered face. Finally, I dug the mud out of my scabbard. After several thick clumps worked loose, the sword at last came free.

I ran my finger over the silver hilt, shining in the spray. Maybe the killer was not just an enemy of dwarves, nor even of men and women, but of all life on Fincayra. Someone who might actually benefit from Valdearg's terror. Someone like . . . Rhita Gawr.

Wiping my face on my sleeve, I frowned. No, no, that couldn't be it. As Rhia herself had chided me, there was no point in creating new enemies. I had enough trouble right now. And yet . . . who else, besides Rhita Gawr, might be cunning enough to find the dragon eggs and ruthless enough to destroy them at birth?

Something soared over my head, darkening the mist. Valdearg! He had returned!

At that instant, a high, piercing shriek sliced through the moist air. It was not, I knew at once, the sound of a dragon. For this sound had assaulted me once before. I could not mistake it.

It was the cry of a kreelix.

I turned skyward just as the bat-like wings appeared out of the mist. The kreelix dove straight at me, its deadly fangs exposed. My hand reached for the hilt of my sword—then froze.

What good was my blade? I could not forget the last time I had faced those fangs, under the Cobblers' Rowan. The shock. The sheer pain. Though I had none of my own magic left, I still had the fear.

Plunging downward, the kreelix opened its blood red mouth. Three deadly fangs arched toward me. Another shriek tore through the swirling mist. The claws raised to slice me to shreds.

Suddenly a dark form bolted out of the fog across the river. Eremon! Clearing the waterway in a great bound, the stag leaped right into the path of the kreelix. With a colossal thud, they met in midair. I jumped out of the way as they came crashing down into the bank. Mud sprayed in all directions.

The two of them tumbled into the river. Eremon gained his legs first and lowered his rack to charge. But the kreelix, shrieking vengefully, lashed out with its claws, ripping the stag's flank. Even so, Eremon plowed straight into the beast, impaling one of its wings. Blood, both red and purple, swirled in the churning waters.

I drew my sword—just as a flash of scarlet light erupted. Above the distant ringing of my blade, I heard Eremon's sharp cry as the kreelix struck again. The great stag faltered, slumping in the middle of the river. I leaped into the spray, swinging my sword as I ran through the waves.

The kreelix whirled around. Like an enormous bat, fangs bared, it swiped at me with its uninjured wing. I dodged—but a bony edge gouged my cheek. As I jabbed my blade at its chest, a river stone slipped under my foot, sending me careening backward. The sword flew out of my hand. Icy water rushed over me.

Before I could right myself, something heavy fell on top of me, pushing me deeper underwater. My ribs collapsed. I gagged, swallowing water, struggling to escape from the mass of fur that crushed my face and chest. My lungs screamed, my mind darkened.

All at once, a strong hand grabbed my arm and pulled me free. Air filled my lungs at last, though I coughed uncontrollably, spewing water like a fountain. Finally, the spasms quieted enough that

I could make out Hallia, in her human form, dragging me from the river. She dropped me, sputtering, at the water's edge, then left immediately.

After a moment, I raised myself on my elbow. Just downriver lay the half-submerged body of the kreelix, the broken shard of an antler lodged in its back. Then a realization colder than the frigid waves washed over me. On the other side of the kreelix lay another body, sprawled on the muddy bank. The body of Eremon.

I rose and stumbled to his side. Hallia, sitting in the mud, was cradling the stag's head upon her lap. Her long face creased in sorrow, she seemed oblivious to the blood seeping into her robe from the puncture in his neck. Wordlessly, she stroked his forehead and his shattered antler, all the while looking into his deep brown eyes.

"My brother," she said softly. "You mustn't die, oh no. You mustn't leave me."

Eremon's chest shuddered as he tried to draw a breath. "I may be dying, my Eo-Lahallia. But leave you? That . . . I will never do."

Her own immense eyes peered into his. "We have so much yet to do, you and I! We still haven't run through the Collwyn Hills in the flower of spring."

His face tightened, and his hoof nudged her thigh. "You know how much I long to run by your side as a deer. And to stand by your side as a man. Yet now . . . I lack even the strength to change back into man form."

"Oh, Eremon! This is worse, far worse, than my dream."

"Here," I offered, starting to rise. "I could make you a poultice that might help."

Eremon's hoof knocked into me. His gaze, stern but kind, seemed to swallow me whole. "No, young hawk. It's too late for such things. Or even for your powers, if you still had them."

I bit my lip. "Whatever powers I once had are just a torment now."

"The kreelix . . ." he began, before taking a halting breath. "It was a kreelix, wasn't it? A magic eater? I thought they had all been destroyed. Long ago."

"So did my tutor, Cairpré."

Eremon blinked. "The bard Cairpré is your tutor? You are blessed indeed."

My brow knitted. "The only blessing I seek is to do something to help you. Now, Eremon."

Ignoring my comment, he asked, "But where . . . did the kreelix come from? Why did it attack you?"

"I don't know. Cairpré thinks someone is raising them, training them to kill."

With difficulty, he swallowed. "The kreelix—it thought you still possessed magic. Or else it wouldn't have attacked you."

I shook my head. "The only magic I possess is what you gave me. It must have sensed that."

Eremon winced. He turned toward his sister. "Forgive me."

Blinking back her tears, she answered bitterly, "I will try."

A wave of spray lifted off the water and settled on the stag with the softness of a candle's glow, caressing his bloodstained body. Another wave of spray came, then another. Almost as if the river itself were grieving, no less than Hallia and myself. Then I noticed that the air around us had begun to quiver, to shimmer, like the veil of mist that separated this world from the Otherworld. In that moment, I sensed somehow that another presence, more elusive than the mist itself, had joined us.

Hallia cocked her head, first in doubt, then in surprise, as she felt something change in her brother's body. His glistening muscles relaxed. His face, newly becalmed, tilted slightly, as if he were listening to someone's whispered words. When at last he spoke, grief still tinged his voice. Yet the old resonance had returned, along with a touch of something else, something I could not quite name.

"My sister, the spirits have come—to take me, to guide me on the Long Journey. Yet before I go, you must know that I, too, have had a dream. A dream . . . about a time when you shall overflow with joy, as the river in spring overflows with water."

Hallia's head fell lower, almost touching his own. "I cannot imagine such a time without you."

His breathing slowed, and he spoke with more effort. "That time . . . will come to you, Eo-Lahallia. And in the days before then, in your moments of fear and in your moments of repose . . . I myself will come to you."

Shutting her eyes, she turned away.

Eremon's hoof quivered, brushing my hand. "Be . . . brave, young hawk. Find the Galator. You have more power . . . than you know."

"Please," I begged. "Don't die."

The deep brown eyes closed, then fluttered briefly. "May green meadows . . . find you."

He exhaled one last time, then lay still.

XIX

THE WHIRLWIND

Swathed in mist, Eremon's blood running down our arms, Hallia and I strained to carry the stag's heavy body over to a protected bend in the riverbank. There a patch of vibrant green grass sprouted, and there we dug his grave in the moist, rich soil. Hallia wove a funeral shawl from shoots of eelgrass, which she carefully draped over his neck. After filling in the grave, I set out to ensure that it would remain undisturbed. Weary though I was, I carried more than a dozen stones to the spot. Hefty ones. Yet as much as my back ached, my heart ached even more.

As I worked, Hallia stood in silence by the grave, an occasional tear drifting down her chin. Although she said nothing, she sometimes clutched her yellow robe or stamped the turf, testimony to the violent storms raging within her. My stone gathering completed, I stood nearby, hardly daring to look at her, let alone comfort her.

At last, without lifting her eyes from her brother's grave, she spoke. "He called you *young hawk.*"

Silently, I nodded.

"It is a name with a meaning for my people."

I said nothing.

Still without looking at me, she continued, her voice sounding far, far away. "There is a story, as old as the first track of the first hoof, about a young hawk. He befriended a fawn. Brought him food when he hurt his leg, led him home when he was lost."

I shook my head. "Your brother had faith in me. More than I do myself."

Her round eyes flitted my way. "In me, too." She sighed heavily. "Soon you will be going, I suppose."

"That's right."

She threw her braid over her shoulder. "Well, if you think I'm coming with you, you are mistaken."

"I never asked—"

"Good. Because if you did, my answer would be no." She kicked at one of the river rocks. "No, I say."

I studied her for a long moment. "I didn't ask you, Hallia."

"No, but *he* did." She glared at the stones. "He asked me. Not with his words, but with his eyes."

"You should not come. You've suffered enough."

Her head bowed. "That I have."

Spying my sword on the bank, I crouched by the river, washing the mud from its blade. Somberly, I replaced it in the scabbard. Then, my feet feeling heavier than the stones I had laid upon Eremon's grave, I stepped slowly over to Hallia. She did not move, merely watching me with her gaze so full of intelligence and grief. A pace away, I stopped.

I felt the urge to take her hand, but held myself back. "I am sorry. Truly sorry."

She did not respond.

For several minutes we stood there, stiff and silent. But for the swirling mist, weaving about our legs, and the churning waters of the River Unceasing, nothing moved, nothing changed. I felt again the profound stillness that I had sensed inside the living stone. And, somewhere deep within, the quiet magic of a deer.

Out of nowhere, a sharp gust of wind struck us. Hallia's robe flapped against her legs. Spray flew off the river, drenching us; mist shredded into nothingness. The wind accelerated—howling, driving us both backward. Hallia cried out as her braid lifted straight up from her head. Hard as I tried to keep my balance, the wind sent me careening on the slick mud. I fell toward the river, about to hit the water, when—

I never hit.

Suddenly I was airborne, carried aloft by the fierce, whirling winds. My tunic flapped and billowed, sometimes covering my face. Hallia's foot struck me as she tumbled through the air nearby, but when I called to her the wind forced the words back into my throat. Spinning wildly, we rose higher into the air.

At one point, through the spiraling mist, my second sight glimpsed the patch of vibrant grass where we had buried Eremon. Just upstream, the remains of Valdearg's eggs lay scattered. Then thick clouds swallowed up everything, even as the wind had swallowed us. The whirling currents screamed in my ears.

Jostled and spun relentlessly, thrown upside down and sideways, I lost any bearings that I might have possessed. My body felt stretched, pummeled, turned inside out. Assaulted—from every side at once. Eyes watering, I could barely breathe amidst the battering winds. Was Hallia doing any better? Wherever this whirling storm was carrying us, I only hoped that we might arrive there alive. Before long, I fell unconscious.

When I awoke, I found myself sprawled facedown on a floor of smooth flagstones. Still whirling, my head pulsed with a roaring sound, as endless as ocean waves. I clung to the stones—they seemed so solid!—for a few more seconds before willing myself to turn over. At last I summoned the strength to roll onto my back. Weakly, my head still spinning, I pushed myself into a sitting position.

Hallia, I realized, lay beside me. Her face looked pale; she breathed fitfully. Her tan-colored hair, no longer tied in a braid, spread across the stones. I reached an unsteady hand toward her, when suddenly I caught myself.

That roaring sound . . . not my head, not the ocean, but voices. Hundreds and hundreds of voices. All around us, all shouting.

The two of us lay in the middle of a great circle of seats, filled with clamoring people. An amphitheater! Although I had never seen one before, I remembered well my mother's descriptions of the Roman amphitheaters during my childhood in Gwynedd. They were, she had explained, colossal arenas for sports—and, sometimes, for sacrifice.

Dizzily, I shook the fog from my second sight, trying to take it all in. The flagstone floor stretched wider than any courtyard I had ever seen, all the way to the rows upon rows of people encircling us. Many waved fists at us, making me feel that their shouts were more likely taunts than cheers.

All of a sudden, a huge pair of doors flung open at the far end of the amphitheater. Out of the darkness galloped an immense black stallion, pulling a wheeled chariot. Seated in the chariot, a muscled warrior raised his burly arms to the crowd. As they bellowed encouragement, he cracked his whip over the horse's streaming mane, driving the chariot directly toward us.

He's going to trample us! The realization shot through me like a bolt of lightning.

Struggling to my feet, I reached under Hallia's arms. Desperately, I tried to lift her onto my back. All the while, above the roaring crowd, I heard the pounding of the stallion's hooves on the stones. Closer drew the chariot, and closer.

At last, shaking with the weight, I managed to lift Hallia off the floor. Glancing behind, I saw the crazed eyes of the horse and the triumphant smile of the warrior bearing swiftly down on us. My heart slammed against my ribs. I took one halting step, then another. The crowd thundered angrily.

My legs buckled beneath me. I collapsed to my knees. Hallia toppled, hitting the floor with a loud moan. I swung my head around, an instant before the chariot crushed us beneath its wheels. Instinctively, I threw myself in front of her.

Just then, the chariot melted into the air. So did the amphitheater, the crowd, the roaring cries. All that remained were the stones, the black stallion, and the warrior himself. Eerie blue lights flickered around the edges of the room, if this really was a room, yet I could see no more. No walls, no ceiling. Only darkness, tinged by the dancing blue lights on the horizon.

With one hand hooked on his gleaming breastplate and the other grasping the whip, the warrior strode over. Grinning down at us, he cackled with evident satisfaction. Then, miraculously, he too began to change. His bearded face grew wider and smoother, as all the hairs vanished. Two triangular ears sprouted, along with a shriveled wart in the center of the high forehead. Across the hairless scalp, wrinkles ran like furrows in a field. Two ancient eyes, blacker even than my own, peered at me. Only the warrior's grin remained, though it was studded with bent, misshapen teeth.

"Domnu," I rasped, my throat suddenly dry.

"Such a pleasure to see you again, my pet." She patted her sack-like robe and began circling us, her bare feet slapping against the stones. "And you gave me such a splendid chance to drive that chariot! The humans, all told, are not much for ideas. But those Romans had a good one there."

She paused, scratching the wart on her forehead. "Or was it the Gaels? The Picts? No matter—humans, of whatever sort. An unusually good idea they had. Even if they lacked the imagination to make it more exciting."

The black stallion stamped his hoof and whinnied loudly. Domnu stopped circling and glanced at the powerful steed. The tips of her teeth showed as her grin widened. Her voice grew more quiet, and even more menacing.

"Are you disagreeing, my colt? Was the excitement too much for you?" She stepped closer and slowly ran her hand down the stallion's nose. While quivering slightly, he continued to hold his head high. "Perhaps you would rather go back to being a chess piece?"

At once, I remembered the chess piece of a black horse that I had seen when I first visited Domnu's lair. He had shown spirit then, as he did now. And he reminded me vaguely of that horse . . . that stallion. What was his name? I chewed my lip, recalling those days, long ago, when I felt my father's strong arms wrapped around me, and the still stronger back supporting us, as we rode around the castle grounds. Whatever else I had forgotten, I could never forget the stallion's prancing gait, his dignified air. And the way he ate apples out of my hand.

As Domnu continued to speak to the stallion, Hallia shifted beside me and opened her eyes. Seeing the hairless hag, she stiffened.

Although a bit of the color had returned to her cheeks, I knew that she was probably still very weak.

"Are you able to stand?" I whispered.

"I . . . don't know." She observed me worriedly. "That wind . . . where are we? Who is that . . . hag? What have I missed?"

"A lot." I gave her a wry smile. "You wouldn't believe me if I told you."

Hallia frowned. Taking my arm, she raised herself to her knees. Her eyes darted to Domnu once more. "She makes me . . . shiver. Who *is* she?"

"Domnu. I think we're in her lair."

"Well, now," interrupted Domnu. "Our second guest is awake." She glanced sharply at the stallion, then slid over to us. Bending toward Hallia, she ran a hand across her wrinkled scalp. "A deer woman, is it?" She clacked her tongue knowingly. "I can always tell by the chin. Bristling bones, I know that shape! So adorably tapered."

Though Hallia stiffened with fright, she did her best to hold her voice steady. "I am, indeed, a deer woman . . . of the Mellwyn-bri-Meath clan." She looked away. "And I beg—no, demand—that you set us free. Imm . . . immediately."

"Demand? Did you say demand?" Once more, the hag started walking in a circle, examining us like a hungry wolf. "Best to make no more demands, my pet. Poor manners, truly poor. I will decide what to do with you in time, just as I will decide how to teach a certain horse a lesson."

At that, the stallion stamped again on the stone floor. He snorted proudly.

Domnu stopped circling. Her dark eyes narrowed. From the

edges of the room, the blue light swelled strangely, crackling like the flames of a heatless fire.

"I understand, my colt." Her voice sounded soothing—and altogether menacing. "You simply need a change. A different perspective on life."

She raised an index finger. Briefly she inspected it, watching the blue light shimmer across her skin. Then she licked it slowly and deliberately. Finally, she held the wet finger before her lips and blew ever so gently.

The stallion reared back, whinnying loudly. He kicked his immense hooves in the air. Suddenly he shrank down into a small, sharp-nosed beast, as thin as a serpent, with dusty brown fur and tiny black eyes. A weasel. The little creature gave us a baleful look, then scurried across the floor, disappearing in the blue flames.

Hallia gasped and clutched my wrist.

Domnu flashed her misshapen teeth. "Poor little colt. This will give him a chance to rest." Her eyes darted back to us. "Of course, I made certain he has no teeth. That way he won't be tempted to use them, shall we say, inappropriately."

"You wretch!" I exclaimed. "That was a terrible thing to do! The horse was only being—"

"Disrespectful." Domnu's face shimmered in the rising blue light. "And I trust that you will not do the same." Thoughtfully, she scratched the prominent wart. "Especially since I plan to feed you a sumptuous meal."

She clapped her wrinkled hands together. Instantly, a full-blown feast appeared on an oaken table in the middle of the floor. Before us lay steaming breads, milk pudding, baked apples, buttered green vegetables, river trout, flasks of water and wine, and an enormous pie that smelled like roasted chestnuts.

My mouth watered. My stomach churned. I could almost taste that pie. Yet one glance at Hallia told me that she felt as mistrustful as I did. We shook our heads in unison. Clambering to my feet, I helped her stand, although she teetered unsteadily. While Hallia looked in the direction of the departed weasel, my own gaze met Domnu's. "We do not want your food."

"Really?" She stroked her scalp. "Perhaps you would prefer venison?"

I scowled. "I would prefer hag."

The blue light at the edges of the room flared, but Domnu watched us impassively. "Surprising, my pets, that you aren't hungry. After all, you have been here for quite some time."

"Some time?" I glared at her. "How long have we been here?"

Domnu started circling again, her feet slapping on the stones. "Oh, how adorable your kind can be when it gets willful! Like little sparrows who are angry that they cannot yet fly! But yes, my pet, it was quite some time ago that my little whirlwind came to fetch you. I was beginning to worry that you might not wake up at all, at least not while I was still in the mood for charioteering."

She scratched a mass of wrinkles by one ear. "I even laid a wager—against myself, there being no one else around just now— that you would never wake up. Though I lost that bet, I also won, if you take my meaning. An admirable outcome." She cackled softly. "I do so love to win."

"How long?" I demanded.

Still circling, Domnu yawned, revealing all her twisted teeth. "Well, now, I should say that it has been at least two days."

"Two days!" I exclaimed. "So I have only three days left!"

"Left, my pet? Do you have some sort of appointment?"

I stepped in front of her, halting her pacing. "I do. An appointment with—" I caught myself, not sure that I should reveal any more. "With someone important."

"Is that so?" asked the hag, with a chilling stare. "Too bad. So too bad. I had thought you might be on the way to meet Valdearg."

I winced. "Yes. That's true. And that is why I was seeking you, Domnu." I straightened my back. "For I have come at last to collect . . . the Galator."

A strange half-grin spread over her face. "How interesting. I was seeking you for the very same reason."

"What do you mean?"

Blue light danced across her brow. "You see, my pet, the Galator has been stolen."

XX

IONN

My knees nearly buckled. "Stolen?"

Blue flames swelled around the room. Wispy shadows, as thin as dead trees, danced across the flagstone floor. "Yes, my pet. The Galator has been stolen. Bones! Breaded bones! Taken from me, its rightful owner."

"No." I placed my fists on my hips. "I am its rightful owner. Not you."

Domnu waved a hand carelessly. "Well, technically, I suppose, you have a claim to it."

"A claim!"

"You might even say that you own it. Still, what is more important, I *possess* it. Or, at least, used to possess it. Whoever stole it will have to return it to me." She squeezed her hand tightly. I heard the distinct sound of bones cracking and splintering, as if she were crushing someone's skull. "And," she added in a low growl, "I will make certain it does not happen again."

Hallia, her doe eyes fixed on Domnu's feet, asked tentatively, "Who . . . would have stolen it?"

Domnu opened her right hand, palm up, and blinked. A silver chalice, brimming with red wine, appeared. Intertwining snakes decorated its rim. She took a slow sip, finishing with a smack of her lips. "The question, my pet, is not who would have done it, but who *could* have done it. My home, while humble, is reasonably well fortified."

My gaze roved over the table arrayed with the feast. Then I looked to the horizon, where the chariot drawn by the stallion had first appeared. Only the ring of blue fire now marked the place. I could hardly believe that I had been convinced I was about to be trampled. Yet it had felt utterly real. No doubt being crushed under those wheels would have felt equally real. "I can't imagine anyone stealing into your lair. Your magic is too powerful."

The hag stopped in the middle of another sip. She glowered at the chalice, which began to melt into a puddle of molten silver, bubbling and steaming, in her palm. Then, with a blink, the remains disappeared. She turned her eyes, which seemed darker than night itself, toward me.

"Just the point, my pet. Whoever stole the Galator was not troubled at all by magic. No, he or she had access to a weapon I have not encountered in many, many ages. A weapon that erases magic itself."

I caught my breath. "You mean . . . *negatus mysterium?*"

Shimmering in the blue light, she nodded. "Because I was confident—too confident—that no more of it remained in Fincayra, I was unprepared. Never again! The person who wielded it simply waited until I left the lair, which I do once every few decades, then pulled loose a few threads of my magical weavings—and walked right in. The *negatus mysterium* erased any signs."

Her bent teeth showed themselves in a sinister grin. "There was one flaw, however." She leaned closer, her voice a hushed whisper. "You may recall that the Galator will only serve its owner if it has been freely given. Which, in this case, it certainly was not."

Running my hand along the leather cord of my satchel, I pondered her words. "So whoever has the Galator cannot use it."

"Precisely, my pet. That mistake is also revealing. It tells me that the thief is someone who knows a good deal about magic, but who is also greedy, arrogant, and impulsive."

I reached inside my satchel and felt the one remaining string from my psaltery. It felt so stiff, so brittle. "I know who the thief is."

Domnu peered at me skeptically. "You do?"

"Yes." Feeling the emptiness within my chest, I nodded. "The same person who stole my powers."

"Explain yourself, my pet."

I traded glances with Hallia. "Before I do, I need your commitment. No treachery this time."

She flashed a mouthful of broken teeth, lit by the flickering flames. "What's wrong, my pet? Don't you trust me?"

"No! And I never will." I watched her warily. "But I might agree to collaborate with you—for a while."

Domnu growled softly. "An alliance, then?"

"An alliance."

"What are the terms?"

My fists clenched. "If together we can regain the Galator, then I can use it to battle Valdearg three days from now. If I should survive, the Galator is yours. I forfeit any claim to it."

Her dark eyes widened. "And if you should not survive?"

"Then it's yours, as well. You may have to argue with Valdearg about it, but I won't be around anymore to trouble you."

"*Hmmm.* Tempting." She studied me severely. "One more term should be added, however. If you can, with my help, regain the Galator, you must show me something."

Puzzled, I cocked my head. "What could I possibly show you?"

The hag hesitated, patting her hairless head for several seconds. "Oh, nothing serious, really. Just a trifle."

"What?"

She bent so close that our noses nearly touched. "I want you to show me how the pendant—especially that green jewel in its center—works."

I stepped backward, almost bumping into Hallia. "You—you don't know? With all your powers?"

Domnu hissed. "Would I ask you if I did? I only know what any wandering bard could tell you. That its powers are truly vast. And utterly mysterious."

Remembering Cairpré's description, I quoted, *"Vast beyond knowing."*

"Quite so. No doubt I could divine all its secrets in a little time. Say, a millennium or two. But someone who knows you made me think you might be able to help me do it faster. Bones! Boiling bones! What was his name? That little fellow who is always playing games with Rhita Gawr."

"Dagda." My face reddened. Little fellow! "His battles with Rhita Gawr are no game."

The hag cackled quietly. "Such naïveté! Charming, my pet, charming." Taking no heed of my contempt, she continued. "One day, perhaps, you will learn that everything is a game. A serious game, perhaps, such as charioteering. Or a meaningless game, full of frivolity—such as life."

I planted my boots, grinding my heels on the stone floor. "You'll never convince me of that."

She waved at the air, her hand awash in blue light. "It doesn't matter. I doubt you will live long enough to learn any better. Even so, I will take the risk that Dagda's remark was true. He told me that, one day, the half-human named Merlin would truly master the power of the Galator."

Surprised, I caught my breath. "Well, I accept your term, though I doubt that prediction will come true. How can it? In all the time I wore the pendant, feeling its weight on my chest, I learned only this: Whatever its magic really is, it has something to do with . . . an emotion."

Suddenly unsettled, Domnu tugged on the folds of her neck. "What emotion?"

"Love."

She made a face like someone who had swallowed curdled milk. "Bones! Are you sure?"

I nodded.

"Well . . . as I said, the risk is mine. I'll just need to find some other way to unlock its power. So there we are, my pet. Allies—for the time being."

"Wait." I glanced toward the flickering lights. "I, too, have an additional term."

The hag eyed me with suspicion. "What is it?"

"Before we go any further, you must return that stallion to his original form."

Hallia started. Her brown eyes gazed at me in astonishment— and, though I couldn't be sure, a touch of gratitude.

"The horse?" asked Domnu. "Why should I?"

I sucked in my breath, remembering the feeling of running upon my own hooves, my own four sturdy legs. "Because you need my help."

The hag grunted. "I suppose I do. All right. Though I doubt that fool beast has learned his lesson yet."

She flicked a finger toward the edge of the room. Suddenly a loud neigh sounded, followed by galloping hooves. The black stallion ran over, keeping his distance from Domnu. Cautiously, he approached Hallia, nuzzling her outstretched hand. Then, his tail swishing, he sidestepped over to me. Gently, I laid my hand on his gleaming coat, feeling its silken surface. He whinnied softly in response.

"He knows you," observed Hallia.

I stroked his black mane, inhaling the horse's familiar smell. Slowly, the edges of my mouth curled upward. "As I know him. His name is . . . Ionn. Ionn y Morwyn. He was my father's horse, and my own first friend."

Domnu shrugged. "How touching. Very well, then. I might consider throwing the horse into the bargain. A sturdy beast, but he's been nothing but trouble to me from the day I, well, rescued him from that drafty old stable."

Ionn gave a loud snort, but she didn't pay any attention. "What I really need is something more docile and obedient—a goblin, perhaps—for my chessboard. So I suppose if you agree to our little alliance, the stallion is yours."

Feeling Ionn's warm breath on my neck, I nodded. "Except that he isn't mine. Or anyone else's, for that matter. This horse belongs to himself. And only to himself."

Ionn nuzzled my shoulder. I continued to stroke his mane, recalling the times I had clung to it as a child. Then, on an impulse, I took an apple from the bowl on the table. The stallion nudged it with his nose, breathing warm air once again on my hand. Wrapping his lips around the fruit, he took his first bite, crunching loudly. Hallia watched, a spare smile on her face.

"So be it, my pet. I will set the horse free."

I watched Ionn take another bite, then turned back to the hag. "Then we are allies."

Domnu reached for one of the still-steaming loaves of bread on the table. Tearing off a chunk, she gave half to me and half to Hallia, who took it reluctantly. "Here. If we are going to be allies, even temporarily, you will need your strength." She pulled off another chunk and popped it into her mouth. *"Mmmm.* Not bad, if I do fffay fffo myfffelf."

Ionn finished the last of the apple, rubbing his soft nose against my wrist as he chewed. At the same time, I took a bite of the bread. Instantly, my mouth filled with its rich, roasted flavor. Before I had even swallowed, Ionn butted my shoulder with his nose. Grinning, I reached over to the bowl and gave him another apple. As he ate, so did I. In time, Hallia too began to nibble.

Together, she and I moved toward the oaken table. With a clap of Domnu's hands, three wooden chairs appeared. Hallia and I fell to the food, eating and drinking ravenously, until we could hold no more. Domnu, for her part, ate the entire pie in just a few seconds, dribbling chestnut sauce on herself. Then, seeing my look of disappointment, she waved her hand. A new pie, speckled with blueberries, suddenly filled the dish. Somehow both Hallia and I found room for hefty slices.

At last, Domnu pushed back her chair. "Now tell me about this person who stole your powers. And why you believe it's the same vermin who took the Galator."

With the back of my hand, I wiped some of the buttery sauce

from the trout off my chin. "I speak of Urnalda, enchantress of the dwarves."

Domnu scoffed. "That old sorceress of the tunnels? She has the arrogance and the greed, to be sure. But she lacks the patience, the cunning, and most of all the understanding of magic. I doubt she could wield *negatus mysterium,* dangerous stuff that it is, without destroying her own magic in the process."

"She used it against me!" I stood, my hands pressed to my ribs. "All my magic, all my power, is gone now." I swallowed. "She even took my staff."

The hag's ancient eyes examined me. "Not true. I perceive magic in you, even now."

Sadly, I traded looks with Hallia. "You must be sensing the magic that was given to me by . . . a friend. Yet that magic allows me to do only one thing."

"Which is, my pet?"

Hallia shot me a warning glance.

"To know . . . a kind of glory." I drew a slow breath. "Though even that won't last much longer."

Domnu's scalp furrowed more deeply. Behind her, the blue flames writhed and twisted, throwing shadows over her burly hands. "Neither will you, I expect. You are quite determined to confront this dragon of yours, I can see that clearly. Well, now, tell me. Do you recall that prediction about you I made when we last met?"

I shuddered, still hearing the sting of her words. "You said that I would bring ruin, utter ruin, to Fincayra."

"That's right, my pet. Don't take it too hard. Besides, I now think my prediction was a bit too harsh."

"Really?"

"Yes." Shadows fluttered like ghouls across the tabletop. "Not because the notion itself was flawed, mind you. But because I now sincerely doubt that you will live long enough to cause much more trouble."

I could only grimace.

"In any case," she went on, "we must consider how to use your remaining time most productively." The flames surrounding us sputtered and crackled. "No, no, I think you would only be wasting what little time is left by seeking out Urnalda."

"But why? I'm sure she's the one."

The hag shook her head, causing ripples of blue light to flow like waves across her scalp. "There is, I suppose, a chance you are right. I sincerely doubt it, though. Still, you have given me an idea. Bones! I should have thought of it sooner. There is a place—an oracle of sorts. It can answer any question, any question at all, posed by a mortal creature. That rules me out, I am afraid. But it ought to work for you."

Uncertainly, I brushed the stray hairs off my forehead. "Where is this place? Is it difficult to get there? My time—it's so short."

"Not difficult at all, my pet. And no whirlwind this time! I could send you there by Leaping." A low cackle filled her throat. "Or, if you like, I could use a chariot. More time-consuming, but ever so much more exciting." Seeing my expression, she frowned. "All right. Leaping, then."

"I'm still not sure. If Urnalda does have the Galator, it could take all the time I have left to win it back."

Domnu reached for the flask of wine, opened her mouth as wide as a crevasse, and poured all the liquid down her throat. "Ah, my pet, don't you understand? If Urnalda does not have it, then you will have used up all your time for nothing. If, however, she does have it, the oracle will tell you that straightaway. This way, you can be certain who really is the thief." She crushed the flask in her fist, spraying shards of glass on the stones. "And that is something—breaded bones, that is something—I would dearly like to know."

Slowly, I gave a nod. "All right, then. Tell me about this oracle. What sort of person is there?"

"Not a person. Not exactly. The oracle lies far to the south, near the sea, in a place surrounded by cliffs—steep, smoking cliffs."

At this, Hallia stiffened. She started to say something, but the hag cut her off.

"It's so simple, my pet! All you need to do is ask it your question." She glanced toward the flickering lights. "That is, after you have surmounted a minor obstacle."

I cringed. "What sort of obstacle?"

Blue light exploded in the room, swallowing everything.

PART THREE

XXI

THE BIRTH OF THE MIST

Salt. On my lips. In the air.

Suddenly I realized that my legs and back felt wet. Thoroughly wet. I shifted, when something rough scraped the side of my neck. Startled, I sat up—as a bright purple sea star fell from my shoulder, landing beside me with a splash.

Tide pool! I was sitting in a tide pool. A strand of kelp clung to my arm; a sea cucumber, slimy and bloated, draped over my hip. And there, smirking at me, sat Hallia. She leaned against a gnarled piece of driftwood, her back to the waves stroking the shore of black, crystalline sand. Trying to stifle a laugh, she quickly turned aside.

"In the name of Dagda!" I cursed, lifting myself out of the shallow pool. As I stood, water coursed off my tunic and splattered my boots. "Of all the places to land . . ."

Hallia's eyes flitted toward me—then veered away. "You'll dry out," she said quietly, pausing for a long moment to watch the undulating wall of mist beyond the waves. "This place holds more heat than you know."

Unsure what she meant, I rubbed the sore spot on my neck. Though the sting of the sea star was fading, its smell was not. And rubbing made it worse. Much like garlic but stronger, the smell wafted over me, pushing aside even the ocean's briny breath. Hoping to wash it off, I bent down to the tide pool and splashed some water on my skin.

"Just wait a bit," said Hallia, still looking at the mist. "A purple brittlepoint's odor won't last very long. You're lucky it wasn't a yellow one. Their smell can take days to die down. And this beach is full of them."

Annoyed, I peered at her. "How do you know so much about sea stars? And this place?"

She turned her eyes, softer than the mist itself, toward me. "Because this is the place of my childhood. Before my clan, the Mellwyn-bri-Meath, left for the woods of the west."

"Your . . . childhood?" I stepped, boots sloshing, closer to her. "Are you sure? This island has so many beaches."

"Not with sand like this." She ran her fingers through the dark crystals. Then her gaze lifted to something behind me. "Nor with cliffs like those."

I spun around to see a line of sheer cliffs, as black as the sand at our feet. Ominous they stood, like a stand of dead trees. Despite the strong light from the sun, still well above the horizon, the cliffs wore only shadows upon shadows. From several points among their crags, thin trails of smoke climbed skyward.

I shivered, from more than the wet tunic on my back. "The smoking cliffs. The ones Domnu talked about."

"Where lies the oracle—among other things."

Using her big toe, Hallia poked a cockleshell, turning it over on the sand. A long, gray leg instantly emerged from the shell and started to push sideways. In a few seconds, the cockle flipped itself back over—with a squirt of seawater for good measure. Watching this, she smiled wistfully. "It was a good place to live. Full of . . . companions. Even now."

"Companions?" I glanced again at the forbidding cliffs, then at the dark stretch of shore. "Beyond the shells and sea stars, there's no one here but us."

"Oh, no?" She hesitated for a long moment. Finally she shook her head, catching the sunlight in her unbraided hair. "My people are here."

"But I thought you said they left."

"They did—except for those whose tracks had already melted into the sand."

I drew a deep breath of salty air, more confused than ever. "I don't understand."

She waved at the cliffs. "Use your deer eyes, Merlin. Not your man eyes."

Turning, I allowed my second sight to spread over the cliffs. To probe their shadows. To feel their edges. The slapping of the waves behind me slowly faded, transforming into a different sound—somehow nearer, somehow farther away. Thrumming. Drumming. Like an ever-beating heart, an ever-pounding hoof.

In time, I began to discern a faint tracery of lines woven across the vertical slopes. The lines ran in all directions, bending with every surge and scoop of the cliffs. Could they be ancient trails? Worn by countless hooves over countless years?

And . . . hollows. Caves. Darker than the shadows. Full of mystery, as well as something more.

I nodded, understanding at last. "Your ancestors are still here."

With the grace of a doe, Hallia rose to her feet. "That they are, buried in the caves, and a part of me with them." She sighed. "In my heart, I still cling to this shore, just as much as those blue mussels cling to the rocks over there. In my dreams, I find myself floating through this mist—like the silver jellyfish, so delicate, that swims through the shallows, forever breathing the water that becomes its very body."

Her words encircled me, enveloping me like the mist itself. "Why then did you leave?"

"Because of the cliffs. The old lava mountain they surround began to rumble, and then to smoke." Her eyes darted like fretful gulls across the shoreline. "Though it never spewed fire, as it did in Distant Time, the mountain released . . . other things. Evil things."

Under my eye, the tender skin started to throb. The mention of the fire mountain, most likely—reminding me of those flames of my own making, flames that had scarred my face forever. I reached up to stroke my skin, when my hand froze. This scar under my eye hadn't come from those flames. No! It had come from an older wound, years before.

How could I have forgotten? On that long-ago day, on a deserted beach much like this one, a wild boar had attacked—and I was its prey. I could still hear its snarl, still see its slashing tusks, still feel its hot breath. And, with every throbbing pulse, I could still remember my shock at discovering that it was really not a boar at all, but the wicked warlord of the spirit world: Rhita Gawr.

Hallia nudged my shoulder with her own, just as I had seen her do once, as a doe, to Eremon. "You are troubled, I can tell."

Despite the moist air, my throat felt parched. "Those evil things . . . from the mountain. What were they?"

She frowned, then stooped to pick up a moon snail on the sand. Pensively, she ran her finger over the round, spiraling shell, the color of cream. "Something tells me you already know. Spirits—angry ones. Seeking death, not life, for anyone who lived here."

As I nodded, her frown deepened. "They came out of the cliffs, the caves, the sea itself, it seemed. No one knew why. We only knew that sickness and pain followed in their tracks." She winced, remembering something. "And that they had come only once before."

"When was that?"

Gently, she placed the shell on the rim of a barnacle-crusted rock. Before straightening, she paused to touch the flower of a pink sea ancmone, limply waiting for the higher tide to return. At last, she stood again and faced me, her eyes now less frightened than sad. "Eremon could have told you. He knew all the ancient stories."

I wrapped my arms around my ribs, hoping to warm myself. "I miss him."

"So do I," she whispered. "So do I."

I watched as her tongue moistened her lips. "How is that tooth healing?"

"It still hurts a little," she said sadly. "But not so much as other places."

"You don't have to tell that story if you don't want to. I just had the feeling . . ."

"I'll try."

Turning her long chin toward the waves, and the billowing mist beyond, she started speaking in a slow, solemn cadence. "In the time before time, all spoken words could be seen and touched and held. Every story, once told, became a single, glowing thread—a thread that wove itself into a limitless, living tapestry. It stretched from these very cliffs all the way down to the sea, across this shore, and under the waves, where it lay beyond reach, beyond knowing. The tapestry—alive with colors and shapes, shadowy places and bright—was called by many names, but to the deer people it was known as the Carpet Caerlochlann."

She watched a crab, decorated with a ragged frond of kelp, strut across the driftwood by her foot. "The Carpet grew more luminous, more richly textured, with each passing season. Until . . . it grew so lovely that it caught the interest of one who wanted it for himself. Not to savor its stories—to feel its layers upon layers of woven yearnings, passions, grievings, and delights—but to own it. Possess it. Control it."

"Rhita Gawr," I said, touching my aching scar.

"Yes. Rhita Gawr. He sent his spirit warriors to haunt the cliffs, chasing away the deer people, poisoning any who dared to remain. Then he took the Carpet Caerlochlann as his own. It is said that on that day, when the sun began to rise, it was so stricken with sorrow that it could not bear to return. So from that moment on, all of Fincayra was cast into darkness."

Waves rolled onto the shore, one after another, nearly slapping our feet. A pair of cormorants soared out of the mist, flapping noisily before splashing down in the shallows. One of them plunged the full length of its neck into the water and came up with a writhing green fish in its beak. Hit by the golden sun, the fish flashed like a living emerald.

"There is sunlight now," I said softly.

"There is, yes. Because the great spirit Dagda confronted Rhita Gawr and won back the tapestry of tales. No one knows just how he succeeded, though it is said that he had to give up something terribly valuable—some of his own precious powers—to do it."

A new kind of cold gripped me, reaching deeper than the skin beneath my sopping tunic. "And what, after paying so dearly, did Dagda do with the tapestry?"

Hallia's round eyes turned to me. "He gave it away."

"He what?"

"Gave it away." She looked toward the slumbering sea, hidden by the vaporous curtain. "First, using the trail of a falling star as his needle, he pulled loose all the threads of story. These he wove together with threads of his own, made partly of air and partly of water. When finally he finished, the new weaving held all the magic of spoken words, and more. It was not quite air, not quite water—but something of both. Something in between. Something called . . ."

"Mist," I finished.

She nodded. "Then Dagda gave the magical mist to the peoples of this island. He wrapped it all the way around the coastline. So that every beach, every cove, every inlet would touch its mysterious vapors. And so that every breath taken upon these shores would mingle with its magic."

Shyly, she shrugged her shoulders. "So that is how, in the tales of my people, Fincayra's eternal mist was born."

For a long moment, neither of us spoke. A gull screeched overhead, while clams squirted by the tide pools. Beyond that, we heard only the waves slapping the shore, sucking the black sand as they pulled back to the sea. Then the lowering sun dropped behind a cloud, and I shivered.

Hallia scrutinized me. "You're cold."

Another shiver. "And wet. What I really need is a fire. Just a small one. Say, if we gather up some of this driftwood—"

"No." She shook her head, tousling her auburn hair. "It will attract *them.*"

My eyes widened. "Spirits?"

She glanced at the cliffs, which loomed even darker than before. "They might have departed. It's been many years. All the same . . . it frightens me."

"A small fire, that's all." I flapped my arms. "Just so I can dry out."

"Well . . . if you must."

Without another word, we began picking up shards of driftwood. Higher on the shore, above the clusters of mussels, I found an old tangle of seaweed that had dried into a mass of brittle stems. Pulling it apart with my fingers, shivering all the while, I made a rough-hewn nest. Then, striking two sharp rocks above the kindling, I tried to make a spark. My first several landed not on the nest, but on the wet sand. Finally one struck a stem. Gently, I breathed on it, coaxing it to burn. In time, a thin trail of smoke drifted skyward.

Before long, Hallia and I were warming ourselves before the crackling flames. "As much as I miss having hooves," I observed, "hands can be useful."

She gave a somber nod. "Eremon liked to say that hooves can make speed, while hands can make music."

Remembering my own disastrous attempt to make music—so long ago, it seemed—I grimaced. "Some hands, anyway."

"You have tried?"

I broke some driftwood over my knee and laid the pieces on the fire. "I've tried."

Hallia watched me, as if she hoped I might say more. When I didn't, she scooped some sand in her palm. "Music, real music, is a kind of magic. As elusive as the mist."

Slowly, I drew out of my satchel the charred remains of my psaltery. Holding the remains of the oaken bridge, I twirled the string, blackened and stiff. I tried to imagine it as part of a whole instrument again, cupped in my hand, with all the gleaming strings intact. But the vision exploded into flames, crumbling into charcoal. Gone: whatever magic this string once possessed. Just like whatever magic my own fingers once possessed.

"Cairpré once asked me," I mused aloud, "whether the music lies in the strings . . ."

"Or in the hands that pluck them?" Hallia grinned at me. "My own mother, who taught me how to play the willow harp, asked me the same question."

"And did you answer it?"

"No."

"Did she?"

"No." She pulled a barnacle off a shard of driftwood, then tossed the wood into the flames. "But she did say, while we sat on a rock on this very beach, that an instrument, by itself, makes no music. Only sound."

She furrowed her brow. "I can't remember her words exactly, but she said something else, too. That musical instruments need to tap into something more—something higher. That's it. She called it *a power still higher.*"

I jumped at the phrase.

She eyed me. "What's wrong?"

"That's what I'm going to need if I'm ever going to stop

Valdearg. *A power still higher.* It could mean the Galator. Or it could mean something else." Using the last of the shards, I shoved the burning coals together. "Whatever it is, I don't think I have it."

Hallia studied me, half her face aglow from the flames. "Maybe not, but you do have something."

I looked at her skeptically.

"You have whatever it took to make Domnu give that stallion back his natural form. And, just as important, to set him free." She turned toward the pulsing waves. "That was a noble thing to do. Almost . . . a stag-like thing."

I lifted the flap of my satchel and replaced the psaltery string. "Maybe I have done at least one thing right, then. I only hope that hag keeps her word and sets Ionn free."

Hallia shook her long strands of hair. "I don't trust her any more than you, believe me! She does need your help, though, if she's going to get back that pendant. That's why she told you about the Wheel."

"Wheel?"

"The oracle. The one in the smoking cliffs." Her face tightened. "It's called . . . the Wheel of Wye."

I squeezed her arm. "You know about it?"

"Not much. Just that it's hidden somewhere up there." She paused. "And that it's a place of fear—and has been long before the spirits came to the mountain."

"Do you know what Domnu meant by *a minor obstacle?*"

"No. And I don't want to find out." She drew a halting breath. "There is, though, a village near the cliffs where you might learn more. It's a brutal place. Filled with m—" She caught herself. "With that *kind* of men. Who don't even notice their own tracks, who would kill a deer just for sport. Not like . . . well, another man I know."

For an instant, the fire glowed bright on her cheeks—and, it seemed, on mine. Suddenly she scowled. "That village . . . I've never been there. And never want to! But for you, it's different. It was the place—in my childhood, at least—where most oracle seekers started their climbs into the cliffs. Someone there might know something useful."

Sensing she was preparing to say good-bye, I felt saddened—even as I felt grateful for her suggestion. "Going there, I suppose, could save time."

"Though it's a rough place, and could end up costing you time." She sighed. "The biggest risk to your time, though, is simply finding it, tucked away in its hidden valley. Unless you know the right trails, you might search for days among the folds of cliffs, and the maze of hillocks on their western edge."

She paused, her lower lip trembling. "Which is why . . . I'm going to take you there myself."

My heart leaped.

"The trip will still take time, though. Even more since we can't use our deer forms. Too much risk of hunters from the village."

I looked her full in the face. "Thank you, Hallia."

"It's only what . . . my brother would have done."

"Let's go, then," I declared. "While there's still daylight. Just let me put out this fire."

With my boot, I crunched on the remaining coals. Yet as soon as I lifted my foot, they sprang back into flames. Puzzled, I glanced at my boot. Once again I tried to stamp out the fire; once again it revived. I kicked the largest of the burning embers into a nearby tide pool. It sputtered and sizzled, but continued to flame. Steam rose, mingling with the mist.

"We must leave," she said urgently. "I only hope we'll be leaving alone."

XXII

A CHILL WIND

Hallia guided me over the slippery, mussel-laden rocks to a sharp cleft at the base of the nearest cliff. There we found a thin, winding trail, covered with dust as black as the cliffs themselves. Wordlessly, we followed it inland for some distance, before turning left on another trail, then right on another. Soon we had made so many turns that I would have lost my bearings completely but for the constant presence of the cliffs towering above us.

All the while, as we wormed our way through the sheer buttresses and piles of black rock, we stayed alert for any signs of the mountain spirits. In time, the sounds and smells of the sea began to fade. The trail we were following gradually widened a bit. To our left appeared a string of stubbly fields, while to our right the dark cliffs loomed, separated from us by a row of steep, rocky hillocks. The sun, partly shrouded by a line of clouds, hung low to the west, casting golden rays on the grasses streaked with the auburns and reds of autumn.

By a field where four or five sheep grazed, heedless of us, Hallia stopped. Cautiously, she surveyed the lengthening shadows. "I don't know which worries me more," she said, her eyes darting from side to side. "The absence of spirits—or the presence of men."

"I'm worried about something else," I said grimly. "Time! There's just three days left before I must face Valdearg—with or without the Galator. Even if this oracle can help me find it, I still have to get it back somehow. And learn how to use it."

She gave her flowing hair a shake and began combing its tangles with her fingers. "And one thing more, Merlin."

My eyebrows lifted.

"You still have to get back to the dwarves' territory—no little bound from here. While you can, if you choose, run like a deer, you'll still need to allow at least two days for the journey. Which leaves you only one day to find the Galator."

Pondering her words, I scraped the ground with my boot—the same boot I had used to try to save the baby dragon. I had failed in that attempt. Would I also fail in this one?

A rock suddenly clattered down from the cliffs above. Hallia started. Her hand tugged anxiously at her hair. "The spirits . . ."

I held her gaze. "You don't have to come any farther, you know. You've already done more than I would have asked."

"I know." Her back straightened. "Even so, I shall stay with you a little longer. To the village. But there I must leave you." She glanced at the shadowed cliffs. "And wish you whatever luck is left in this land."

So very much, I wanted to tell her thanks. And something more, something beyond words. Yet my throat had closed as tight as a fist.

As her hands went back to combing her tangled hair, she turned and started slowly down the trail. I stared past her toward the rocky hillocks and the smoking crags behind. The sun's rays, piercing the gathering clouds, had deepened from gold to orange, yet the cliffs seemed darker than ever. Darker than my second sight could fathom.

In silence, we walked. The trail swung straight into the hillocks, which pressed so close to our sides that at times the mountain itself disappeared from view. While Hallia's bare feet made only the slightest shuffle on the pebbles and dust, my boots crunched with every step. Although the trail continued to grow wider, broadening into a rough road, the shadowy rock piles seemed to press all the closer.

As she maneuvered deftly around a yellow-spotted snake, Hallia gave me a worried look. "The Wheel of Wye, as an oracle, must have strong magic of its own. But it may not be stronger than Rhita Gawr's spirits. That might even be why he sent them here—to destroy it, or make it serve his purposes."

I kept striding. Shadows deepened all around us. Under my breath, I replied, "I only hope that he himself is not among them."

She inhaled sharply. "You really think he might be?"

"I don't know. It's just that . . . well, I can't shake the feeling he's somehow more involved than we know. Not just with the spirits' return, but with other things, as well. The kreelixes, for example. Why did they come back just now? And the outbreak of *negatus mysterium*—strong enough to steal the Galator from right under Domnu's warty brow. Maybe even, though I can't explain why, the murder of all those baby dragons."

She studied me doubtfully. "That's like saying the crying of a fawn is connected to the stirring of oak leaves in the wind."

"Exactly," I declared. "For connected they are! I don't understand why or how. Just that, somehow, they are."

Her face pensive, she continued along the rock-strewn road. "You sound almost like . . . someone else."

A moment later, we rounded a bend—and suddenly halted. Before us, lit by the reddening rays, rose three columns of smoke. Not from the cliffs, but from chimneys. The village.

Hallia tensed, one foot twisting anxiously on the pebbles. "I'm . . . frightened."

I took her arm. "You don't have to go any farther."

She shook free. "I know. But I'll decide when I'm turning back. Not you."

Together, we continued walking. The high-walled hillocks on both sides receded, opening into a compact valley. There, scored by shadows, sat a ramshackle settlement, made of the very slabs that dotted its stony field. The huts, seven or eight in all, looked like nothing more than square piles of rock. The roof of one had fallen in, but no one seemed to care enough to repair it. But for the smoke streaming from the chimneys, the sheep gnawing at the few tussocks of grass, and the pair of huddled figures leaning against the wall of the largest building, the whole village could have been mistaken for the rock outcroppings around it. Rising sharply from the far end of the valley, the mountain surged into smoking crags, dark and foreboding.

Hallia rolled her head, sniffing the air. "You see what I was saying about this place? Just look at it! Whatever people live here haven't joined with the land. Never have. See there? Not a single garden, or flower box, or even a bench to sit upon. Most of those huts don't have any windows."

I nodded. "The kind of place where people come to escape from trouble. Or maybe cause it."

A few raindrops splattered us. I glanced at the thick bank of clouds now obscuring the horizon. Arms of clouds, writhing like dark serpents, stretched toward the cliffs. The wind blew cold and hard out of the west, promising more rain shortly. There would be no sunset tonight—and probably no stars for some time.

Grimly, I pondered the cliffs. "I can't hope to climb up there in a storm. Whether or not I can learn something useful, I'll need to wait out the worst of it in the village. As soon as it starts to clear, and some stars emerge, I'll leave. Until then, I'll just say I'm a traveler passing through."

"Two travelers," declared Hallia. She blew a long breath. "Though I'd rather find shelter in the rocks, believe me. No matter how hard it rains."

"Are you sure?"

She lifted her chin a bit higher. "No, but I'm coming anyway."

The chill wind shoved us along the road, which skirted the edge of the village before continuing up the narrow valley. More clouds rolled in, obscuring all but the nearest huts. More quickly than I expected, the rain swelled into a shower, then a downpour. Thunder echoed off the crags, pounding like celestial hooves. By the time we reached the larger building, sheets of rain slapped against the stone roof. The two huddled figures we had seen from a distance had already gone inside, leaving the roughly planked door ajar.

After shaking the water from my hair and wringing out the sleeves of my tunic, I peered inside. Not much to see. Just a peat fire sputtering in the hearth, a few spare tables and chairs, and a bent, white-haired fellow emerging from another room. This was, apparently, some sort of tavern. The old fellow, who wore a waiter's apron, was carrying a clay bowl in his hands. From the room he was leaving, someone bellowed at him—so loudly that he nearly dropped the bowl. Meekly, he nodded, plunging the tips of his sagging moustache into its steaming contents.

"My broth!" roared a man from a table by the fire. "Bring my dog-damned broth!"

Hurriedly, the old waiter brought over the bowl. The man tore it away, planted his feet on the wall beside the fire, then drained the broth in three swallows. He tossed the bowl to the floor, where it shattered into pieces. Even as the old fellow stooped to clean up the mess, the man shouted at him again.

"Fetch some more peat for the fire, will you? I'm wet and cold, can't you see? What sort of rat's hole inn is this that you freeze your guests like corpses?"

The old fellow, his white hair all askew, holding the chips of pottery in his apron, headed toward the adjacent room. He stumbled past the other man who had come in from the rain, now seated in a dimly lit corner, tearing roughly at some dried meat. Although the hood of his black cloak obscured his face entirely, his manner conveyed the same surliness as the man by the fire.

With a frown at Hallia, I pulled open the door. Its squeal was drowned out by the cacophony of the rain on the roof, but the heads of both men immediately turned our way. Even though the hooded man's face remained in shadow, I could almost feel the harshness of his gaze. Hallia, close behind me, hesitated in the doorway.

"By the corpse's death," grumbled the man by the hearth. "Close the dog-damned door!" His eyes, like his coarse beard, glowed red in the firelight. "You'll give me a dog-damned fever, you will."

She looked for an instant as if she were on the edge of bolting, but stepped inside and shut the door. I nodded toward a rough-hewn table at the opposite end of the room. While it sat not far from the other man, whose black hood still dripped from the rain, he seemed likely to be a better neighbor than the ranter by the hearth. As we moved toward the table, the white-haired waiter returned, bending even lower than before under the weight of a few clumps of peat. He barely glanced at us as we passed.

Suddenly the hooded man leaped to his feet. A rusted dagger glinted in his hand. Before I could draw my own blade, he kicked over the table, knocking me backward into Hallia. We fell in a heap on the floor.

The man, bundled in his heavy cloak, scurried past us. Even as we regained our feet, the creaky door slammed shut. I ran after him, pulled open the door, and scanned the rain-soaked road, the stone huts, the dreary field. No sign of him anywhere.

Pushing the wet locks off my brow, I turned back to Hallia. "He's disappeared."

"Why would he do that?" she asked, shaken. "We didn't threaten him."

"Ye came too awfully close, me dear." It was the white-haired man, having rid himself of the load of peat. Still, he hunched so low that his wrinkled brow came no higher than the middle of Hallia's chest. "Ye disturbed his privacy, ye see."

She scowled. "Such a friendly village."

The old man gave a tense, wheezing laugh. "So friendly, me dear, it don't even have a proper name. Or any longtime residents, but for master Lugaid, who owns this public house, an' me, old Bachod. An' a few lame sheep." He glowered at the bearded man by the fire. "It's a mean-hearted place, me dear, I can assure ye that. Jest a place worth avoidin', if ye can."

With a heave, I righted the table. "Do you mind if we sit here a little while? Just to dry off."

Bachod's white hairs, toppling over his ears, wagged from side to side—along with his greasy moustache. "As long as ye pay before ye eat anythin', master Lugaid shouldn't object." He pulled out a rag and began wiping the table. "Jest mind who ye sit near, if ye wish to stay healthful."

"We will." I brushed some moldy cheese off a chair, then sat down next to Hallia. "By the way," I asked, as nonchalantly as I could, "where does that old road out there lead? Surely not up into the cliffs."

The old man continued wiping. "Ah, that little pathway is older than meself, older than the rocks perhaps. It jest curves about this valley like a coilin' snake, not leadin' anywhere." His raspy voice lowered a notch. "Some say it was the ghosts who made it."

"Ghosts?"

"From up the mountain. Ye haven't heard of 'em, me lad? Well then, ye needs to know, that's certain, since ye're journeyin' hereabouts." He ceased wiping and glanced around fearfully, as if the chairs and tables themselves might be listening. Finally he rasped, "They're angry. An' so very vengeful. Yer life is safe, perhaps, in this little valley. But anywhere on the mountain . . . well, ye'd rather be pierced by a thousan' spears before lettin' 'em take ye."

Nervously, he tugged on his moustache. Then he turned to Hallia. His voice lowered ominously. "Death—that'd be a kindness, though, compared to what they'd be doin' to yer heart, to yer innards, an' worse yet, to yer everlastin' soul, if they found ye was . . . a deer person."

Her eyes swelled to their widest. In a flash, she bolted for the door, threw it open, and vanished into the rain.

I glared at Bachod. "You old fool!"

He shrunk away from me. "Jest wanted to be helpful, I did."

Tempted as I was to give him a fright of his own, I turned and sprinted after Hallia. Just as I reached the doorway, I caught a glimpse of her dashing behind the hut with the fallen roof. Beyond, darker than even the sky itself, I could see the ragged edge of the cliffs rising above the valley.

"Hallia!" I cried, charging after her. Mud sprayed from my boots, as rivers ran down my neck and arms. Thunder slammed against the mountainside.

Sliding to a halt by the collapsed hut, I peered into the torrent. Nothing. Nothing but rain.

At that instant I heard a whisper just behind me. "M-e-e-erlin."

I whirled around. There, under an overhanging slab of rock, all that remained of the crumbled roof, cowered Hallia. Ducking under the slab, I joined her in the hollow. I placed my arms around her sopping shoulders, holding her shivering body close to mine.

Several minutes passed. The downpour did not relent. At last, though, her shivers subsided. She began to breathe more normally. I felt her relax, leaning her head against my shoulder. Rain splattered all around, as a chill wind sliced through our clothing. Yet somehow I did not feel cold.

All at once, Hallia stiffened. Before I could move, the blade of a dagger pressed between my shoulder blades.

XXIII

DAGGERPOINT

Steady now," growled the voice behind me. The dagger pressed tight against my back.

I felt Hallia standing by my side, as alert as if she were facing a pack of wolves. Water streamed off the overhanging slab that sheltered us, splattering my left arm. Trying to remain calm, I sucked in my breath. "We have no wish to harm you, good sir. Let us go in peace."

"Fancy words! You must have been mentored by a bard."

Despite the knife, I started. Something about the phrasing, if not the voice, sounded vaguely familiar. Yet I couldn't quite place it.

"Tell me the truth," the man in the shadows demanded. "Have you also learned to play the psaltery?"

Heedless of any danger, I whirled around. "Cairpré!" I threw my arms around him.

"Well met," declared the poet, tossing back his black hood.

Hallia gasped. "You know this . . . ruffian?"

The gray mane bobbed as Cairpré nodded. "Well enough to know that I don't like to use a dagger for anything more dangerous than slicing bread." He slipped the blade in its sheath. "I do hope I didn't give you a fright."

"Oh, no," snarled Hallia, her eyes darting over the shadowy hollow. To my chagrin, she edged away from me. "I had simply forgotten, for a moment, about the treacherous ways of men."

Cairpré's eyes, deeper than pools, regarded her thoughtfully. "You are a deer woman, I see. Of the clan Mellwyn-bri-Meath, if I am not mistaken."

She bristled, but said nothing.

"I am Cairpré, a humble bard." He bowed his head slightly. "I am pleased to meet you. And my heart is pained, for I can see that my own race has brought suffering to yours."

Her doe-like eyes narrowed. "More than you could imagine."

"I am sorry." Cairpré regarded her for another moment, then turned to me. "My disguise was necessary. As was that little scene in the tavern, when I feared you might come close enough to recognize me. Bachod, the old waiter, is—"

"A fool," I declared.

"Perhaps." He wiped a raindrop from the tip of his nose, as sharp as an eagle's beak. "Yet he knows more than he lets on, good fellow. Though his learning comes not from books, he is really, I think, a bard at heart. *Though speech be unlearn'd, The wisdom be earn'd.*"

He glanced again at the black cliffs. "He has already helped me more than he knows, by sharing a few old stories about this land. But to avoid raising any suspicions, I've kept my own identity secret. So Bachod thinks I'm just a wandering bard. He has no idea who I really am, or what brings me here."

The cold wind strengthened, and with it, the downpour. Thunder reverberated again and again among the craggy cliffs. As Hallia and I both drew deeper into the hollow, trying to avoid the drenching gusts, I tried to catch her eye. Yet she avoided my gaze.

Shielding his brow from the rain, Cairpré peered out of the overhang at the massive clouds that had converged above the valley. "The storm is worsening, I fear. We may be caught here for some time."

Still disbelieving we were together again, I shook my head. "What *does* bring you here, old friend? Are you, too, searching for the Galator?"

The poet's expression darkened. He moved to avoid a new trickle of water from the slab above us. "No, my boy. Not the Galator."

"What, then?"

"I seek the person responsible for the return of the kreelix."

Hallia tensed, as did I. "The kreelix? What have you learned?"

"Precious little, I'm afraid." Gathering his cloak, he sat down on the wet stones, motioning for us to join him. I did so, while Hallia remained standing apart. "Suffice it to say that shortly after you and Rhia departed, I set out myself—to learn whatever I could. Kreelixes have been gone for ages! Their return threatens the life—not just of you, my boy, though that's weighed heavily on my mind—but of all creatures of magic. Indeed, of this whole island."

His bushy brows drew together. "Rags and rat holes, it was hard to leave Elen! Yet I knew that my path could be dangerous, almost as dangerous as your own. Even so, she wanted badly, very badly, to come with me. If she hadn't already promised to wait for Rhia in the forest, I could never have stopped her."

Sadly, I grinned. "Rhia's promise to come back was the only thing that kept her from staying with me, as well."

"No doubt. You two, as brother and sister, couldn't be closer. *So thoroughly bound, As roots to the ground.*"

In the shadows, Hallia shifted her weight. And, though I couldn't be certain, she seemed to edge a tiny bit closer.

Cairpré's fist clenched. "Devourers of magic! I've spent many hours wondering who or what could have brought even one of them back." A sizzling blast of lightning struck the mountain, followed by a crash of thunder. "And I've concluded that there could be only one source so wicked, so cruel, to have done it."

Before he could say the name, I did. "Rhita Gawr."

Grimly, he observed me. "Yes, Merlin. The nemesis of anyone—and any land—he can't control." His head, gray hairs dripping, swung toward Hallia. "That's why he brought his terrible spells to this place. And why he tormented your clan into leaving your ancestral home."

"But . . . why?" she whispered from the shadows. "This was our land. Our home."

The poet waited for another roll of thunder to pass. "Because he needed no interference for a long time—long enough to breed and train the kreelixes. And your people knew too many of this mountain's secrets. You might have gotten in his way. For to bring back those beasts, he needed to tap the mountain's volcanic power. To unleash the *negatus mysterium* within its lava. That's always been the case. Clan Righteous, the people who bred kreelixes long ago, often made lava mountains their hideaways for the same reason."

Lightning struck the cliffs, etching our faces. I remembered, with a shudder, the emblem of Clan Righteous that Cairpré had described once before: a fist crushing a lightning bolt. "So do you think," I asked hesitantly, "that Rhita Gawr has returned?"

"I cannot say. He may still be too enmeshed in his battles with Dagda, relying instead on mortal allies. Or," he added gravely, "he may be nearer than we know." The deep pools beneath his brows surveyed me. "Now, my boy. You said you're seeking the Galator?"

I gazed out of the overhang into the darkening night, the wailing wind, the endless rain. "To use its power, if I can, to stop Valdearg."

Slowly, he nodded. "As your grandfather did, long ago. Yet— why here? Is it hidden among the cliffs?"

"No. But an oracle is—the Wheel of Wye."

"The Wheel! Rags and rat holes, my boy! If the Wheel of Wye exists, and I'm not sure it does, it could be every bit as dangerous as the dragon himself. Why would you ever risk such a thing?"

"I have no choice."

"You always have a choice. Even when it seems otherwise." He laid his hand on my shoulder. "Tell me where you have been since we parted."

As rain slashed against the stone above our heads, I took a deep breath and began my tale. I told of my trek with Rhia, and my narrow escape from the living stone. My confrontation with Urnalda— and her treachery. The poet's hand squeezed my shoulder tightly as I described the shock of how she destroyed my powers. And my staff. I went on, telling of my escape, of Eremon's wondrous gift, and of our discovery of the mutilated eggs, the ghastly remains of Valdearg's offspring.

Then, to the surprise of both Cairpré and Hallia, I described how I had found the last surviving hatchling—and tried to save its life. All through that long night. And how, with no magic left in my hands, I had failed.

Hallia, as gracefully as a falling leaf, sat down beside me. "You really did that? You never spoke of it."

"I didn't do anything worth telling about."

"You tried." Her eyes glistened in the waning light. "To save a life you didn't need to save. Not the sort of thing most . . . men would do."

"Perhaps not," observed Cairpré. "But it was the sort of thing a wizard might do."

I bit my lip. Then, as much to change the subject as to finish my tale, I continued. Briefly, I sketched the attack by the second kreelix—and Eremon's sacrifice. I described (though it made me feel nauseated) the terrible whirlwind. And, at last, our encounter with Domnu. As I felt Hallia's warm breath upon my neck, I explained the disappearance of the glowing pendant, and the hope, however faint, that the oracle might help me find it again in time.

After I concluded, the shaggy-haired bard watched me solemnly for a moment. The last hint of twilight ran along the ridges of his wet brow as he spoke again. "Rags and rat holes, my boy. You do seem to attract your share of difficulties."

Hallia managed a spare smile. "That he does."

I struck my own thigh. "I should start for the cliffs right now! Storm or no storm! Whatever hours I spend huddled here are wasted."

Hallia started to speak, but a sudden clap of thunder cut her off. Finally, she asked, "You would risk climbing a sheer rock wall, slick with rain, in the dead of night? With spirits of evil near at hand? You are more foolhardy than brave."

I started to rise. "But I must . . ."

"She is right, Merlin." Again the poet's hand squeezed my shoulder, coaxing me back down. "Here. In the time we have together, at least let me tell you what I know about the Wheel of Wye."

Reluctantly, I nodded.

Gazing at the gloom beyond the dripping edge of the overhang, Cairpré ran a hand through his wet hair. "If indeed the Wheel exists, and you can manage to find it, the legends say that you will face a choice. A difficult choice."

"The obstacle," said Hallia. "The one Domnu predicted."

Impatiently, I shifted on the stones, wiping some drops of water off my chin. "What choice?"

"You will find that the Wheel itself has not one voice, but several. One, and only one, of those is the voice of complete truth. All the others are to some degree false. If somehow you choose the correct voice, you will be allowed to ask any question and learn the answer. If, however, you choose the wrong one—you will die."

With a groan, I shook my head. "Is that all?"

"No." Cairpré paused, listening to the wind whistling on the crags. "The legends say that the Wheel of Wye will answer only one question of any mortal. So, if you get that far, you will be faced with a choice every bit as difficult as the first: the choice of your one question. Choose well, my boy. For after the Wheel has answered, it will reveal no more to you forever."

Hallia bent close to my ear. "What will you ask, if you are given the chance?"

For a moment, I pondered in the darkness. "The question I want to ask—long to ask. The question that haunts me more than those spirits up there: Is there any way I could regain my powers? Even if I'm never able to follow the pathway of Tuatha. Even if I'm still destined to die in the jaws of that dragon. Those powers were . . . me." My head drooped. "And yet I can't ask that question. For the fate of Fincayra, it seems, hinges on my asking something else: Where is the Galator?"

I blew a heavy breath. "So the truth is . . . I really don't know what to ask."

I could feel, more than see, Cairpré's gaze. "Seek your answer within, my boy. For the choice is different for each different person. Take, for example, your sister, who longs to fly like a canyon eagle. No doubt she would ask how the Fincayrans, in ancient times, lost their wings—and how they could find them again."

Working my stiff shoulders, I nodded. "And what about you?"

"I wouldn't ask where the kreelixes are hiding, for I think I can learn that on my own. Thanks to old Bachod, who still has more to show me about this place—if this storm ever ends, that is. I'm closer than ever now. *Around the bend, My trail shall end.* No, the question that torments me the most, the one I would ask the oracle, is how to *fight* them."

His frown deepened. "I couldn't find anything about that in the texts. All I know is that the weaponry of magic, applied directly, is futile. The ancient mages who battled them must have found something else—something as ordinary, yet as powerful, as air itself. The trouble is, though, nothing but magic seems strong enough to defeat a whole mass of them. And a mass, I fear, is what we will have to face before this is over."

I listened to the thunder echoing over the mountainside. "If only I understood that phrase, the one at the end of the prophecy."

"Not the one that predicts that, if you do fight Valdearg, both of you will—"

"No, not that. *A power still higher.*"

He nodded, stroking his chin. "It could mean the Galator. Or *negatus mysterium,* I suppose. Or . . . something else altogether."

Gently, I spoke to Hallia. "Before I go, tell me. What would you ask the Wheel?"

Her voice so soft I could hardly hear it above the storm, she answered. "Whether, in this world or another, I might ever find . . . the joy in Eremon's dream. How could that ever be? Without his hooves running beside my own?"

The mention of his name suddenly gave me an idea. "It would be much easier for me to climb the cliffs," I said slowly, "with four legs rather than two."

She stiffened. "That's true." A rainy gust swept over us. "And it would be easier still if you had someone with you—someone who knew the trails."

"No, Hallia."

"And why not?" Despite the bravery of her words, her voice quavered. "You would rather go without me?"

"I would rather know you're safe."

"Merlin. I am coming."

"But you—"

"Are the only hope you have! Hear me. This mountain has many trails, many caves. But only one is right."

Knowing she spoke the truth, I could only nod. Slowly, all of us rose to our feet. We stood there, as silent as stones.

Then Cairpré clasped our hands. In a hoarse whisper, he said, "May Dagda be at your side. And at Fincayra's, as well."

XXIV

THE CLIMB

Anyone who could have seen through the sheets of rain that night might have glimpsed two figures dashing from the ruins of the tumbled hut—at first on two legs, then on four. At the start I felt only my own wetness, and the weight of my sopping tunic and drenched boots. Then, seconds later, the weight began to fall away. I felt warmer and drier than I had all day long. The floppy tunic dissolved, replaced by coarse, thick fur. The boots disappeared, changed into sturdy hooves. My back lengthened, as did my neck. The pounding rain joined with a new and deeper pounding.

Racing across the soaked field, I spotted a pair of sheep ahead. I did not go around them, as I would have only a moment before. Instead, I leaped from the turf and sailed over them, as easily as a drifting cloud.

For I could, once again, run like a deer.

Hallia and I bounded up the road toward the end of the valley, splashing through puddles and leaping across gullies that flowed like rivers. Oh, the new strength in my shoulders and hips! The new suppleness of my body! As I ran, the driving rain seemed less to wash off me than to part and fall around me. My nose tingled with aromas of seawater, gulls' nests, and cliff lichen. Best of all, I could truly hear again—not with my ears, but with my very bones.

In time the road narrowed until it was nothing more than a winding gully. Rocks huddled at the sides like crouching figures; water coursed over our hooves. Hallia, more surefooted than I, took the lead. Her ears swiveled constantly, ever alert. Together, we began to pick our way up the increasingly steep slope.

The wind howled constantly, as rain slashed against my nose, my eyes. Bounding over some rocks and around others, we climbed steadily higher, the torrent raging around us. Now that I was no longer running, water rushed over me, flowing down my ears and back and rear-angled knees. I felt as if I'd stepped into a waterfall. My tail, compact as it was, moved constantly, shifting my weight just enough to help me balance on the slippery rocks.

Despite the darkness, I could see better than I had expected. My eyes discerned the jutting edges of outcroppings, the faint shadows of what might have been caves. Even so, I felt grateful for the frequent flashes of lightning as we made our way slowly upward. Often the wind gusted unexpectedly, nearly knocking me over. Several times the rocks under my hooves suddenly wrenched free, sliding down the slope. Only the quick instincts and sturdy legs of my stag's body saved me from falling.

All the while, I couldn't rid myself of the feeling that we were not alone on this stormy slope. Someone, I felt certain, was watching. From those caves, perhaps.

Hallia, climbing just above me, leaped from a long, narrow slab to a flat ledge. Without warning, the slab broke loose. Grinding against the rocky slope, it slid straight at my hind legs. I had no time to do anything but leap. The slab grazed me slightly, but I landed on a sturdier spot, my hooves beside Hallia's own.

Her black nose nudged my shoulder. "You're more a deer by the minute."

I felt as if I'd sprouted a new point on my antlers. "I've been watching you, that's all."

Another round of thunder rolled down the cliffs.

She stiffened, her ears erect. "They're here. Close by. Can you feel them?" Before I could even nod, she bounded away, hooves clattering on the rocks.

Higher we pushed, over steeper and steeper terrain. The wind blew colder, chafing our hides, as the rain took on the sharp edges of sleet. Soon ice appeared, under ledges and along cracks, making the footing more treacherous than ever. Slowly, we struggled upward—one hoof at a time, one rock at a time.

Hallia turned to the right, following a barely visible trail. I felt it more than saw it, my hooves fitting into subtle grooves worn by many hooves before. Meanwhile, the temperature dropped still more. Even as we worked our way upward, sweating with effort, the chill air made us shiver.

We reached a tall pile of rocks, leaning like a dying tree, just as the first hailstones smacked against the slope. As well as our backs. In seconds, the hail—bigger than acorns—started pouring down. Striking like hundreds of hammers, the pellets inundated us. I yelped as one struck the tip of my nose. Hallia pressed close to me as we shrank next to the jumble of rocks.

All at once, the entire pile gave way. Rocks smashed down the slope, nearly taking us with them. Pummeled by hail, we bolted higher. The wind screamed—as did something else, something more like high, shrieking laughter.

A cave loomed ahead, dark against the whitening slope. Instinctively, we dashed toward it—when several pairs of eyes appeared, glowing like torches. More laughter! We veered away, straight into the wind, our hooves sliding on the icy rocks. Thunder pounded, drowning only briefly the raucous laughter from the cave.

Hail! Battering us, biting our hides. My shoulders ached from cold; my ears heard only that hideous sound.

Just ahead of me, Hallia suddenly swerved at the edge of a deep crevasse. Like an unhealed gash it cut across the slope, blocking our ascent. Standing on its lip, she glanced back at me, eyes wide with fright. I knew instantly that she hadn't expected to find the crevasse—and didn't know where to cross it.

Side by side, we tried to work our way along the edge. But the crevasse grew only wider. Only in the instant of lightning strikes could we even see its opposite side. Then . . . yes! It melted away at the base of a sheer outcropping. Muscles straining, we climbed upward. Unstable rocks broke loose under our hooves. Clouds of white came with every frosted breath. Finally, we reached the top— only to find ourselves staring down into the same crevasse as before.

Laboriously, we backtracked, trying to keep our balance on the wind-whipped face. Tiny icicles began forming on my eyelashes, blurring my vision. My lungs stung as the temperature dropped further. Snow started mingling with the hail, coating the treacherous rocks.

At the base of the outcropping, Hallia leaped over a crusted slab. As she landed, her hooves skidded in the snow. Helplessly, she tumbled down the slope, rolling over the rocks. Just at the edge of the crevasse, she managed to plant her hooves and arrest her fall. In the flash of lightning that followed, I saw her leap away, a trail of blood running down her thigh.

A moment later, I reached her side. "Are you hurt?"

"N-n-not badly," she answered, as a brutal shiver coursed through her body. "But I'm lost, Merlin! This crevasse . . . I don't remember it! And we must find a way to cross it soon—or head back down."

"We can't do that!"

"Then we'll die," she cried over the wailing wind. "There's no way to—"

Another clap of thunder cut her off. Then more laughter rang out, piercing us like hunters' arrows. The skin under my eye began to throb—whether from the battering of hailstones or the presence of Rhita Gawr, I could not tell.

The hail slackened, but more snow, thick and wet, fell on us. Rocks, and the gaps between them, were fast disappearing under the blanket of white. In a few moments, the entire slope, and any hope of finding the oracle's cave, would be utterly buried.

Suddenly, a brilliant flash lit the mountainside—revealing a shape, bold and broad, standing beside the crevasse. Both Hallia and I caught our breath. Though it was difficult to see through the swirling snow, it looked almost like a figure we knew well. Almost like . . . a stag! Yet I couldn't be sure. Were those antlers atop its head, or horns, or something else entirely? Before the lightning vanished, the figure turned and charged off, skirting the edge of the crevasse.

"Eremon!" cried Hallia, leaping after him.

"Wait," I called. "It could be just a trick!"

But the doe paid no heed. She bounded off, cutting through the swelling drifts. I ran behind, following her tracks, only hoping we weren't chasing death itself.

Along the edge we raced. Sometimes we veered so close that I could hear rocks, kicked loose by our hooves, skittering down into the depths. The crevasse, even in lightning, showed only shadows—and no place narrow enough to cross. And as the snow deepened, so did my fears. If the wicked spirits meant to trap us, to strand us without any hope of finding our way, this was just the way to do it.

Abruptly, Hallia stopped. My hooves skidded, and I nearly slammed into her from behind. We stood, panting, on a slab jutting into the crevasse. Nothing but darkness loomed before us. The figure—whatever it was—had disappeared.

"Where," I huffed, "did it go?"

"Eremon. I'm sure it was him. He jumped from this spot. Then . . . vanished."

I shook the snow off my rack and leaned into the dark abyss. "It's a trick, I tell you. We can't jump into that."

Her round eyes met mine. "There's a ledge over there, I'm sure. That's why he jumped when he did! Come—it's our only chance."

"No!" I stamped my hoof. "It's madness!"

Ignoring me, she crouched, shuddered once—and sprang. Her legs exploded, her long neck stretched forward. Snow spewed my face as she faded into the darkness. I heard a thud—then nothing.

"Hallia!"

"Your turn," came her cry at last, her voice nearly smothered by the storm. "Come, Merlin!"

I crouched, my heart slamming against my ribs. I tried not to look down, but couldn't help myself. The shadows within the crevasse seemed to reach for me, to snatch at me. "I—I can't. It's too far."

"You can! You are a deer."

A shiver ran up my flank. "But I can't see the other side . . ."

Another gust of snow slapped me, almost throwing me off the edge. Under my hooves, the slab teetered, ready to fall at any instant. Without thinking, I pushed off with all my strength. I flew through the air, suspended by nothing but whirling snow, and landed with a thump on a ledge beside Hallia.

Her shoulder rubbed against my own. "You flew! Really flew! Like the young hawk of your name."

As lightning again seared the sky, I raised my eyes toward the cliffs. For the first time since the storm began, I could see their outlines, thrusting upward like enormous icicles. "Do you really think that was Eremon? Or, perhaps, Dagda himself in the form of a stag?"

Her ears cocked, one forward, one behind. "Let's hope it was Eremon. Because if Dagda is here, then so is Rhita Gawr." She blew a frosted breath. "Besides, I felt him near. More near than I know how to say."

My head beside hers, I whispered, "Then it must have been him."

More lightning. I turned back to the cliffs, gleaming from the flash. They were completely robed in white, but for the dark spots of caves. "The storm," I observed, "might be letting up."

"You may be right." She peered through the thinning veil of snow at the slopes above. "Come! I think I know where we are now."

She bounded off, following a slight indentation in the snow. Picking our way through the drifts, kicking away clumps of ice with our hooves, we moved higher into the crags. From somewhere overhead, I heard the faint cry of kittiwakes. At the next blaze of lightning, I thought I glimpsed one of the birds swooping out of the clouds just above us.

At that instant, the wind shifted. As it flowed over us, it carried a new smell. Smoke—sulphurous smoke. And also a new sound. An eerie, warbling sound. Half sighing, half wailing. A shudder ran through my long body. More spirits!

Hallia froze, as rigid as the rocks. Her ears pricked, then rotated slightly. "That sound—it's so different from that horrid laughing."

"It could still be . . . them."

"Or it could be the oracle."

All at once, she darted higher on the slope. Fast. So fast that I could barely keep up with her. Chips of ice broke under our hooves, while snow sprayed in our wakes. Relentlessly, we pushed up the cliffs. All the while, the haunting sound drifted toward us, now louder, now softer.

A wave of fog, smelling of sulphur, swept down the mountain. Like a phantom avalanche, it rolled over us, burying us completely. Although I kept climbing, I could no longer see Hallia. She had faded away—just like, I realized, the eerie wailing. I started to call for her, when suddenly I bumped into her flank.

She turned sharply. "We must have passed it."

Quickly, she led us back down the slope, pausing only to sniff the air or swivel her ears one way or another. Gradually the sound grew louder, closer. All at once, she halted. The fog before us parted, revealing a feeble glow among the whitened rocks.

A cave! Unlike the others we had seen, this one seemed to be lit from within. Or was that just an illusion? What unnerved me even more, though, was the continuous wailing that poured out of its bowels. For a long moment we stood there, listening. There could be no doubt, I knew with a shiver. The sound came not from wind, nor from sliding rocks—but from voices. Pained, tormented voices.

XXV

ONE VOICE
OUT OF MANY

Together, we planted our hooves upon the ice-crusted rocks at the lip of the cave. From deep within, voices sighed and called, wailed and pleaded. Though I could not make out any words, the voices' tone of anguish and longing could not be mistaken. Hallia and I traded anxious looks. Was this, in fact, the passage to the Wheel of Wye? Or some sort of trap laid by the mountain spirits? And was there any way to find out—except by entering?

I could see in Hallia's eyes that she had reached the same conclusion as I. In unison, we strode forward into the cave. Heeding our silent command, our bodies melted into different forms. Where two deer had stood only an instant before, an unshod young woman and a booted young man stood now. My own sigh joined with those of the voices, for I suddenly felt too vertical, too stiff, too much like wood and not enough like wind.

Wordlessly, we moved deeper into the cave, ducking under a row of icicles that hung like bars across the entrance. The cave did not descend, but rather plunged straight into the face of the cliffs. The air felt thick and humid, as if we were walking inside a cloud. A smoky, sulphurous cloud. At the same time, it felt warmer than I would have expected, reminding us that the lava that had formed these crags so long ago still coursed beneath the surface.

As we continued, plunging deeper into the mountain, the wavering light grew stronger, filtering toward us from somewhere ahead. What, I wondered, was its source? No doubt we'd learn before long. Thousands upon thousands of black crystals coated the floor, walls, and ceiling. Even through my boots, they poked and jabbed at my feet. I marveled at Hallia's ability to walk over them with such ease. She strode as gracefully as a doe crossing a bed of moss, her toes curling gently over the facets.

With every step we took, the black crystals glowed more brightly. Their facets glinted like so many eyes—staring at us and winking at one another as we moved past. Even without my own magic, I could sense that these crystals possessed some strange magic of their own.

Always, I have loved caves. Crystal caves especially. Their quiet depths, their mysterious shadows, their gleaming facets. As we moved deeper, the black crystals created ever more intricate patterns. Circles, waves, spirals—as well as more random designs. While most were black, a few gleamed yellow, pink, and purple. Above our heads draped a row of stalactites, lavender in color. And so ancient in years! They hung like the whiskers of Distant Time itself.

I paused, looking closer—and jumped. There, clinging to the base of one of the stalactites, was a dark, bony creature. Though I knew in an instant it was just a bat, it resembled too much another kind of creature, one I never wanted to meet again.

As the light within the cavern grew stronger, so did the voices. And their torment swelled at the same time. Whether moaning, pleading, or cajoling, they shared a common edge of agony. Yet . . . I couldn't make out any of their words. Only their emotions. If, indeed, they were the many voices of the Wheel of Wye, my stomach churned at the prospect of choosing one—and only one—out of all of them.

The silver light flickered on Hallia's face. "Can you understand them?"

I shook my head. "Not at all. Only . . . the pain." A brittle crystal snapped under my heel. "How will I know which one to choose?"

She slowed, touching a curved arm of crystals protruding from the wall. "Do you remember what Eremon said to you just before he . . . left us?"

"Yes," I answered grimly. *"Find the Galator."*

"No, no. After that. He said, *You have more power than you know.*"

Despondently, I dragged my boot across a bulge of glinting crystals. "He meant his own gift to me—the deer's power."

She scowled at me. "He meant more than that, Merlin. You do have—well, a certain kind of magic. And power. Yes, even now."

I looked at her skeptically. "What kind?"

For several seconds, she considered me. "I'm not sure what to call it. But whatever its name, it was enough to inspire his gift. Enough to make you want to try to help that newborn dragon, even if you couldn't possibly save her. And it just might be enough to help you know what to do at the oracle."

Slowly, I exhaled. "I want to believe you. I really do."

Pace by pace, we marched farther into the cave. Gradually, the passage bent to the left, then grew wider, as well as taller. As we rounded the bend, the ceiling abruptly vaulted high above our heads. Glittering walls of stone arched to meet it. The light in this immense chamber shone intensely bright, reflecting on the crystals. Still, I couldn't find the source.

All at once I understood. The crystals themselves! They were sparkling, glowing with a silvery light of their own.

Directly opposite us, covering almost the entire wall, hung a great, glistening wheel. Slowly, very slowly, it spun, its continual groaning joining the chorus of voices that now clamored in our ears. While the voices themselves were still incomprehensible, they clearly came from somewhere near. Just where, I couldn't tell. Like frogs calling from a hidden pond at night, the voices swam around us, swelling and fading, without ever revealing their source.

We stood there, amazed, watching the wheel turning endlessly on its axis. It appeared to be fashioned from some sort of wood, though its color looked darker than any wood I had ever seen. Each of its five broad spokes, as well as the rim, showed numberless facets, as if whatever hand had fashioned them had carved the surrounding crystals as well.

Five spokes inside a circle . . . just like the star inside a circle that had been carved into my staff. My lost staff! How clearly I remembered that night, long ago, when Gwri of the Golden Hair had descended from the starry sky to meet me on a windswept ridge. The symbol, she said, would remind me that all things, somehow, are connected. That all words, all songs, are part of what she called *the great and glorious Song of the Stars.*

I shook my head. That shape now reminded me of all that I had lost. My staff. My powers. My essence.

At that instant, I noticed three or four dark patches on the floor of the chamber. No crystals glowed, no light radiated, at those spots. Curious, I moved closer to the nearest one. Suddenly, my blood turned to ice. A mass of bones! Splintered and charred by some potent force. From their size and shape I could tell that they were all that remained of a man or a woman—someone who had, no doubt, chosen to listen to the wrong voice.

As I stooped to pick up a fragment of the skull, Hallia seized my arm. "The spokes!" she cried above the reverberating voices. "They're changing."

I gasped, dropping the skull. The facets in the middle of each of the five spokes were, indeed, changing. Gradually, they started to stretch, to lengthen and broaden, drawing themselves together in strange clusters. Some pushed outward into bulbous lumps, while others curled inward to form slashes or pits. The midsections of the spokes started to bulge, as the clusters coalesced and rearranged themselves, burgeoning into larger shapes. Shapes with patterns. Shapes with . . .

Faces. Hallia and I traded glances. For in the middle of each spoke, a face, as distorted as knotty wood, had appeared. While the wheel continued spinning, the faces grew more defined. One by one, they opened their dull yellow eyes, stretched their lips, and turned their gazes on us. As their mouths opened for the first time, each assumed one of the disembodied voices in the chamber. At the same time, the voices adopted the language of Fincayra.

"Free me!" moaned a wide, squarish face that had just risen to the top of the wheel. "Free me and truth shall be yours." As the wheel slowly turned, the face contorted, growing even wider than before. It released a deep, prolonged groan. "Free me! Have you no mercy at all? Freeeee meeeee."

"Ignore that—such a shame, such a shame—voice," snapped a second writhing face on a lower spoke. "He will lead you—what a pity, what a pity—astray. The true voice—such a disgrace—is not his, but mine!"

"Free me, please. Free me!"

"Oh, do be—what a crime—silent."

The sharp nose of a third face jabbed at us. From the pinched mouth came a wrathful hiss. "Don't lissssssten to thossssse voicessssss! Lisssssssten to me, ssssso you may sssssurvive."

Hallia started to whisper something to me, when a fourth voice cut her off. "Woe to you, who seeks to live; Woe to me, who yearns to give." From a lopsided face with deep-set eyes, the anguished voice wailed: "Choose the right, and it is I; Choose the wrong, and you shall die."

"Ssssssuch nonsssssssensssssse!"

"Free me, I beg of you—"

"Stop, plee-ee-ease," squealed a fifth voice, sounding like a dog with a broken leg. "I am the only-y-y voice of truth! You must belie-ee-eve me-ee-ee."

Full of uncertainty, I took a step closer to the revolving wheel. My gaze roamed around the crystalline chamber, from the turning faces, to the worried eyes of Hallia, to the piles of bones at my feet. Then, drawing a slow breath, I addressed all five faces at once. "I have come here," I declared, "to find the truth."

"Plee-ee-ease choose me-ee-ee."

"Choose me! Free me!"

"Sssssilence! You musssssst choose me or you will die."

"One of five shall give you life; All the rest give only strife."

"You must—such a dilemma, such a dilemma—choose me!"

As the voices clamored, the silver light from the crystals grew steadily brighter. Raising my voice above the cacophony, I addressed the wheel again. "Tell me, each of you, why I should choose you."

For a few seconds, the faces on the spokes fell silent. Only the groaning of the turning wheel echoed in the chamber. Yet the light from the crystals continued to brighten, until the walls were almost too dazzling to bear. I sensed that I must make my choice soon, or the crystals' swelling power would somehow explode—like a bolt of lightning—reducing me to another pile of bones. I waved to Hallia to retreat into the passage where she might be safer, yet she stood firmly in place, squinting from the light.

"Free me!" cried one voice, shattering the lull. "Free me and I shall love you always! For I, and I alone, am the truth of the heart."

"Sssselect me," promised another. "I can give you sssso many thingsssss more! All the wealth you sssseek, all the power you dessssserve. For I am the sssstrongest truth of all, yesssss! The truth of the hand."

"Choose me—what joy, what joy!" The voice burst into laughter, then suddenly started wailing wretchedly. "I am—such sorrow, such sorrow—the truth of the mind. All that I know, whether merry or grim, soothing or painful, can be yours, all yours."

"Plee-ee-ease," begged the next voice. "I can shower you with wonder, with mystery-y-y! For I shall always be-ee-ee the truth of the unknown."

The last voice, merely a whisper, offered only this: "Truth of the spirit am I; Wisdom and peace I supply."

By now the light had grown so bright that I could no longer even look at the spinning faces, let alone the crystalline walls. The crystals themselves had begun to buzz, as if they could barely contain their swelling power. In seconds, the entire chamber had started vibrating. I knew my time was almost gone.

Concentrating, I forced myself to think. The voices spoke for different kinds of truth—each one important, each one precious. Like the separate parts of the story circle that Hallia, Eremon, and I had created together on the day we met . . .

Truth of the heart, the mind, the hand, the spirit, the unknown. How could I possibly pick only one? What was the truth of the spirit without the truth of the heart? And the heart without the mind?

My thoughts raced, even as the voices, the walls, the wheel all roared at me. The floor shook beneath my feet. What had Cairpré told me? *One and only one, is the complete voice of the truth.*

But which one?

Heart . . . Hand . . . Unknown . . . Mind . . . Spirit . . . which to choose? The walls bent and swayed. I could barely keep my balance. The crystals burned like stars.

Stars! That phrase again flowed through my memory: *the great and glorious Song of the Stars.* All words, Gwri had said, played some part in the song. All words, all voices . . . Could that be the answer? Perhaps the voice of truth was *not* one of the voices I was hearing after all! Perhaps it was another voice entirely—the only voice that could be called *the complete voice of truth.*

"All the voices!" I cried. I raised my hands to the revolving wheel, shouting at the top of my lungs. "All the voices are true!"

Instantaneously, the walls and floor stopped shaking. The light from the crystals dimmed; the buzzing ceased. The Wheel of Wye, however, started spinning faster than ever before. Soon it became a blur, then a shadow. At the same time, the clamoring voices became less distinct. The faster they spun, the more they melted together. When, at last, the wheel was nearly invisible, the voices had merged into a single, resonant tone. Then the oracle spoke—in one unified voice.

"Aaask whaaat youuu wiiill."

Hallia stepped to my side. "You did it, Merlin! But remember, now. You have only one question."

I pushed some straggly hairs off my brow. "I know, I know."

But which one to ask? I had come here, originally, to find the Galator. And yet, with all my heart, I wanted to find my own powers again. They might give me at least a chance against Valdearg. Perhaps I wouldn't even need the magical pendant after all.

I chewed my lip. Tuatha, so long ago, had carried both his own powers and the Galator when he faced the dragon. The problem was—which one did he need most? Or, perhaps . . . which one did Fincayra need most?

"Aaask nooow."

Working my tongue inside my mouth, I turned back to the spinning Wheel of Wye. This choice tormented me even more than the first. How could I be victorious without the pendant? Yet how could I be myself without my powers?

"Aaask nooow."

"Great wheel," I began, my throat suddenly dry. "I seek the powers of . . . the Galator. Where can I find them?"

"Thooose pooowers aaare veeery neeear." The wheel spun all the faster. *"Youuu caaan fiiind theeem iiin—"*

Something as fast as lightning shot out of the passageway behind us and struck the axis of the wheel. Scarlet light exploded in the cavern, or perhaps just in my head. As the axis splintered, an ear-splitting crack rocked the chamber, fading into a distant rumble that seemed to emanate from far beneath us. The voices halted, as did the wheel itself. The five faces on the spokes froze in lifeless stares. Dumbfounded, Hallia and I gazed at the black shape that had lodged like an arrow in the middle of the axis.

A kreelix.

XXVI

THE END OF ALL MAGIC

Are ye lookin' for somethin', me dears?"

We whirled around to see an old man, standing behind us in the entry to the chamber. Bachod! The glowing crystals around him shone no less than his eyes. For this Bachod looked altogether different from the haggard waiter of the tavern. He stood perfectly straight, his arms folded upon his chest, watching us in the way an owl observes its prey before swooping down to crush its skull. Yet I couldn't mistake his crackling voice, limp moustache, and white hair that brushed the shoulders of his robe.

Crouching by his side, ready to spring at an instant's notice, rested another kreelix. Even with its wings folded on its back, its massive body filled much of the passageway. As it opened its blood red mouth, baring its three deadly fangs, Hallia and I shrank back. I nearly tripped over one of the piles of bones.

Bachod smirked. "I'm so sorry yer little conversation with the turnin' wheel never finished, me dears. Me furred companion, ye see, jest couldn't stop itself in time. Ye needn't worry, though. It won't be botherin' ye anymore."

"You stopped it!" I cried. "Ended its magic! Just when it was going to tell me where to find—" I caught myself before saying more.

Bachod shook his head, swaying his white locks. "Mayhaps I can help ye, me lad. Save ye some time an' trouble." He reached into the folds of his robe. With a flourish, he pulled forth a pendant on a leather cord. Its jeweled center flashed with a stunning green radiance.

"The Galator!" I started toward him, when the kreelix's vicious snarl stopped me. "How—how did you get it?"

"I stole it," answered Bachod with pride. "With some help from a cunnin' friend of mine."

My cheeks burned. "You mean Rhita Gawr!"

His dark eyes glinted with satisfaction. "He taught me about *negatus mysterium,* ye see. An' how to breed an' train the kreelixes to do our work."

"And what work is that?" demanded Hallia, her voice shaking with rage.

"The work of destroyin' magic!" Bachod tossed the glowing pendant into the air. It twirled, sparkling, then fell back into his hand. Gripping it tightly, he sneered, "Magic's the plague of this island. Always has been! Whether from wizards, or pendants, or oracles like this turnin' wheel. It's all evil, an' dangerous, an' worst of all, against nature."

He turned to the kreelix crouching beside him. "That's why these beasts are so useful. For destroyin' the plague." With a glance at me, he chortled. "Or them who spread it—like young wizards."

I almost grabbed a bone from the floor and threw it at him. "So you were the one who tried to kill me."

"Twice, yes—our beasts tracked ye down. Ye may have escaped those times, but never again." He tugged on his sagging moustache. "Me friend, the one ye mentioned, seems to be feelin' a bit angry with ye."

My boot ground into the crystals of the floor. "As I am with him."

"That's yer concern, not mine. Me own concern is magic. Nothin' less than the end of all magic, me dears, can bring lastin' peace to this island. An' that's the work of us who understands."

"Us who understands," I repeated scornfully.

With his free hand, Bachod drew a curved sword from his belt. The blade glinted in the light of the crystals. Seeing it, my heart thundered. For at the base of the blade, burned in black, was an emblem of a fist crushing a lightning bolt.

"Clan Righteous?"

"Yes, me lad! There's only three of us—two bein' up on the cliffs right now, tendin' to the kreelixes—but ye can expect more precious soon." He smiled grimly. "Precious soon. Fer when the word gets out that we're freein' the land from magic, most of Fincayra will rise up to join us."

"You're wrong," I declared. "About Fincayra—and about magic, too. Magic is a tool. No different from a sword, or a hammer, or a cooking pot, except that its powers are greater. And like any other tool, it can be misused. But whether it's ultimately good or evil—well, that depends on the person who wields it."

Hallia nodded. "And don't think wizards are the only ones with magic. No! It lives in quiet places, too—from the hollow log of a tiny light flyer to the meadow grazed by deer people." Her eyes seemed to sizzle. "You have no right to destroy all that . . . and so much more."

Bachod grimaced. "I've every right. Every right, ye see! An' when Rhita Gawr an' I are finished, Fincayra will have no magic left."

"No!" I glared at him. "It will have no *defenders* left. Don't you see? You've been duped, old man! Rhita Gawr is just using you. That's right. To help him wipe out all those who might have any power to stand against him."

He waved his hand contemptuously. "Magic has twisted yer mind."

"It's true," I protested. "Listen! Rhita Gawr could just walk in and declare this world his own if there were no wizards, no Galators, no . . ." I caught myself. "No dragons." I glanced at Bachod's boots, knowing that his heels would show slashes from the sharp stones of this floor, just as Eremon had predicted.

"It was you, wasn't it, who killed the young dragons?"

Bachod smirked. "Of course, me dears. I hadn't planned on wakin' up their father jest yet—but it's jest as well. Havin' him burn a few towns will remind people about the plague."

He studied his sword, flashing in the light of the crystals. "Valdearg's time will be comin' soon enough. Jest as yers will! An' yer friend the bard, a few minutes from now, when I meet him fer a little, ah, stroll up the cliffs." His smirk broadened. "He thinks he's been learnin' about the kreelixes from me, ye see. That he has, me dears, but jest a little bit. All the while I've been learnin' more from him. Much more. He's told me plenty already about the hidin' places of magic."

With that, he grabbed the cord of the Galator, allowing the pendant to swing freely. Sparks of radiant green reflected on the walls of the chamber, dancing with the silvery glow of the crystals. Bachod's grin broadened. "But first, me dears, ye get to watch me destroy this wicked thing." He clucked in anticipation. "I've been so waitful fer the right moment, an' I do believe it's now. With ye both as me audience."

"No!" I cried. "You can't!"

"The Galator is as old as Fincayra itself," pleaded Hallia.

Bachod had already begun uttering a command to the kreelix. The beast's pointed ears stiffened and its shoulders tensed. The dagger-like claws raked against the floor of the cavern. It turned to the Galator, luminous and mysterious, and exposed its fangs.

"Now ye shall see true power," promised the white-haired man, swinging the pendant. "The power of *negatus mysterium.*" He chortled softly. "Watch, me dears, as this green glow dies ferever."

Just as he started to utter the final command to the kreelix, I leaped at him. The kreelix screeched, sending a blaze of scarlet light rebounding off the walls of my mind, as well as the cavern. Simultaneously, Bachod toppled over backward. The Galator flew through the air, landing somewhere near the motionless wheel. Even as I fell to the floor, Hallia, springing like a deer, was at my side. Before we could press the attack, however, the kreelix swatted us with an enormous, bat-like wing.

We hurtled into the crystal-covered wall. Sharp facets tore our legs and gouged our backs before we rolled to a halt. Barely had we regained our feet, when a sudden tremor jolted the chamber, knocking us down again.

Several crystals on the ceiling flickered, then exploded, showering the wheel with flaming embers. At the same time, a second tremor rocked the chamber. A great chunk of black rock broke loose from the ceiling, smashing into the crystalline floor only an arm's length from my head. The wheel itself shuddered and creaked as the axis fell away completely. The whole structure tilted forward, tottering precariously on its rim.

Bachod struggled to his feet, then kicked the kreelix in the side.

It snarled, but didn't lash out. "Ye foolish beast! Yer power struck the crystals instead! An' who knows what that could—"

The Wheel of Wye crashed to the floor. Spokes and rim shattered, sailing in all directions. More crystals exploded overhead. Jagged cracks snaked across the walls of the chamber. Then—vents of steam burst open, hissing and snapping. Hotter grew the air, and hotter still.

A sly grin on his face, Bachod mounted the back of the kreelix. "So ye want the Galator, me dears? Well, it's yers ferever more! See how long its magic keeps ye safe now."

The kreelix spread its wings, flapped, and shot into the passageway. At the same instant, another section of the ceiling broke loose. With a burst of sparks, it landed on the remains of the wheel. Flames leaped, blazing with a fury that I had not seen since the fire that had cost me my eyes. I turned to Hallia, even as the wall behind us cracked and buckled, spraying us with chips of stone. Then, to my horror, a sizzling, orange liquid—brighter than the flames around us—started bubbling out of the cracks. Lava.

"Go!" I commanded. "You can still escape in time to warn Cairpré. Run like a deer!"

She glanced up at the crumbling walls. "What about you?"

"The Galator! I've got to find it before—" The wall arching over us shifted, groaning like a dying beast. A spurt of lava erupted from a crack. "Before it's lost for all time."

Hallia seized my arm. *"You'll* be lost for all time if you don't flee now!"

I pulled free. "I, too, can run like a deer. Remember? Please, Hallia. I'll be right behind you."

Her brown eyes, glowing with a light as rich—and unfathomable—as the Galator's, studied me. "All right, but be quick! Even a deer can't run through lava."

"Then, if I have to, I'll fly. Yes—like a young hawk."

She grinned fleetingly, even as she leaped to her feet. Dodging a patch of flaming, sputtering crystals, she dashed for the door. She melted into a tan-colored streak that bounded, hooves pounding, down the passage.

Hastily, I sprang to the spot where the Galator had fallen. A spark struck the back of my neck, burning my skin. I brushed it away—just as a plume of fire erupted by my boot, scorching my leg. Blood from the crystals' scrapings dripped down my forearm. Yet none of this mattered. Only the Galator mattered.

Plunging into the wreckage, I leaped over a smoldering crystal. Wildly, I turned over every piece of fallen stone I could find, searching for the pendant. Then I realized that a broken fragment from the wheel's rim now covered the place where it had fallen. Planting my boots, I tried my hardest to lift the fragment.

It wouldn't budge. Again I braced; again I lifted. The piece shifted only slightly before slipping out of my grasp. A new segment of the ceiling toppled, crashing on the very spot where Hallia and I had sat just a moment before. Crystals sprayed across the floor. More rumbling shook the collapsing walls. The heat was so stifling I could barely breathe.

I planted my feet at a different angle, hoping for better leverage. Wrapping my fingers around the heavy fragment, I pulled. And pulled. My legs shook. My back strained. My head felt as if it would burst. At last, the piece lifted ever so slightly. With a final groan, I shoved it aside.

Not there! I raised my arms, cursing. Where else could the Galator be?

At that instant, an enormous crack slashed across the floor under my feet. Sulphurous smoke belched out. As I leaped aside, the ceiling exploded in a new storm of sparks. Then, to my horror, I spotted a gargantuan slab of rock working loose above the entry to the chamber. I hesitated, scanning the floor one last time, then threw myself into the passage.

Rolling over the crystals, I turned for a final glance at the crumbling walls. Suddenly I saw a flash of green at the far end of the chamber. The Galator! I started to plunge back in again, when the enormous slab tore loose. It smashed to the floor, sealing the opening. A curtain of molten lava flowed over it.

I reeled as if the slab had fallen on top of me. *Gone. The Galator was gone.*

My eyes clouding, I started to stumble down the smoke-filled passageway. Another tremor, more violent than the rest, rocked the cliffs. Vents split open, gushing superheated steam. I pitched to the side, slamming into the wall. *A deer. I must run like a deer.* With all my remaining strength, I tried to run, to become a deer before it was too late.

Nothing happened. I ran harder, my lungs screaming. Nothing happened.

The power! It had vanished! By the new depth of emptiness in my chest, I knew that Eremon's gift had at last abandoned me. He had warned me that it would run out unexpectedly. But why now?

A row of flaming crystals from the roof of the passageway split open, raining sparks and jagged chips on my head. Another section of wall erupted as I passed. I stumbled forward. My head rattled no less than the rocks. All of a sudden the floor buckled beneath me, knocking me sprawling.

I lay there, facedown on the crystals. Though they jabbed and singed my skin, I felt too weak to rise. I could not run like a deer. I could not even run like a man. Here I would die, buried in lava along with the Galator.

XXVII

VERY NEAR

Something hard thudded against my back. A piece of rock, no doubt. Or debris from the shattering crystals. I did not roll over.

A thud came again. And with it, a sound, mixing with the crashing and grinding of the collapsing passageway. A sound I had heard, it seemed, ages ago. A sound like . . . a horse whinnying.

I flipped over. The eyes of a stallion, as coal black as my own, greeted me. Ionn!

His great hoof, raised to strike me again, lowered to the crystalline floor. He shook his mane and whinnied. Half dazed, I raised myself to a crouch. Ionn nudged me with his nose, urging me to stand. I threw an arm around his mighty neck, straightened up, and hoisted myself onto his back. In an instant, we were careening down the passage.

Stone walls broke apart, melting into lava as we passed. The whole passage now glowed brilliant orange—the color of the mountain's deepest fires. Arching forward on the stallion's back, I held on as tight as I possibly could, my fingers clawing at his neck. Crystals flared and sizzled. Steam spurted, barely missing us. Yet Ionn never faltered. His hooves pounded against the quaking floor.

Moments later, we burst out of the passage into daylight. The sun—not lava—cast light on me. Ionn started picking his way down the treacherous face of the snowbound cliffs. From behind, I heard a rumble that gathered into a thunderous roar. Turning around, I saw a fountain of molten rock gush out of the glowing passageway.

Above, the cliffs were disintegrating. As lava flowed over them, great boulders exploded into ashes or simply melted away. Snowdrifts burst into steam. Crevasses tore open, splitting the crags. Caves, whether or not inhabited by spirits, collapsed in flames. Dark columns of smoke belched into the sky, while savage tremors rocked the mountain to its very roots.

Ionn continued to work his way downward, staying just ahead of the streaming lava. Icy rocks, kicked loose by his hooves, clattered down the face. Over the quaking slabs and promontories, he followed a trail of his own making. He managed to avoid the wide crevasse we had crossed during the ascent, skirting its edge for some distance until it narrowed and finally faded away. Often he twisted suddenly to stay clear of a glowing lump of lava, sizzling on the rocks, or leaped to the side to find better footing. Yet bit by bit he made progress, pushing farther down the mountain.

At length, the slope grew less precipitous. The ground beneath us didn't tremble so violently. Mosses and grasses appeared between the cracks; a few scraggly pines clung to the mountainside. Although I knew that soon they would be covered by molten rock, the glimpse of green gave me a spurt of hope that we might yet escape.

Into what? Into the valley and fields that I could see below, warmed by the golden hues of the sun? I knew better. My destination lay far beyond, in the land of the dwarves. And the late afternoon light meant that I had barely two days left to get there.

The thought made me cringe. What did time matter now, anyway? I had no Galator—and no powers of my own. Only the prospect of facing a wrathful dragon alone. And yet, to my own surprise, I still felt sure I must try.

Over the continuous rumbling, I heard a shout. I turned, but saw only the narrow, overhanging edge of a crevasse, marked by a pair of twisted pine trees. The shout came again. Then I noticed, just beyond the pines, a pair of hands and a head topped with shaggy gray hair. Cairpré!

"Ionn!" I cried. "Stop here!"

The stallion halted abruptly. Even so, he looked at the oncoming rivers of lava and whinnied excitedly. I slid off his back. As fast as I could, I ran past the pines, then onto the jutting edge. Cairpré hung there, straining to hold on. Locking both of my hands around his wrists, I heaved with all my strength. I could hear the rumbling around us growing louder. At last one leg lifted over the lip of rock, then the other.

His face white with exhaustion, the poet gazed at me weakly. "Can't . . . stand up."

"You must," I urged, hauling him to his feet. He slumped against me, unable to stay upright.

Without warning, a flying lump of lava struck the trunk of one of the pines. Its resiny wood exploded in flames, as the entire top half of the tree split off, collapsing across the overhang. A wall of fire leaped into the air, roaring furiously, cutting us off completely.

As I stared into the scorching flames, another wall of fire ripped across my mind. *The blaze . . . my face, my eyes! I can't cross that. Can't!*

I staggered, nearly stepping off the edge of the overhang.

"Merlin," panted Cairpré. "Leave me . . . Save yourself."

His legs buckled completely. I struggled just to stand. Beyond the blazing tree, I heard the approaching roar of descending lava. And, in my ear, the labored breathing of my friend.

From somewhere I could not fathom, I found the strength to lean his limp body over my back. With a groan, I lifted him and tottered ahead into the flames. Fire slapped my face, singed my hair, licked my tunic. A branch caught my arm, but I shook free. Stumbling, I fell forward.

Onto solid rock. Ionn whinnied, stamping impatiently. Oncoming lava spat at us. I heaved Cairpré over the horse's broad back, then mounted myself.

Ionn bounded off, widening the gap between us and the molten river of rock. The slope became less steep, giving him sounder footing. Still, it was all I could do to keep both myself and the unconscious poet on his back. Downward he pushed—until, at last, the slope merged into the rocky hillocks. Moments later, we came to the edge of the narrow valley. Ionn instinctively avoided Bachod's village, crossing onto the higher ground on the valley's opposite side.

Behind us, the cliffs continued to glow with orange lava. Above, the sky darkened with clouds of smoke and ash. An immense column of steam rose in the distance, perhaps from lava flowing into the sea. Yet the mountain's tremors had all but ceased. The eruption, it appeared, had spent itself. The land grew steadily quieter.

By a small spring, bubbling through a ring of ice, we rested. I doused Cairpré's head in the spring, which at first made him cough but soon encouraged him to drink. Before long, he had revived enough to talk, and to share some of his salted meat, though his face remained quite pale. Nearby, Ionn tugged at some clumps of grass.

The poet eyed me gratefully. "That was a test of flames, my boy. The mountain's as well as your own."

I tore at a slice of meat. "The greater test is still to come." I hesitated, almost afraid to ask the question most on my mind. "Did you see Hallia?"

The poet hesitated before finally responding. "Yes. I . . . saw her."

"Is she all right?"

Somberly, he shook his gray mane. "No, Merlin. She is not."

I swallowed. "What happened?"

"Well, when the eruption first started, I was a good way up the slope, waiting for Bachod." He paused, weakly running his hand across his brow. "We were supposed to meet there. He was late, and I was growing concerned. The lava mountain seemed to be waking up. All of a sudden, he appeared. Riding on the back of one of those infernal creatures! Rags and rat holes, I was a fool to trust him."

He grimaced. "I did my best to escape, but he finally chased me to the edge of that precipice. Clumsy me—I fell over, barely catching myself. *The vision grows dim, Though ever more grim.* He dismounted, drew his sword on me—when suddenly Hallia bounded over the crevasse. Seeing her, Bachod cursed and leaped onto the kreelix again. Off they flew, chasing her up the slope."

My jaw dropped. "Up the slope? But the lava . . ."

"She knew just what she was doing. If she led him down into the more level terrain, she would have had fewer places to hide. Higher on the slope, she could avoid him longer, buying me a little more time."

"Buying your life with her own," I added bitterly. "So either Bachod got her, or the lava did."

"I fear so. Neither of them came back. But Bachod, I presume, survived. He probably just left me for dead and went about trying to save as many of his kreelixes as he could. Their hideaway, I'm sure, was somewhere up in the cliffs."

He twisted a willow shoot with his finger. "I'm sorry, my boy. Dreadfully sorry. I haven't felt this wretched since . . . I parted from Elen."

The pain in his voice seemed to echo somewhere inside me. For several minutes, we sat in silence, hearing only our own thoughts and the swirling waters of the spring. In time, Cairpré offered me a few slices of dried apple. I chewed for a while, then told him about my discovery of the Wheel of Wye's true voice, my choice of a question—and the incomplete answer. His fists clenched as I described the destruction of the oracle, as well as the Galator.

As I concluded, a slight breeze wafted over us, fluttering my charred tunic. "If I'm going to face Valdearg, I must leave soon."

"Are you sure you want to do this, my boy?"

I splashed some cold water on my face. "Yes. I only wish I knew what to do when I get there. If, that is, I can make it past Urnalda. After the way I escaped from her, she'll probably want to punish me herself before turning me over to Valdearg."

The poet broke an apple slice in two. "I've been thinking about your last encounter with her. It doesn't make sense that she, as a creature of magic herself, would use *negatus mysterium* against you."

"She sees me as her people's archenemy! Or, at least, as their only shield against the dragon. And she's arrogant enough to use any weapons she might have against me."

He frowned, but said nothing.

"If only there were some way I could convince Valdearg that he shouldn't be fighting me—but Bachod, who killed his young, and Rhita Gawr, who made it possible."

Cairpré gnawed on the dried fruit. "Dragons are difficult to convince, my boy."

"I know, I know. But doing that could be my only chance of stopping him from devastating everything! I certainly can't defeat him in battle. Not without the Galator."

"It's just possible that the wheel, like most oracles, might have meant more than one thing by what it said."

I leaned closer. "What do you mean?"

The poet's eyes lifted toward the cliffs, glowing now both with trails of lava and the light of the setting sun. "I mean," he answered slowly, "that it said the powers of the Galator were very near. That could have meant the Galator itself was near—as, indeed, it was. Or it could have also meant *its powers* were very near. Nearer than you knew."

"I still don't understand." Rising, I stepped over to Ionn. The stallion raised his head from the tufts of grass and nickered softly. Running my hand along his jaw, I pondered Cairpré's words. "We knew so little about the Galator's powers—except that they were great."

He stroked his chin. "Were they any greater, do you think, than whatever power brought you and Ionn back together after so many years? Than whatever power gave you the strength to carry me through those flames?"

"I don't know. I only know that any powers I can find, I'm going to need." Drawing in my breath, I pulled myself onto the stallion's back. He gave his head a bold shake as he anticipated my command. "Let us ride, my friend. To the land of the dwarves!"

XXVIII

GALLOPING

Down the narrow valley we rode, and into the night. Ionn's massive hooves thundered in my ears, reminding me of the erupting mountain we had fled. As he pounded over the stones, weaving among the hillocks, his black mane no longer glowed with the reflected light of lava. How often, as a child, I had clung to that very mane . . . I wondered whether this ride, out of one set of flames and into another, would be our last.

Air, as cold as the first breath of winter, rushed over me. Tears streamed down my cheeks from my useless eyes. Though I told myself they came from the wind, I knew they also came from the memory of the many faces I might never see again. Cairpré. Rhia. My mother. And another face, full of intelligence and feeling, with brown eyes that shone like pools of liquid light.

As Ionn galloped, I glanced back at the cliff walls, streaked with bands of orange. I shuddered to think that, somewhere up there, lay the lifeless body of a doe. Whether Hallia had been destroyed by the kreelix or by the onslaught of lava I would never know. It gave me no comfort to imagine that now, at least, she had rejoined her brother.

Ahead, the remaining rays of twilight faded, revealing a few quivering scenes—a twisted tree here, a pair of tilting boulders there. Behind, heavy clouds of ash, darker than night itself, rose into the sky. The rumbling cliffs soon vanished, obscured by the hillocks, which themselves started to diminish as the valley widened. In time, stretches of thick, ragged grass replaced the meager tufts that had interspersed the stones. The valley opened into an expanse of rolling grassland that I knew to be the eastern reaches of the Rusted Plains.

My arms embraced Ionn's broad neck, while my legs pinched his heaving chest. Galloping, galloping, we drove across the plains. Night deepened around us. But for the occasional howl of a wolf in the distance, the only sounds were the relentless pounding of the stallion's hooves and the continuous surging of his breath. Once or twice I almost dozed, but awoke with a start just before I tumbled off his back.

As dawn's first light dappled the grasses, Ionn whinnied and veered to the north. Minutes later, I glimpsed the sparkling surface of a braided stream ahead. Ionn slowed to a trot, then pranced to the water's edge. Stiffly, I dismounted. On unsteady legs, I stepped to the stream and thrust in my whole head. Even with the frigid water washing over my ears, I could still hear the pounding of hooves.

We drank deeply. Finally, we lifted our heads in unison. While I stretched my neck and back, Ionn frisked a bit, seeming to shake the weariness from his bones. I beckoned him toward some tall clusters of grass, but he moved there only reluctantly. I could tell that he, like myself, knew that our time was fast disappearing. Only after he saw me pull some shriveled berries from the vines on the bank did he, too, take time to eat. Soon he nudged my shoulder to mount again.

Onward we rode. The plains rose and fell like gentle waves, tinted with the yellows and tans of autumn. Following the arc of the sun overhead, we pushed westward. By the time the ridges of mist-shrouded hills lifted on the horizon, late afternoon light painted the grasses. As the plains stretched before us, I continued to scan the vista, searching for the fog-filled banks of the River Unceasing. There, I knew, lay the outer edge of the dwarves' realm.

Despite the continual thumping of Ionn's back against me, I felt always aware of the emptiness within my chest. What I would give to sense my old powers coursing through my veins again! To grip the shaft of my staff again.

Was there any chance that Urnalda might be convinced to restore my lost powers? I grimaced, knowing the answer. If she hadn't believed me before I humiliated her—escaping from her very grasp—she would surely not believe me now. Her wrath toward me no doubt rivaled the dragon's. Besides, I doubted she could restore my powers in any case. Cairpré's doubts notwithstanding, I could feel in my depths that they had been utterly destroyed, no less than the Galator itself.

The grasslands seemed to stretch on forever. Another day ended, marked by another sunset. Deep into the night we pressed ahead, with no moon to light our way. I could feel Ionn's muscles straining to keep running. My own back and shoulders ached; my head swam with dizziness and exhaustion.

Sometime after midnight, a new rushing sound mixed with the wind. We pitched forward. Suddenly the stallion neighed and turned sharply. Panic flooded me, along with the fear that Ionn had stumbled. Then a cold wave slammed against my right leg, splashing the side of my face.

The River Unceasing! His mighty frame leaning into the current,

Ionn waded deeper into the waterway. Turning, I viewed with my second sight the ragged mounds lining the bank behind us. Though I caught no more than a whiff of the stench of rotting flesh, that was enough to rekindle the memory of the devastated eggs—and the last of the hatchlings. Somewhere nearby, I knew, her immense young body lay rotting. And not far away, the body of Eremon lay under a mound of river rocks. Through the surging water and chilling spray Ionn pushed, though not fast enough for me.

At last, the stallion clambered up the far bank, his hooves slapping against the mud. Spray, luminous in the starlight, glistened on his coat. I stroked his neck. "Let us rest, old friend. You need it, as do I. But not here. Find us a secluded spot down the river, where no dwarves or dragons are likely to disturb us."

Moments later, we came to a patch of fragrant fern. I dismounted and crumpled to the ground. Though I glimpsed some edible mushrooms, I was far too tired to eat them. With my back hunched, my head between my knees, I fell into a fitful sleep. I dreamed of running through an endless field of fire, with no chance to rest, no chance to escape.

The sun was already riding high when Ionn's wet nose nudged my cheek. With a start, I awoke. Whether from perspiring in my dreams or from the misty air, my tunic was soaking wet. Worse, it was nearly noon. Nearly half a day's travel, I remembered well from my first run as a deer, lay before us. After a brief meal of mushrooms for me and fern stalks for Ionn, we set off again.

Through the meadows and stands of cedar we rode, following the staircase of plateaus into the heart of the dwarves' realm. As the sun dropped lower, the air grew smokier and the signs of recent burning more common. Alert for any dwarves, I scanned the charred fields and scorched rocks that had replaced the verdant lands along the river. No trace of them . . . yet.

The setting sun spilled crimson over the ground as a tall, pyramid-shaped hill came into view. The place where Valdearg would land. "There," I pointed out to Ionn. "That's where we go. But tread carefully. The dwarves could be—"

At that instant, a tumult of shouts filled the air. From behind boulders and bushes, from out of trenches and gullies, leaped an army of the stocky warriors. Waving their spears and slashing their swords, they formed a line between us and the hill. Ionn's ears flicked forward. Galloping ever faster, he bore down on them.

As we neared, more dwarves joined the barrier, their beards and helmets glowing red in the sunset. Now their line was at least four deep. Short as they were, they stood as firmly as oak trees planted in our path. Yet the stallion's speed did not slacken.

Out of the middle of the line jumped a paunchy dwarf wearing a conical hat and a black cloak. "Stop!" Urnalda cried, swirling her cloak about her. "This be my command!"

Ionn only galloped harder. I leaned forward, peering straight into the eyes of the enchantress who had stolen my best hope.

Seconds before the great hooves trampled her, Urnalda raised her staff, as if preparing to stop us by magic. But before she could, Ionn abruptly changed direction, swerving to the right. Somehow, I managed to stay on. He plunged toward a thin section of the line and, with a powerful leap, sailed right over the heads of the awestruck dwarves.

Soon the angry shouts faded behind us. The pyramid-shaped hill loomed closer. Then, without warning, a violent rumbling filled the air.

XXIX

BATTLE TO THE LAST

Like a landslide on high, the rumbling rolled out of the sky, overwhelming Ionn and myself, shaking the charred ground beneath us. An outcropping of rock on the summit of the pyramid-shaped hill broke loose, clattering down the slope. Ionn reared back, arresting his gallop, as we both turned toward the source of the sound.

Valdearg, wings outstretched, plunged at us with incredible speed. Caught by the rays of the setting sun, he looked at first like a clot of crimson against the smoky sky, though soon armored scales of green and orange showed along his tail and wings. Then, as he banked to one side, his terrible claws flashed brightly. Closer he came, and closer, until we could see the smoldering yellow of his eyes.

Writhing columns of smoke poured from his flared nostrils. Beneath his nose, the scales had been so blackened that he seemed to wear a thick moustache. Immense slabs of charcoal clung to the rims of his orange ears, flaking off every time the ears twisted. Several of his claws sported black humps, resembling knuckles. More lumps of charcoal, I thought at first—until the truth struck me like a hammer: They were skulls, burned in the fires of his wrath, worn like so many decorative rings.

As if entranced, we did not move as the dragon descended.

Waves of rumbling rolled over us. If the sky itself had ripped apart, I thought, the noise couldn't have been louder. I was wrong. Soaring straight at us, the dragon opened his cavernous mouth. Row upon row of dagger-like teeth glinted in the reddish light. The gargantuan chest rippled and contracted, releasing an explosive roar so loud that I almost toppled from Ionn's back.

The roar broke our trance—fortunate indeed, for along with it came an enormous, twisting tongue of flame. Ionn whinnied and bolted from the spot. The fire blasted the ground just behind us, splitting the very rocks with its heat. While flames singed my back and Ionn's flank, we galloped away.

"Quick," I cried. "Behind the hill!"

The stallion drove for the pyramidal hill, even as another deafening roar struck our ears. Ionn barely had time to dodge behind a boulder, shaped like an immense fist, before more licks of flames flooded over us. As we cowered behind the wall of stone, blazing fingers curled over the top and around the sides, scorching all they touched. Only the boulder's thickness saved us from being reduced to heaps of ash.

The flames had hardly dissipated when I cautiously lifted my head to check the dragon's whereabouts. He had just landed! He drew his wings to his back and slid his titanic form, nearly as huge as the hill itself, across the ground. Strangely, he was turning—not toward us but to the side. In a flash, I understood why.

I slapped Ionn's neck, and he charged for the rim of the hill. At the same instant, the dragon's massive tail uncoiled. Like a hideous whip, its barbed tips waving, the tail sliced through the air. It slammed into the fist-shaped boulder, sending chunks of stone in all directions. Shards rained on us as we rounded the hill's edge just in time.

"Grandson of Tuatha!" The dragon's voice, deeper than thunder, exploded against the slope. "You murdered my children!"

As Ionn continued to run behind the hill, I bent forward. "Wait. I must answer him."

Although he slowed to a trot, the stallion gave a loud neigh, shaking his head vigorously.

"I must, Ionn."

Again, he protested.

Sadly, I stroked his neck. "You're right—it's madness for us both to go back. Here, I'll dismount, so at least you can run to safety."

Before I could lift my leg, Ionn reared back, forcing me to grab his mane more tightly. He whirled around, turned his muzzle toward me, and scanned me with a dark eye. With a loud snort, he trotted back to the edge of the hill.

From astride his back, I peered cautiously around the charred rocks. Drawing a deep breath, I called as loud as I could to Valdearg. "Your rage burns deep, great dragon! But you must hear me. I did not kill your offspring!" I waited for the wave of rumbling to cease. "It was another man—who serves Rhita Gawr. And who brings the kreelix, the magic eater, back to our land. His name is—"

A torrent of flames erupted, cutting me off and driving me back behind the rocks. "You dare to deny your crime?" Valdearg's voice shook the air, as his tail smashed against the ground. "Even your evil grandfather did not try to hide from his deeds! You do not deserve to bear the title of wizard."

The emptiness in my chest almost throbbed. Grimly, I led Ionn back to the hill's edge. "You speak truly. I don't deserve it. But I did not—did not—murder your young."

The dragon's yellow eyes flashed. Smoke billowed from his nostrils. "And I did not come to hear your prattle about kreelixes and Rhita Gawr. Ages ago I fought the last of all the kreelixes—a battle to the death. His death, not mine! Now I shall do the same to you. And you shall die nine deaths, one for each of my slain children."

"I tell you I didn't kill them!"

"Liar! They must be avenged!"

With that another roar rocked the smoky skies, the charred ground, and all between. The mammoth tail lifted and swept toward me. Ionn needed no command to break into a run. The tail slammed full force into the side of the hill, sending up a shower of broken rocks. I turned just in time to see an enormous slab, heavy enough to crush a dozen people, topple over onto the midsection of the tail. It struck the green scales and bounced harmlessly away.

Ionn galloped with all his strength, trying to put as much distance as possible between ourselves and Valdearg. As we neared the far side of the hill, I glanced to the rear just as the massive head came into view. The dragon's eyes, as bright as suns in the waning light, glared at me. More flames shot out. Fire nipped at Ionn's hooves as we rounded the bend.

Using the hill itself as our shield, we avoided one assault after another. Back and forth Ionn ran, his legs churning, his ears attuned to any sound. For although we could not see our attacker behind the hill, we could still hear him maneuvering, roaring, or slapping his huge tail against the rocks. If his vast bulk slid one way, we dashed the other. We paused, breathless, whenever we could no longer hear him, then galloped off again as soon as he stirred.

Deep into the night the pursuit continued. Once Valdearg tried to take flight, hoping to surprise us in the darkness, but even then the noise of his approach gave him away. Yet I knew that, with enough time, he would surely outlast us. Ionn was bound to make a mistake, to stumble or misread the sounds. And one mistake was all that the dragon needed. Or was he merely toying with us, prolonging his moment of vengeance?

As dawn's first rays caressed the slope, dousing the rocks with gold, I could see that Ionn was tiring. Globules of sweat clung to his lips and mane; his shoulder muscles quivered. He ran laboriously, hardly lifting his hooves.

If only I could do something more than cling to the back of this brave stallion! But what? The prophecy had forecast a terrible battle, fought to the last. Yet, what kind of battle was this? It was merely a pursuit—with a certain outcome.

For a long moment, as the sun lifted over the horizon, Valdearg did not move. Then, suddenly, he started sliding over the rocks, crushing them beneath his weight. Immediately, Ionn bounded in the opposite direction. He rounded the corner at a gallop, then halted so fast that I rammed into his uplifted neck and nearly flew over his head. We were face-to-face with Valdearg! The sound we had heard must have come from loose rocks tumbling down the slope.

Ionn reared back, kicking wildly. But at the same moment, the monstrous tail lashed out. The barbs coiled swiftly around my chest, crushing my ribs, then carried me into the air. In an instant, I hung suspended before Valdearg's snout.

A blast of hot air scorched me as he gave a disgusted grunt. His voice as immense as his open jaws, he demanded, "Why do you not fight me, young wizard? Why do you only flee?"

Barely able to breathe, let alone speak, I rasped, "I have . . . no powers."

"You have powers enough to murder hatchlings still in their eggs!" The yellow eyes blazed. "Well, grandson of Tuatha, you shall flee no more."

"You must . . . believe me," I protested. "I didn't . . . do it."

"Shall I begin by biting off one limb at a time?" His purple lips parted as he wrenched a skull off one of his upraised claws. His jaws compressed, crunching the skull completely. "No, I have a better idea. I shall roast you first."

The rumbling gathered, swelling deep within his chest. It grew steadily louder, while flames started licking his nostrils. At the same time, the tail's grip on me tightened. My lungs couldn't breathe. My heart couldn't beat. The jaws opened wide, as an avalanche of fire rushed toward me.

All at once Valdearg's ears pricked and he cocked his head slightly. The flames shot past, searing my boots but nothing more. Valdearg released a sudden cry of surprise—and his tail released its hold. I thudded to the ground. Ionn raced to my side as I gasped for air. Wrapping one arm around the stallion's neck, I struggled to rise—and to see what had distracted the dragon.

Approaching us on the charred terrain, half hobbling and half flying, came a truly strange creature. At first all I could see was an ungainly mass, as ragged as a storm-lashed sapling. Then I glimpsed a flash of iridescent purple, a crumpled fold of leathery skin, a pair of bony shoulders. And, atop the head supported by a thin, gangly neck, a pair of ears—one of which thrust out to the side like a misplaced horn.

The baby dragon! She had survived!

In a flash, her enormous father spun around, nearly swatting Ionn and me with the bony tip of his wing. He lumbered over to the hatchling, stopping just short of her. His belly rumbled with a steady, soft drone, almost like the purr of an oversized cat, as he placed his snout upon the ground.

Cautiously at first, then whimpering excitedly, the baby dragon allowed his warm breath to blow across her scales. For a long moment they looked at each other, the yellow glow of his eyes melting into the orange glow of hers. Finally, he unfurled his massive wing so that she might crawl into it. Folding its edges around her like a blanket, Valdearg drew his baby near. She gave a contented squeak and huddled closer.

Craning his neck, the dragon lifted his colossal head. To the skies rose a sound unlike any sound heard in Fincayra for ages upon ages, since the birth of Wings of Fire himself. It was a mixture of deep rumbling and high, swirling, ringing notes that flew skyward with the grace of arrows. It was a complex melody, a magical tapestry woven with the lore of generations of dragons. It was, more than anything else, a song of celebration.

Ionn and I listened, transfixed, as Valdearg's song continued for an hour or more. The hatchling, curled tightly inside her father's wing, lifted her own snout from time to time. Her ear, as plucky as ever, stretched out to the side. She seemed to be listening to the song as carefully as ourselves, but with native understanding far beyond our own.

In time, the great dragon lowered his head. Moving with the power of a huge wave surging over the sea, his neck swung toward me. As soon as his gaze met my own, the spell of his song disappeared. Fear raced through me. He was coming after me again! I leaped on Ionn's back, grasping his mane, ready to ride once more.

Just then the baby dragon squealed. The shrill cry arrested me, as it did her father. His orange ears swiveled; his lips curled in puzzlement. She squealed again, this time flapping her little wings frantically. He rumbled, then quieted, as she made several sharp, chirping sounds.

At length, Valdearg's yellow eyes turned back to me. "It seems, young wizard, that some of what you told me was true." A dark cloud of smoke rose from his nostrils. "You are not the man who murdered my children."

Ionn tossed his head, nickering with relief. I gave the side of his neck a pat.

"Yet some of what you said was false: that you have no powers. My daughter here says otherwise." He glanced at her with obvious affection. "She says you saved her by your magic."

I shook my head. "Not with my magic. With my herbs, that's all. It's different."

"Not so different as you think." His huge tail lifted and wrapped around itself, forming a knot of orange and green scales that flashed in the sunlight. "For whatever the magic is called, it has given me back my child."

XXX

WHEN ELEMENTS
MERGE

A high-pitched shriek pierced the sky. Like Valdearg, the hatchling, and Ionn, I looked up. And in that instant, my blood froze.

Not one kreelix, but many—at least a dozen—were plunging toward us out of the smoky clouds. Their mouths, gaping, showed their deadly fangs. And on the back of the leader rode the hunched figure of Bachod, his white hair streaming behind him.

Bachod waved his arm to the kreelixes. Angling their bat-like wings, they immediately fanned out in a wide arc. With an ear-shattering series of screeches, they dived downward. Ionn whinnied and snorted, stamping his hooves angrily. My sword rang bravely as I drew it from the scabbard, though I knew well its limits against *negatus mysterium*. In an instant, the kreelixes would be upon us.

Suddenly Valdearg's tail uncoiled and shot upward. The monstrous whip snapped as it struck one of the kreelixes. The beast screeched and fell lifeless from the sky.

Like a raging swarm of hornets, the remaining kreelixes converged on the great dragon. Diving and swooping, they bore down on him, fangs bared, trying to get close enough to strike. Immense though he was, he moved with dazzling speed—spinning, rolling, and flashing his tail. Yet as long as he remained on the ground, the kreelixes would hold the advantage. At first I wondered why he didn't take to the air, where he could be just as mobile as they.

Then I remembered: the baby dragon. He was protecting her! Deep in the folds of his wing she cowered, safe for the moment. But as long as he held her wrapped in one of his wings, he could not fly. And staying on the ground made him far more vulnerable.

Ionn paced, whinnying anxiously, as we looked on. Though I brandished my sword and shouted at Bachod and the kreelixes, they ignored me. Nothing I did drew their attention away from the flailing dragon. Ionn reared back, kicking at the air, then galloped in a circle around Valdearg. Still the attackers paid no heed. Bachod didn't even look our way.

All at once I understood. Since my deer magic had now vanished, they could sense that I possessed no power! Where I might have been at least a mild threat to them before, I was no threat at all to them now. The empty feeling in my chest ached like never before.

The words from the prophecy of *The Dragon's Eye* echoed in my mind. *Lo! Nothing can stop him Except for one foe Descended from enemies Fought long ago.* A new realization gripped me. Perhaps the prophecy never meant me at all! Perhaps the dragon's ancient foe, the enemy who would either kill him or be killed in the process, was a kreelix!

But if that was the case, what could the rest of the prophecy mean? Would all the kreelixes perish, or just some of them? And what about that phrase—*a power still higher?* Something that could make elements suddenly merge: air into water, water into fire . . .

Roaring and spitting flames, Valdearg continued to hold off the attackers. His eyes, themselves practically aflame, seemed everywhere at once. The ground beneath us shook with the slamming of his tail. Dust and smoke climbed skyward. His one free wing batted constantly at the air above the wing enfolding the cowering hatchling. In all his days of terror, I felt sure, never had he been more worthy of the name Wings of Fire.

Now three burned kreelixes lay as smoldering heaps on the ground. The remains of two more, smashed by the tail, had been trampled in the fray. Still, seven kreelixes, including the one bearing Bachod, remained. They swooped and hovered, always seeking a chance to bury their fangs someplace—anyplace—not shielded by scales. The most exposed target, I suddenly realized, was his wing. Curled tightly around his infant, the wing's leathery folds lay unprotected.

Maybe, with the dragon's immense bulk, it would take more than one gash to destroy him. The thought gave me a spurt of hope. Then I bit my lip, remembering Cairpré's warning that even the smallest contact with the kreelix's fang could end the power—as well as the life—of any magical creature, no matter how large.

At Bachod's command, the kreelixes climbed upward, so high they were nothing more than tiny black dots in the shreds of smoke. Barely, I could see them arrange themselves into a new formation— like the head of a spear. An instant later, they screeched in unison and soared straight at their enemy. Viscerally, I knew they were aiming for Valdearg's wing. And only one of them needed to strike home. The baby dragon, sensing the same thing, whimpered and nestled deeper into the folds.

As they shot toward Valdearg, who seemed now less like a wrathful monarch than a protective parent, he released a defiant roar. Bracing for the assault, he swung his massive head toward me. For a fraction of a heartbeat we gazed at each other. Yet even in that brief instant I could not miss the look that I had never before seen in those glowing eyes: the look of fear.

Twisting Ionn's mane in my hands, I strained my mind to think of something, anything, I could do to help. But what? In seconds, the kreelixes would reach their target.

The baby dragon whimpered, shrinking farther into the wing. How, I wondered, had she revived? Was it possible that I had really given her something more potent than the herbs from my satchel?

Without thinking, I reached inside the satchel. My finger pricked something sharp. The string from my psaltery! What had Cairpré once said it might bring? *High magic, like nothing you have ever known before.* I pulled out the string, warped and blackened by Urnalda's fiery summons. Might it somehow call forth magic even now? From hands without any magic of their own?

I glanced at the sky. Wings folded against their backs, the kreelixes sped downward. Now I could see Bachod riding the leader, the point of the spearhead. And surrounding him I could see seven snarling mouths, seven sets of fangs.

In desperation, I plucked the string. It twanged, releasing a puff of soot—then fell silent. I heard no music. I felt no magic.

Then, out of the very air around me, I heard a voice.

It was Rhia, reminding me: *Remember all the life around you, and all the life within yourself.* Then, joining her, came the ancient, grinding voice of the living stone. *What is this strange magic within you, young man? How can you resist me? A stone's power springs from all that surrounds, all that connects.* The hag Domnu cut in. *My pet,* she declared, *I feel magic in you even now.* Finally, the resonant voice of Eremon called to me. *You have power, Merlin. More power than you know.*

All the life within yourself . . .

This strange magic within you . . .

I feel it even now . . .

More power than you know . . .

The kreelixes screeched, only an instant away. I looked up to see Bachod leering, his eyes fixed on Valdearg's bulging wing that shielded his child. The great creature roared for the last time.

The voice of Cairpré joined the others. *Seek your answer within, my boy.* Then came the many voices, blended into one, of the Wheel of Wye: *Thooose pooowers aaare veeery neeear.*

A wrenching thought struck me. Perhaps I never lost my powers after all! Perhaps Urnalda merely tricked me into believing that! And yet . . . even if I still had magic, how could I use it now? The kreelixes would just consume it, destroy it. Cairpré had said that magic, applied directly, was futile. That the best weapon was something indirect. What was his phrase? *Something as ordinary, yet as powerful, as air itself.*

Air itself! Even as Valdearg's tail lashed out to strike as many kreelixes as it could, my mind raced through the many virtues of air. Bearer of breath. Of wind. Of sounds and smells. Of water.

Water! Was there any way . . .

The dragon's tail struck two of the kreelixes, sending them spinning. Yet he had missed Bachod, now only a fraction of an instant away from striking. Valdearg, unable to whip his tail again in time, was helpless.

With all my strength, I willed the air surrounding the kreelixes to chill. To freeze. The psaltery string in my hand suddenly rang out—like a chime within my very chest. The old emptiness vanished, replaced by a surge of power that I knew to be my own.

Concentrating all my thoughts on the air, I tried to draw away its heat. The air around Ionn and me instantly shimmered with new warmth. I perspired, less from the heat than from the strain.

At the very moment of contact, the air above Valdearg transformed into a mass of ice, encasing Bachod and the rest of the kreelixes. They had no time even to shriek, although my head reeled from the scarlet explosion of *negatus mysterium* being released. The enormous block of ice fell squarely on the dragon's back, just below his folded wing.

As the block of ice crashed to the charred terrain, Valdearg bellowed in anger and pain. He released a torrent of flames, so hot that the frozen block erupted in a conflagration of hissing steam and sizzling bodies. Seconds later, all that remained of the incinerated attackers was a pool of water, blood, and fur, licked by tongues of sputtering flames.

Ionn neighed triumphantly. Casting his head about, he frisked and capered. For my part, I dismounted and moved closer to the steaming pool. My mind was filled with the vision of elements having suddenly merged. For air had indeed turned to water; water to fire.

A high-pitched squeal arrested my thoughts. I started, for it sounded almost like a kreelix. In a flash I realized that it was, instead, the baby dragon. She had emerged from the protective wing, her stubborn ear still protruding. Yet my stomach turned to see the expression of grief on her face. And again to see why.

Valdearg, emperor of the dragons, lay still, his head resting heavily on his foreleg. No smoke curled from his nostrils, while his rumbling sounded thinner, frailer, than before. Although his green and orange scales still gleamed in the light, they seemed somehow to have lost their luster. Yet most telling of all was the dimness of his eyes. While they continued to glow, their light seemed as fragile as the flickering flames at the edge of the steaming pool.

Ionn joined me as I stepped nearer. There, at the base of the wing that had shielded the hatchling, I saw a telltale trickle of blood flowing from a small puncture. While a wound of that size might not normally have been even noticed by a dragon, this wound had come from the fang of a kreelix. The hatchling, whimpering softly, stroked the spot with one of her floppy little wings.

"He is dying," declared a familiar voice.

Ionn and I whirled around. There, facing us, stood a large-eyed doe. Her tan-colored fur was streaked with mud, while her legs bore several scratches and scrapes. Her mud-caked ears cocked toward me.

"Hallia," I whispered through the lump in my throat. "I thought . . . I thought you were dead."

"You underestimate me." She gave a slight snort, pretending to be insulted. "Deer know a few tricks of dodging pursuers, you know. Even kreelixes." Her deep brown eyes observed me. "You know a few tricks yourself, Merlin. I only arrived a moment ago, yet that was time enough to see what you accomplished."

I winced. "And did not accomplish." Turning back to Valdearg, I watched him gazing weakly at his offspring, now curled beside his belly. "My powers have returned, but an instant too late."

Solemnly, I approached the dragon. Warm air flooded over me with each of his rasping breaths. His yellow eyes, now half closed, turned in my direction.

"Grandson of Tuatha," the great creature rumbled. "I was wrong. You deserve to be called . . . a wizard."

My tongue, as dry as wood, worked in my mouth.

He tried to lift his head, then slumped back. "Neither the kreelixes nor I . . . survived this battle. At least I had the joy . . . of roasting them in the end." His bulk shook with an anguished cough. "My child, though! What of her? Who will teach her . . . to feed herself, to fly, to master her own magic? Who will . . . show her how to find my hollow, our ancestral home? Who will help her to know . . . the high destiny of a dragon?"

Wishing I had my staff to lean against, I shifted uneasily before answering. "I know very little about dragons. And less about their magic. But I do know the way to your hollow, and my heart would be gladdened to guide her there."

I glanced at Hallia, who now stood on the blackened turf not far from the hatchling. Their eyes, one pair circles of radiant brown and the other pair triangles of glowing orange, were fastened upon each other. Perhaps it was their shared magic, or their shared experience of loss, but I felt certain that these two beings were communicating, speaking to each other in some silent language.

"Your child will be cared for," I declared.

The dragon's eyes glowed brighter, then faded rapidly. "Never have I feared anything or anyone," he rasped. "Until today. Yet what I feared during the battle was not an attack of kreelixes, but the death of my little one." Another cough racked his body down to the barbs of his tail. "And now . . . now I find myself fearing something else."

"What?"

"Death. My own death! A dragon craves life, devours it. Swallows it in great, heaping mouthfuls! He is not slain easily—and does not die tranquilly. He resists . . ." He paused, trying to stifle a cough. "To the last." His baleful eyes, now dull yellow, scanned me. "Yet now I can resist no more. And now, young wizard, I am . . . afraid."

Slowly, I stepped closer to the immense face. My hand extended to touch the prominent brow above one eye. Without knowing where the words came from, I said, "Just look for the light, Wings of Fire . . . Walk there. Fly there. Your child will be with you. And so will I."

With that, Valdearg heaved a final breath, releasing a final wisp of smoke. The light in his eyes extinguished. They closed forever.

XXXI

A POWER STILL
HIGHER

An endless moment followed. We stood as silent as the charred lands around us, as still as the dead dragon. Only the hatchling stirred from time to time, nuzzling the lifeless body of her father.

Finally, Hallia stepped closer to the baby dragon. As she walked, her deer form melted away, replaced by that of a sturdy young woman. All the while, her soulful eyes remained fixed on the hatchling. As she drew nearer, the creature's lavender tail uncoiled and thumped anxiously against the ground. Hallia began to sing a slow, soothing melody, full of images of green meadows and sunlit streams. By the time she had reached the baby dragon's side, the tail fell still. With a single, graceful motion, she sat down, singing all the while.

Following suit, Ionn and I joined them. The stallion, his black coat gleaming in the midday sun, tossed his head in greeting. The baby dragon—half again as tall as Ionn, though much scrawnier—hesitated at first, then responded in kind. When she tossed her own head, though, orange-colored droplets sprinkled the rest of us. Hallia and I traded glances, knowing they were tears.

Hallia stopped singing. Cocking her head to one side, she studied the creature with sympathy. "Your loss is even worse than mine, young one. At least I knew my brother well. So well that I can still hear his breathing as well as his thoughts, almost before I hear my own."

Gingerly, I reached out and stroked the baby dragon's uncooperative ear. Although it protruded as stiffly as a branch, stretching longer than my forearm, it felt amazingly soft. Tiny purple hairs covered its entire length. The dragon whimpered quietly, then lowered her snout toward my feet. Without warning, she grasped one of my boots in her jaws and jerked it toward her, knocking me flat on my back.

Hallia grinned. "She recognizes you."

Despite the ache in my back, I could not keep from grinning myself. "Even more, I think, she recognizes my boot. I used it to feed her when we met before."

The baby dragon tugged again, pulling the boot free. It was, I realized, the same boot that I myself had chewed upon long ago when I had visited her father's lair. Before I could reach to take it back, the hatchling tilted back her head and swallowed it whole. I cried out, but too late. The boot was gone.

Ionn released a snort that resembled a hearty laugh. Suddenly he stiffened. His ears pricked forward. He swung his head to the side, stamping the ground with his hoof. Hallia leaped to her feet. Both of us followed Ionn's gaze.

A band of short, squat figures was approaching from around the edge of the pyramidal hill. Shields and breastplates flashed in the sun. In the center of the group strode a figure bearing a staff, wearing a peaked hat over a mass of unruly red hair. Urnalda.

Though my anger boiled just beneath the surface, I held my

tongue. Despite the lack of my boot, I threw back my shoulders and stood as tall as I could.

Urnalda's earrings of shells glinted as she came near. I could not read the look in her eyes, but her clenched jaw seemed both grim and unremorseful. As the band came within a few paces of us, she slowed and raised a stubby hand. The other dwarves, grasping their axes and bows, halted.

The enchantress stepped forward, examining the corpse of the fallen dragon. She flinched slightly upon seeing the baby dragon nestled there, but said nothing. Her gaze fell to the steaming pool, clotted with the blood and hair of Bachod and the kreelixes.

At last, she turned to me. "I see that your powers be restored."

My eyes narrowed. "They never left, as you know. You only tricked me into believing they were gone."

"That be true." The earrings clinked as she nodded. "The only way a magic-robbing spell can work be if the victim completely believes that his powers be destroyed. Then he and everyone else around him be fooled. It all be part of Urnalda's plan."

My hand, still holding the string from my psaltery, closed into a fist. "And was wiping out all but one of Valdearg's offspring also part of your plan?"

"No," she replied coldly, twirling the tip of her staff in the blackened soil. "Yet that be not a bad result."

"What about the kreelixes? Did your plan account for them? Thanks to your help, they slayed this dragon—and would have gone on to slay you and me and every other creature of magic on Fincayra." My voice lowered to a growl. "In your arrogance, Urnalda, you almost opened the door to Rhita Gawr! It was his plan, not yours, that was guiding your actions. You did it unwittingly, I think, but you still served as his tool."

Her face, normally pale, flushed deep red. "Bah! I never be wrong," she declared. Her eyes lowered for just an instant. "It be possible, though, that I be temporarily deceived."

She extended her hand, palm up. A flash of light split the air, causing several of her dwarves to leap aside, tripping over themselves in the process. There, in her hand, rested my staff. She spat out a few words and the staff floated, twirling gracefully, over to me.

Eagerly, I clutched its shaft, embracing it like the outstretched hand of an old friend. My second sight ran over all the familiar markings—the cracked stone, the sword, the star within a circle, and the rest. All the wisdom of the Seven Songs. Now, at last, I felt completely restored.

Urnalda watched me, playing with one of her shell earrings. "That be for doing what you did to help my people."

Knowing that was as close to an apology as I would ever get from her, I hefted the staff. "Consider my promise fulfilled."

She tilted her head toward the huddled form of the baby dragon. "Now there be only one task remaining. Let us, together, destroy the last of those despicable beasts."

"Wait now," I declared. "The old dragon's death could be an opportunity. That's right—to bridge the ancient divide between the dragons and ourselves. Hard as it will be, couldn't we try to treat her as our fellow creature? Maybe even as our friend? It's possible, at least, she might come to do the same for us."

"Fellow creature? Friend?" she scoffed. "Never! I be seeing far too much of dragons' wrath for that! You may be finding your powers, but you be losing your mind." She clapped her hands. "Guards! Raise your weapons."

Instantly, the dwarves flanking her nocked their arrows and lifted their double-sided axes. They stood poised, awaiting her next command.

I jammed my staff into the ground, splintering a slab of charcoal. "Hear my words, all of you! That dragon shall live." Glaring at Urnalda, I took a single step closer. My head leaned toward hers. "If you or any of your people should ever try to harm that dragon, through whatever means, for whatever reason, you shall face my own wrath. The wrath . . . of a wizard. What happened to those kreelixes over there will be nothing compared to what will happen to you."

For a long moment, the enchantress glowered at me. The air between us sizzled, crackling with tiny sparks. Then, without another word, she turned and strode off the way she had come. Hurriedly, her band of squat warriors stowed their weapons and followed, marching as fast as they could to keep pace with her. I watched as they rounded the bend and disappeared behind the hill.

Ionn nudged my arm. I stroked his neck, still staring at the spot where I had last seen the tip of Urnalda's peaked hat. All of a sudden, Hallia cried out. The stallion and I spun around to see her pointing at the steaming pool, bubbling with the remains of the kreelixes.

Out of the vapors, a shape was forming. A face—with no hair, misshapen teeth, and a wart in the middle of the forehead. I braced myself, knowing it was the image of Domnu. As the hag's mouth creased in a grisly smile, blue flames licked the edges of the pool.

"Well, my pets, you survived. I wouldn't have predicted it." The flames swelled, gathering around her eyes. "Even my little pony over there survived."

Ionn's hoof thudded against the ground. He neighed defiantly.

The vaporous form, vibrating with the rising steam, wrinkled her scalp. "Now, what about our bargain?"

I shook my head. "The Galator is lost. Buried under a mountain of lava."

Blue flames leaped from her eyes. "You wouldn't think of betraying me now, would you?"

"No," I replied. "Unlike some people, I don't go back on my word." I indicated the simmering pool beneath her. "But the thief who stole it from your lair won't bother you again."

Domnu scowled, her whole face writhing. "Bones. Boiling bones! Gone before I had any chance to play with it! Well . . . so be it. I really didn't like the color of the cursed thing anyway. Farewell, my pets."

Instantly, the pool erupted in a swirl of blue flames. When, a moment later, they faded into the rising steam, the face of the hag had vanished. I continued watching the pool, leaning against my staff.

Hallia's resonant voice broke the stillness. "Merlin?"

I turned to face her. How it delighted me to see those eyes again! I felt a new surge of gratitude that she had escaped harm. And, to my surprise, something else, deeper than gratitude.

"Do you recall," she asked softly, "that moment in the oracle's cave, when I said you had a certain kind of power?"

"I do. And I also recall you couldn't put any name to it."

She nodded slowly. "Well, now I can. Call it the power of understanding. Of leaping across barriers, finding meaning in tracks. And as strong as a dragon, or a kreelix, or even a Galator may be, hat's something even stronger. For all their power, it's really a ower still higher."

Twirling the string from my psaltery, I almost smiled.

"Don't forget, though," she added with a nudge. "Even a great wizard needs two boots, not just one."

I wiggled the toes of my bare foot. "Unless, of course, he can run like a deer."

She watched me thoughtfully. "Or fly . . . like a young hawk."